Praise for

THE SCORPION TRAIL

"Larry D. Sweazy's Josiah Wolfe books promise to stand among the great Western series. Think The Rifleman in the deft hands of a Larry McMurtry or a Cormac McCarthy."

—Loren D. Estleman, Spur Award–winning author of
The Book of Murdock

"Larry D. Sweazy takes you on a fierce ride . . . This crisp, well-written story returns you to the West as it really was— and you'll like being there."

—Cotton Smith, author of *Ride for Rule Cordell* and
past president of Western Writers of America

"Larry D. Sweazy writes a lively blend of mystery, action, and historical realism."

—John D. Nesbitt, Spur Award–winning author of
Gather My Horses

Praise for
THE RATTLESNAKE SEASON

"Combines the slam-bang action of a good Western with the sensitivity of style and depth of character that used to be the hallmark of literary fiction."   —Loren D. Estleman

"A character-rich story about a Texas Ranger haunted by dark memories, on the hunt for a former comrade-in-arms turned killer."

—Elmer Kelton, seven-time Spur Award–winning author

"There's a new fresh voice in the pages of Western fiction . . . His powerful, authentic voice rings steel tough . . . A must read for the Western fan."

—Dusty Richards, Spur Award–winning author of *Wulf's Tracks*

"Larry D. Sweazy's novel is a fast-paced, hard to put down book, chock-full of unforgettable characters you will be glad you met . . . a page-turner."

—Robert J. Conley, author of *The Cherokee Nation* and
vice president of Western Writers of America

Titles by Larry D. Sweazy

Josiah Wolfe, Texas Ranger Series

THE
COUGAR'S
PREY

A Josiah Wolfe, Texas Ranger Novel

LARRY D. SWEAZY

BERKLEY BOOKS, NEW YORK

THE BERKLEY PUBLISHING GROUP
Published by the Penguin Group
Penguin Group (USA) Inc.
375 Hudson Street, New York, New York 10014, USA
Penguin Group (Canada), 90 Eglinton Avenue East, Suite 700, Toronto, Ontario M4P 2Y3, Canada
(a division of Pearson Penguin Canada Inc.)
Penguin Books Ltd., 80 Strand, London WC2R 0RL, England
Penguin Group Ireland, 25 St. Stephen's Green, Dublin 2, Ireland (a division of Penguin Books Ltd.)
Penguin Group (Australia), 250 Camberwell Road, Camberwell, Victoria 3124, Australia
(a division of Pearson Australia Group Pty. Ltd.)
Penguin Books India Pvt. Ltd., 11 Community Centre, Panchsheel Park, New Delhi—110 017, India
Penguin Group (NZ), 67 Apollo Drive, Rosedale, Auckland 0632, New Zealand
(a division of Pearson New Zealand Ltd.)
Penguin Books (South Africa) (Pty.) Ltd., 24 Sturdee Avenue, Rosebank, Johannesburg 2196,
South Africa

Penguin Books Ltd., Registered Offices: 80 Strand, London WC2R 0RL, England

This is a work of fiction. Names, characters, places, and incidents either are the product of the author's imagination or are used fictitiously, and any resemblance to actual persons, living or dead, business establishments, events, or locales is entirely coincidental. The publisher does not have any control over and does not assume any responsibility for author or third-party websites or their content.

THE COUGAR'S PREY

A Berkley Book / published by arrangement with the author

PRINTING HISTORY
Berkley edition / October 2011

Copyright © 2011 by Larry D. Sweazy.
Cover illustration by Bruce Emmett.
Cover design by Lesley Worrell.
Interior text design by Laura K. Corless.

ISBN: 978-0-425-24394-7

BERKLEY®
Berkley Books are published by The Berkley Publishing Group,
a division of Penguin Group (USA) Inc.,
375 Hudson Street, New York, New York 10014.
BERKLEY® is a registered trademark of Penguin Group (USA) Inc.
The "B" design is a trademark of Penguin Group (USA) Inc.

PRINTED IN THE UNITED STATES OF AMERICA

10   9   8   7   6   5   4   3   2   1

This book is dedicated to Ron Clark,
a bright, shining example
of a public school teacher
who lit the way.

ACKNOWLEDGMENTS

The adventure of writing a novel may start in a dimly lit room, alone at a desk, but there is no question that the adventure quickly turns into a bright journey filled with new friends, acquaintances, and happy accidents. I offer my humble thanks to the people who helped me along the way as I wrote this novel.

I greatly appreciate the time Bob and Kathy Muller took to introduce me to Tim and Patty Redmond, and their herd of longhorns. It was a fine summer day that I won't soon forget.

Jim Friedt taught me the art of net casting, and standing knee-deep in the ocean on another perfect day (and evening) greatly contributed to my understanding of saltwater fishing.

Special thanks, as always, goes to John Duncklee, for his help with the Spanish language, and his constant encouragement. *Gracias, mi amigo.* Any mistakes are my own.

I enjoyed a day of research with fellow writers Phil Dunlap, and William "Lavista Bill" Bell, at the Pleasant Valley SASS (Single Action Shooting Society) meet. Special thanks to all of the members of the Pleasant Valley Renegades, and Jerry "Nomore Slim" West, for welcoming us and sharing their knowledge and enthusiasm about the guns of the West. Any mistakes concerning firearms are my own.

I am extremely lucky to have a talented group of friends and colleagues who offer encouragement and help in every phase of writing the Josiah Wolfe novels. Thanks to Jeff; Liz and Chris; my agent, Cherry Weiner; my editor, Faith Black; and the entire Berkley production team, for all that you do to make my novels an enjoyable experience for the readers of this series.

Finally, there is no way I could ever thank my wife, Rose, enough, for her sharp eyes and ears. She is my first reader, and we have loads of fun talking about the characters in my books like they are members of our family. Not only am I a better writer for her presence, I am a better human being because of her of love. Thank you . . .

AUTHOR'S NOTE

The Josiah Wolfe books are a continuing work of western fiction, set against historical events that often include historical characters. Accuracy of research is something I strive for in each book. But this is fiction, after all, and sometimes the story or a timeline of actual events dictates a little interference on my part to serve a more dramatic, or storytelling, purpose.

For historical works concerning the Texas Rangers and the Frontier Battalion, the following books may be of interest to the readers of this series and have served me well as I conducted my continuing research: *Lone Star Justice: The First Century of the Texas Rangers* by Robert M. Utley (Berkley, 2002); *The Texas Rangers: Wearing the Cinco Peso, 1821– 1900* by Mike Cox (Forge, 2008); *Six Years with the Texas Rangers, 1875–1881* by James B. Gillet (Bison Books, 1976).

Online resources such as www.texas.gov, the *Handbook of Texas*, and the *Texas Ranger Dispatch* magazine, have also been helpful in portraying the Texas Rangers as historically accurate, and as honorably, as possible.

PROLOGUE

———✦✦✦✦———

May 1862

The Virginia highlands looked like the bellies of sleeping giants to Josiah Wolfe. Every day for the last six months had been a new adventure, one more foot set outside of the boundaries of everything he had known and understood all his life. Until he had mustered in Tyler and joined the Texas Brigade, specifically the First Infantry, Josiah had never once set foot outside the state of Texas.

He had barely been out of the confines of Tyler and Seerville, the small town just miles from his father's farm that had been his home from the day of his birth. But now, after months of military training, marching, and train rides, the smell of battle was in the air just outside of Eltham's Landing in Virginia.

Wood smoke lingered in the air, mixing with the scent of a spring morning; thousands of white, yellow, and purple wildflowers coated the ground, and Josiah hardly knew any of the names of the flowers. Not like home. The alien flowers made him miss the bluebonnets and Indian paintbrush, and the fresh smell of the piney forest not far from his cabin.

He knew the early wildflower season was nearly over now that it was May in Texas. Thinking of home was a frequent exercise for him, but he pushed the sad thoughts away by staying busy or remembering his anger at his father for not seeing him off to war. But that was the past. There was no need to fret over things that couldn't be changed, not with the certainty of a real fight coming any moment.

Josiah was numbed by duty, by the marching and drills, the regularity of soldiering life. So far, he found life in the army suited him. He liked every minute of the day, filled by someone else's orders, and the camaraderie was a welcome change in his life, since he had been an only child, raised alone with no brothers, sisters, or even nearby cousins.

His stomach was full. There'd been a mess of bacon, beans, and biscuits to start the day. The musket he'd been assigned was cleaned and ready to go, empty of a load, since the command had yet to be given. If anything was lacking in his preparedness, it may have been the courage that was hiding deep in Josiah's spirit.

He was most certainly afraid of what was coming, but he didn't dare show it to any of the fellas around him. They were afraid, too. Josiah could smell the aroma of fear in the air through the smoke.

Killing had never come easily to him, even when it was a squirrel, though he'd gotten used to that pretty quickly. But killing another man was something else—even without a strong basis of religion like some of the boys that had joined up in Tyler—killing would be a hard task to face. But he knew he'd have to kill a Yankee, whether he truly believed in the cause or not. Politics were left to smarter men than him, and though he said nothing, Josiah was not sure he completely understood, or condoned, the reasons for war. But . . . he was a son of Texas, and he had chosen to stand and fight with the side the politicians had decided on.

A few days before, General Joseph E. Johnston had unexpectedly withdrawn his Confederate troops from the Warwick Line during the night, at a battle in Yorktown. The move caught the Union by surprise, and they couldn't mount a pursuit quick enough. Johnston was headed toward Richmond, by way of West Point, traveling up the York River. He stopped to regroup in Barhamsville. The Yankees had caught up, coming ashore on light pontoon boats. They'd even built a long wharf that floated, bringing in heavy artillery.

But still there'd been some small rounds of fire from the pickets set up on the bluffs, shooting down at the Yankees as they prepared for battle.

Josiah served under General John Bell Hood.

Hood's reputation as a brave man was unequaled, and he was aggressive to the point of recklessness, as far as some of the men were concerned. Not Josiah. He'd watched the general and found his style of leadership inspiring. Hood knew the area around the small town they'd lit into; he'd studied at West Point, nearby, albeit with a modest record, according to the gossip Josiah had been privy to. Hood was a tall, slender man, with a chest-length beard, a high forehead, and a thick head of dark brown hair, and he rode a horse of the same color, sitting high in the saddle, a proud, stiff man, certain in his rank and manners.

The call to assembly came quickly after the sun broke over the bluffs. A brigade had been sent up to protect the road into Barhamsville, but the Texas Brigade was being sent to the skirmish line on the north side of the landing road.

Hood rode up and down the line, his horse prancing in front of the troops. "I don't want a man to load his weapon until the command is given, is that understood?"

"Yes sir!" the troops said resoundingly.

Josiah was three rows back, craning his neck, as subtly as he could, so he could clearly see what was going on.

"Ain't that crazy."

Josiah glanced over and saw standing next to him an unusually skinny boy of no more than eighteen, who spit and then scowled at the general. "Why's that?" Josiah whispered.

"General's afeared of a man taking a shot at one of his own across the way. You's can see the gray caps clear as a candlelight in a cave. I'm already loaded."

Josiah looked to the woods. It was full of brush and bramble, covered by a tall canopy of tender new leaves that barely let any sunlight hit the ground. He felt a cold chill run up his spine. The boy, John Deal, was a corporal just like him, and he was openly disobeying General Hood's order.

"I'd load up, too, Wolfe, if'n I was you."

Josiah shook his head no. He understood Hood's order, knew how hard it was to see in the woods on a calm day. He couldn't imagine the difficulty of seeing the right target during a battle.

"Suit yourself then," Deal said. "I ain't gonna die today."

Hood gave the command to march, and the brigade headed into the woods.

Marching came easy to Josiah, his musket in hand, ready to load. His hand was sweating, making the gun slick in his grip, and his heart was beating so loudly he thought everyone within earshot could hear it. There was no turning back now.

About fifteen paces into the woods, they encountered an enemy picket line.

A Yankee jumped up and drew General Hood into his bead as he advanced. John Deal must have seen the gunman, because he pushed through the rank, stepped firm once he was clear, and fired at the Yankee just in time, killing him with one sure shot.

General Hood could hardly scold the boy since he'd just

saved his life. The command to load was quickly given, and the infantry prepared to engage the Yankees.

Josiah couldn't believe what he was seeing. If John Deal hadn't disobeyed orders, the general would have been dead before the battle even began. It was something he wouldn't soon forget.

The air was quickly full of gunpowder, and the clear sky reverberated with the thunder of firing shots. He realized then that he could die at any second. And life at any rate would never be the same.

Josiah followed the general's order, loaded his musket, then took his position.

It was only a matter of seconds before he sighted a target, a blue cap easing along the picket, a glimmer off the Union bayonet giving away his position.

Josiah eased his finger onto the trigger, took a deep breath, waited, then waited another second, until he saw flesh, the blink of a blue eye and a forehead, then pulled the trigger with all his might.

He did not wait to see if the shot was successful. He knew it was. The Yankee was dead, or dying, and Josiah Wolfe had fully joined the War Between the States.

CHAPTER 1

March 1875

Josiah Wolfe sat outside the cantina on a hardwood chair, a beer in one hand and a cigarette in the other.

The smell of the cigarette didn't entice Josiah, since he'd never acquired a taste for tobacco. Beer either, as far as that went. But at the moment, what enticed Josiah Wolfe didn't matter, nor did the taste or implication of vices that he'd never picked up—but he held them in his hands and touched them to his lips anyway.

Nobody in the cantina, or in all of Corpus Christi for that matter, knew him as Josiah Wolfe. To everyone he encountered, Josiah was a lowly hide trader named Zeb Teter, a man who had a quick reputation for his inability to hold his liquor but knew how to cut a deal with the Mexicans like the hard bargainer he professed to be.

No one knew he was a Texas Ranger. Or at least he hoped no one did. He was on a special mission, assigned to him by Captain Leander McNelly, as a spy, his main job to cultivate a network of paid informants to report back on the movement of cattle, the raids, and anything else he could learn about the thefts that were leaving the local ranchers, and the ones to the north, with less profit and angry as hell. The anger was aimed mostly at a man named Juan Cortina, who was heading up the raids and making scads of money to fuel his political and military desires south of the border.

Josiah's face was covered with four days' worth of scruff, and it had been as many days since he'd had a quick bath. He had been gone from home for nearly four months and was fully involved as the new man he claimed to be, Zeb Teter, who had no family matters to consider in the middle of the night—or in the light of day, for that matter.

Josiah's hands smelled of hides, old and new. The tanning process was ingrained in his mind, under his fingernails, on his every breath. Josiah wondered if the dung paste the hides soaked in for two days would ever wash out of his skin. Most people avoided him, sat downwind of him when they could, and for that, he was glad. Less conversation meant less chance he'd slip up. Being a spy was new to him. This was his first mission alone, not riding with a company of Rangers, serving in the Frontier Battalion.

The cantina was on the north end of Corpus, and the ocean was several miles away. Still, a steady and soft wind blew off the waves and pushed a healthy dose of salt air inland, making the air as soothing as a sweet nectar.

The sea air was like a tonic to Josiah. He was surprised how much better it made him feel, sprier, his head clearer. He was only thirty-three years old, but until he came to the seashore, sometimes he felt like he'd lived a hundred years.

It was late afternoon, and the sun was slowly scooting toward the horizon, inch by inch, it, too, seemingly content with the perfection of the calm spring day, not wanting it to come to an end or fall into the inescapable darkness that was destined to come.

There wasn't a cloud in the deep blue sky. Azure. That's what Josiah had heard somebody call the color of this kind of sky once. He didn't know what azure was—but he knew it now when he saw it, and was glad that there was no weather in the perfect sky to threaten the ease of the day. Waiting was a big part of being a spy; at least it had been so far.

The cantina was small, a mere hole in the wall, on a block of buildings constructed of both limestone and wood frames, and most were one storey.

A Mexican sat in the back corner plucking on a guitar, a soft song that was not meant for anything other than to exercise the man's fingers.

Josiah had heard the man play at night when the torches were lit, when the beer was flowing like a rushing stream in spring, and the man played fast and hard, the calluses on the tips of his fingers beet red. The loud music was like honey to flies, drawing in men looking for a good time.

A band usually gathered at night in the cantina, four or five Mexicans playing for their dinner, a crock or two of beer here and there, and a coin or two from a happily drunk patron. Josiah didn't know the guitar player's name but watched him closely when he was in the cantina. He was sure the man was somehow connected to Juan Cortina— there'd been a few times when there were whispers exchanged with a stranger or two, followed by a quick disappearance of both men. Some kind of transaction obviously taking place.

Josiah was the only customer in the establishment. The man behind the bar, Agusto, another Mexican, sat on a stool and stared outside, not paying any attention to Josiah.

Agusto's belly hung over his belt, and there was no gun on his hip, but there was a twelve-gauge shotgun under the bar and probably more firepower hidden about the cantina than Josiah was aware of.

The whole front wall of the cantina opened up to the street, allowing tables to be pushed outside, protected from the sun overhead by long, extending eaves. There were seven rooms above the cantina, the entrance to the upstairs outside, at the back of the building, a rickety set of stairs that showed plenty of wear.

Use of the rooms was less for sleeping than for private entertainment with one of the many women who worked the floor of the cantina when business was good. Agusto held the keys, charged a price, but did not manage the girls—someone else held control over them—a man Josiah didn't know, or care to, unless he had to. Agusto was just the gatekeeper.

Josiah had never had cause to inquire about the nightly entertainment. Whores were not a vice to Josiah *or* Zeb Teter, at least not yet. It would happen only if it needed to.

Duty was full of fickle rules as far as Josiah was concerned. Especially spy duty.

Josiah sat just outside the cantina, his attention drawn by the occasional horse or wagon traversing the street. Beyond the soft guitar music, there was not much noise in the surrounding town, no amount of traffic. It was the end of siesta time.

He took a slow drink of the beer. The taste was not unpalatable, a hint of sweetness to offset the alcohol, but drinking beer was nothing that he sought to make a habit of, even if it was a requirement to convince people he was Zeb Teter. Josiah liked to keep his head about him.

The glass of beer was still nearly full, and Josiah had been sitting for an hour, waiting.

When he sat the glass down, Agusto looked up and made eye contact with him. "You take all day to drink that beer, Mr. Zeb, and I don't make no money."

Josiah smiled slightly at being called Mr. Zeb. He had wanted to make sure the barkeep knew his name from the very beginning. Josiah had slid him an extra bit for the first couple of beers to make sure he was taken care of . . . and was remembered as Mr. Zeb, as a generous man.

"You'll make plenty of money once the sun goes down, Agusto. Traders should be coming in."

The barkeep shook his head no. His face was fat, sweaty, and deep brown. A thin black mustache sat atop a set of full, puffy lips. "A bad wind is coming, Mr. Zeb."

"Looks like a perfect day to me," Josiah said.

"Wind is changing. Can't you tell?"

It was Josiah's turn to shake his head no. "Feels the same to me."

Agusto smiled, exposing a mouth full of broken yellow teeth. "The sky will rumble before the day's over, Mr. Zeb. Mark my words."

Josiah nodded then and said nothing. He took another slow sip of beer and stared up at the sky. Something *was* coming, that was for sure; he just wasn't sure what.

The woman was tall for a Mexican. She wore a tight-fitting black dress, the neck cut deep, exposing a generous view of healthy cleavage that no man in the cantina could ignore—not even Josiah.

Long, wavy black hair flowed over the woman's shoulders, and her lips were as red as the fiery sun. Her sultry brown eyes were locked on Josiah, and she ignored every man's attempt to get her attention. She stopped directly in front of Josiah and offered him her hand.

"Would you like to dance, señor?" the woman asked.

Josiah stared up at her. "It's before four o'clock. In the heat of the day?"

The woman smirked and withdrew her hand. "You have no sense of adventure." Her accent was soft, her English easy to understand. She was exceptionally beautiful, and Josiah had never seen her before. He rarely saw any of the girls from upstairs in the cantina during the day, so her appearance was out of the ordinary.

For a moment, Josiah was uncomfortable. He wasn't

quite sure if she was what he was waiting for or not.

"Perhaps," the woman continued, "you would like to dance in private. Are you bashful?"

Josiah forced a smile. "I'm sure Agusto wouldn't mind me stumbling about."

Agusto didn't say anything, just smiled and waved Josiah off, like he was fending off one of the many flies that called the cantina home.

The guitar music had stopped. Josiah hadn't seen the guitar player disappear, but the stool where the Mexican had sat just minutes before was now empty, like he'd never existed at all.

"Looks like we've lost our music," he said.

"We can make our own music, Señor Zeb."

"How come you know my name, and I don't know yours?"

"I am Maria. Maria Villareal."

Josiah nodded and stood up. "After you, Maria Villareal," he said. He'd been given the name Maria Villareal as a contact. She *was* who he'd been waiting on.

The woman flashed him a grin, looked him hard in the eye, quickly, to acknowledge he'd made the right choice, then walked slowly toward the back of the cantina.

Josiah followed, his hand inches away from the Peacemaker he carried on his hip. He had a knife in one boot and a small .25-caliber pistol in the other. He was not entirely trusting of this woman, or of anyone in Corpus Christi for that matter.

The woman rounded the corner first. Josiah lost sight of her for a second and hurried his pace.

When he came to the other side of the building, he walked straight into the barrel of a gun, forcing him to come to a quick, unanticipated stop.

The guitar player was waiting for him, a Walker Colt, a revolver with a nine-inch barrel, cocked and ready to fire.

"You better tell me what you're doing here, Ranger, or you're a dead man."

CHAPTER 2

━━◆✕◆━━

December 1874

Josiah sat alone in a room on the second floor of the state capitol building. There were three empty chairs sitting behind a simple table void of any papers, pens, or anything that might look official. The room smelled musty, like it had been locked up for a long time, and there was a slight chill in the air; a draft circled around his ankles like a set of invisible shackles had appeared out of nowhere to hold him in place. Beyond the temperature of the air, Josiah barely felt anything. He was numb from the inside out.

On the other side of the table, a single-pane window looked out over Capitol Square, then south, down Congress Avenue. The Old Stone Capitol building stood at the end of the avenue, a three-storey Greek Revival building that was less than grand but would have to suffice, considering the budget constraints put on the state by the Panic of '73. Everyone was having to make do, including the Rangers, and all of the government agencies, because of the nationwide financial collapse.

The avenue was lined with buildings, mostly two-storey

but some, including the hotels, were three storeys. It was a clear, sunny day, and daily life was progressing at a normal pace. Wagons were coming and going. A stagecoach sat waiting in front of the old Bullock Hotel, just arriving from Brastop. So far, the winter season had been reasonably dry. Horses kicked up dust on the road as they came and went, even at a slow pace. The sounds of activity were audible but slight. Even though it was midday, a piano banged distantly from a nearby saloon, the sound muffled but unmistakable.

Josiah was wearing his best set of clothes, the ones he reserved for funerals and other important matters. The last time he'd worn them was not so long ago, to a fine dinner that he had been invited to at the Fikes estate. It was the night Pete Feders asked Pearl to marry him in front of every important man and woman in Austin, and she had declined. It was also the night that Feders relieved Josiah of duty with the Frontier Battalion, reassigning him to Captain Leander McNelly's company of Special Rangers. That night was hard to forget, indelibly imprinted in Josiah's mind, as a night of tragedy and pure happiness, as he ended up spending the night making love to Pearl Fikes in the barn. The beginning of the end. Days later, Josiah faced Pete Feders, a gun in his hand, and surprise and regret in his heart. He shot and killed his captain, who had joined up with an outlaw to start a cattle rustling operation.

Now he had to suffer the consequences of his own actions—answer for them in a way that he'd never thought he would. Though during the many sleepless nights of late, even he had questioned if his response had been of pure intention. His own motivations were a mystery even to himself, other than to stay alive—for his son, for himself, and whatever the future held. At that point, he thought he actually had a future for the first time in a long, long time. But he couldn't be sure if the future was all he had been protecting. It was not the first time Josiah had ever killed a man, but it was the first time he ever had reason to question whether he was a cold-blooded killer or not. His feelings for Pearl Fikes were confusing everything in his life.

Footsteps approached down the long corridor. They echoed, causing Josiah to stiffen in anticipation.

The room he was sequestered in was at the very end of the hall.

At first, the steps were distant, but they grew closer at a quick pace, like thunder rolling toward him, announcing the coming of a storm of undetermined severity.

The doorknob turned. Josiah stood up and turned to face those who entered the room.

Captain Leander McNelly looked away from Josiah and pushed by him with an air of discontent.

McNelly was a thin, bony man, with a mid-range beard free of muttonchops, and his black frock coat and pants were free of lint or dust. He was a long sufferer of consumption, but his will was strong, and he managed his company of Special Rangers with the grip of a man not to be mistaken for a weakling. Every man in the company had great respect for McNelly, including Josiah.

The next man to enter the room was Major John B. Jones, who headed up the Frontier Battalion.

Josiah had ridden with Jones and had even, at times, considered him a rival for the affection of Pearl Fikes. Jones was a well-known womanizer, still a bachelor, with rumored acquaintances in more than one Texas town. He wore a perfectly trimmed V mustache and was dressed similar to McNelly, all in black, except the highly starched white shirt. The major always looked very official, always took pride in his appearance, and there was not a whit of soil to be witnessed on his clothes. Even his boot heels glimmered in the late morning sunlight streaming in through the window.

William Steele was the last man in the grim parade and followed behind Jones with heavy footsteps and a noticeable limp.

Steele was the elder statesman of the three, a stout man

who towered over both Jones and McNelly. His beard was grizzled and gray, with wiry hairs poking out in every direction. In comparison to Jones and McNelly, Steele looked like he had just rolled out of bed and jumped into his clothes, which were black, too, but wrinkled. They didn't look like they'd seen the hands of a laundress or a Chinaman since they'd been delivered by the tailor.

Each man had served in the Confederate Army, all in varying capacities, but each in a commanding position, each coming to, or returning home to Texas with a desire to put the past behind him.

For some men, the loss to the Union was harder to take than for others. Josiah wasn't sure which man held any anger toward that subject, nor did he care—he was thankful the War Between the States was long over. The only importance of any of the men's attitudes was simple: Josiah had also served the Confederacy, and was a former military man himself, having spent his entire service in the First Texas Brigade. On a small scale, they all had a shared experience, a brotherhood, that would hopefully make things a little less tense and more equitable for Josiah.

Chairs scooted in as each man took his place. Steele sat in the middle, with Jones to his right and McNelly to his left. Josiah kept standing, waiting to be told what to do next, what was expected of him. This was not a formal military inquiry, but it needed to be treated as such, as far as Josiah was concerned.

Steele had carried a satchel full of papers into the room with him. He dug out a pair of reading glasses from inside his coat, opened the satchel, and cleared his throat. "Close the door, Wolfe. We've seen enough of your shenanigans in the newspaper of late. Hard to say who's out there lurking within earshot." His voice was booming and commanding.

Josiah did as he was told, his mind racing, his stomach nervous. He had never been in trouble to this degree in his entire life. Nor had he, or his escapades, been the subject of direct and vicious coverage in any newspaper. The *Austin Statesman* was having a heyday with the story of Feders's death, painting Josiah as a rogue Ranger, questioning whether he had killed Pete Feders in cold blood for the hand of Pearl Fikes. The social pages had carried the news of the engagement party gone wrong, and it seemed as if every tongue in the city was wagging about the whole affair.

Josiah was certain that Pearl's mother was behind the stories; if not directly, then she was feeding the fire somehow. She had promised him as much, that she would ruin him, and it looked as though she was intent on keeping that promise.

The constant everyday front page stories had left the state government, and the Ranger hierarchy, little choice but to investigate the shooting in a very public way.

The Ranger organization itself had been under constant scrutiny since it had been organized less than a year earlier.

Governor Richard Coke had been under pressure to cut the Rangers' budget, which was already increasingly thin. The Comanche were still attacking white settlements to the north, but to a lesser degree, and that had been one of the main reasons for the Rangers being formally organized in the first place. The Sutton-Taylor feud had been quelled in Dewitt County, McNelly's first assignment, and a major success—but overshadowed by Josiah's actions in South Texas.

There was a growing chorus of fiscally restrained citizens who were questioning the need for the Rangers to exist at all—and if they did, what their function truly was, and how they should be funded. Somehow, Feders's death was being turned into a political debate, another matter Josiah had no experience with and did not desire now. But it didn't matter.

"The Feders killing," as it was being called, was being used as further proof that the Rangers were a renegade bunch of men, set on making their own laws, while they raided the state coffers.

Josiah was not accustomed to being known, to walking down the street and having people whisper behind his back, or utter scurrilous terms like "traitor" or "murderer" as he passed by on the street.

Because of that, over the last few days, since the burial of Pete Feders had been conducted, and as the newspapers drummed a demand for a formal investigation into the death of the Texas Ranger captain, whose record and attributes had been portrayed as flawless in the *Austin Statesman*, Josiah had laid low, staying shut up in his house as much as was humanly possible. He did not dare take Lyle anywhere. He did not want his son subjected to any ill treatment caused by his own actions.

Josiah did as he was told by Steele and closed the door, then returned to the chair and remained standing.

Steele looked over the papers, not giving any notice to anything but what was in front of him.

Jones and McNelly stared at Josiah coldly, not giving one hint of their inclination toward his innocence or guilt. If there was a shared brotherhood among the men in the room, Josiah was not feeling a part of it.

A clock ticked somewhere close by, maybe in the next room, but loud enough to be heard faintly.

Josiah tried to stand as still as he could, nearly at attention, his heels together, his arms stiff to his sides. He tried to look past the men, out the window. A crowd was assembling outside of the capitol building. They had been alerted to the meeting.

He felt a sudden urge to relieve himself but knew he could not move, could not run, even if he wanted to. There was no hiding from the moment he'd found himself in.

CHAPTER 3

William Steele exhaled strongly enough to make the wild hairs of his beard tremble. "We have never met, have we, Ranger Wolfe?"

"No, sir, I don't believe we have."

Steele looked Josiah over, trailing his gaze from head to toe, then waved his hand. "Sit down. This is not a formal trial."

Josiah did as he was instructed, though he would have preferred to remain standing, would have preferred to hold some kind of advantage, height or otherwise, rather than having to face all three men at a lower level. He was at an extreme disadvantage as it was, three against one, his fate in the hands of ambitious men with their own political careers on the line.

"It should be a trial according to those waiting beyond the doors and out on the street," Major Jones said.

"They're after nothing but more blood," Steele answered. "I promised the governor we would put an end to this charade quickly, and that justice would be served, if it has not been already. Make no mistake, I answer to the governor, not to that mob out there, and certainly not to that rag that poses as a newspaper these days. You have an enemy in the press, Wolfe, and you are sorely at a disadvantage."

There were no words that came to Josiah's mind that he could offer Steele in his own defense. The attacks in the newspaper had taken him aback, and being the simple man that he was, he had no idea how to combat the "vile creature" as Steele had called it.

McNelly did not move, did not say a word. He just stared past Josiah, at the door. Jones, on the other hand, fidgeted, looking like he had been admonished. His lips drew up tighter than a clam.

Josiah could hear each breath drawn in and forced out by McNelly, could tell that it was difficult for the captain to even sit there. There was a sadness about the man that was underlying every movement, in every blink of the eye. It was as if McNelly wondered at every moment what his life would have been if he had not contracted the tubercular disease that consumed him, and instead had the lungs of a normal man. Not that his accomplishments weren't notable, they were, especially for a man of his constitution, but still, the question was always there, though never spoken of by McNelly himself, or any of his men.

"Tell me about yourself, Wolfe," Steele said.

Josiah was not prepared for the question. He expected to be asked to recount the events that had led up to Pete Feders's death. "I'm a Ranger," he stuttered. "I hail from here in Austin."

"Relax, Wolfe. I promise you there is no hangman's noose waiting for you at the end of this day. I am aware of your service to the Rangers. I can read what is on your papers: the date you joined, the company you were assigned to, what you are paid. But it says nothing of the man I am about to pass judgment on. I must consider whether you're a man of your word, or a troublemaker, an outlaw hiding behind the law who deserves a trial, a murder charge—to be thrown to the wolves waiting outside—not set free because you were just doing your duty and protecting your own life and the citizens of Texas. You may never have another chance like this again, Wolfe. Now, tell me about yourself, but do not, I warn you, lie to me, or embellish your tale, or I will snatch that chance away from you as quickly as it was offered, and your life will never be the same again. Am I clear?"

"Yes, sir, you are." Josiah tried to relax, tried to regulate his own breathing and slow his racing heart down. "I'm new to the city," he said in an even tone as he quickly calmed himself down, comforted, in a way, by Steele's directness. "I grew up outside of Tyler in a tiny town called Seerville. The railroad came in too far away, and the town's pretty much died out now."

"And that's why you've moved to Austin?" Steele asked.

Jones looked completely bored. He kept checking his watch and glaring out of the corner of his eye at Steele.

"No, sir," Josiah said. "After I came back from the war, I took up being the marshal of Seerville. My folks were still alive, and I helped out on the farm as much as I could, too. It was a small farm, a couple head of cattle, a few goats, chickens, and a plot for corn and a decent-sized garden. It was a simple life that we had, and it was a comfortable place to return to after all that I saw in the East fighting with the First Brigade. There wasn't much to being a marshal, and it suited me pretty well, gave me a little income, since I was getting married and starting a family. I wanted nothing more than to put the War Between the States behind me, if you don't mind me saying so, sir."

Steele nodded. "We've all been trying to do just that for the last ten years, son."

Josiah forced a smile and continued, "One of my deputies, Charlie Langdon, and I fought together in the Brigade.

We were first in, last out. Charlie got a taste for blood and no rules, and I didn't see it until it was too late. He went bad on me, took off on a killing spree and robbing banks as much as he could, whenever he could. I thought he was my friend, but I was wrong. He was nobody's friend."

Major Jones scooted his chair back. "Really, General Steele, what does this have to do with a man killing his captain?"

"I asked Wolfe to tell me about himself, sir, or were you not listening?" The tone in Steele's voice was unmistakable, hard and cold. He came by his name honestly.

Jones ran his finger down the right side of his mustache. "I am late for an appointment."

"That is your problem, Major Jones. We are not done here yet. We are just starting. Go on, Wolfe, pay this man no mind."

Josiah moved to the edge of his seat. Instinct told him to prepare for a fight of some kind, coming from Jones's way. He drew in a deep breath. "About that time, after there was no need for a marshal in Seerville any longer, I began to ride with Captain Hiram Fikes, irregularly, as a Ranger. It was a much looser organization then, sir, as you well know, with little money to pay us, so men came and went, but Pete Feders was always there, riding alongside Captain Fikes. They seemed an odd team, the captain almost ignoring Feders at every move, but Pete never gave up trying to impress the captain, trying to get in his good graces. It always struck me as strange, but I didn't question his motives too much back then. Just noticed. I came to trust Pete. I thought he was a good man to have your back. I was never ambitious, didn't ever want to be a captain, so I wasn't a threat to him, I suppose. That came later, though even when the threat did come, I didn't understand it."

Steele nodded, listening intently. "So you have known Peter Feders for a long time?"

"Yes, sir, before the reign of the State Police, and since the creation of the Frontier Battalion."

"So, you rode with Fikes when he commanded a troop of State Police for the previous governor, as well?" Steele asked.

"Infrequently," Josiah answered. "I had three daughters by then, and my folks had died. I was trying to make a go of the farm. I was never much good at being a farmer, but my wife, Lily, loved that life, and she was none too fond of me being away for long stretches at a time."

"Then how is it you ride with the Rangers now?"

"My wife died, sir. The fevers took my three girls first. One after another. Slow. With the death of each one, I didn't think the pain could be any worse. But I was wrong. After my last girl died, Lily became pregnant again. We were infused with hope, thought that maybe we'd turned a corner, been given a second chance. If you believe in such things. But Lily died in childbirth. That was the worst of the pain, and I nearly went mad. The midwife and I were able to save the baby, a boy, named Lyle. He lived—is still alive—and is the only reason I am here today, standing before you as sane a man as I can be, I believe."

Josiah's eyes had welled up with tears. He hadn't spoken of Lily's death in a very long time, and with all that had happened recently, his emotions were rawer than he realized. He missed his old life. It was just a faint memory now. He could barely hear Lily's voice in his mind. It was as if she had never existed in the first place.

Steele didn't say anything. He let Josiah's words fade away. Neither McNelly nor Jones seemed moved, or had changed his expression. Jones remained impatient, and McNelly remained uncommitted, void of any readable emotion. Both men were being forced to stay where they were, and judgment, for once, was not theirs to dole out.

Josiah wondered what their roles really were, why they

were there at all, as he tried to regain his breath and force himself back into the reality of the moment.

Shouts could be heard outside, "Murderer! Murderer! Hang him! Hang him!" But no one acknowledged the mob, least of all Josiah. He had never been so uncomfortable in his life as the shouts became louder and the crowd swelled out into the street.

"I apologize that there are no curtains on the window. All privacy is lost to us these days," Steele said.

"If I may beg your pardon, sir," Major Jones said, scooting forward in his chair, preparing to stand.

Steele cut him off before he could say another word. "No, sir, you may not. I intend to hear this man out. The world outside of this room would string him up without one iota of a chance to explain himself. I have seen it done. We all have. The newspapers have already convicted him and are out for blood. Now, sit there, Major Jones, and give this man his due. He rode with you in the Lost Valley fight, did he not?"

"Yes, he did," Jones said coldly.

"And did he not conduct himself with bravery and valor when you commanded your troops into that valley and were trapped by the Kiowa?"

Josiah remained quiet, but the conversation had garnered McNelly's attention. He leaned down and watched Jones very closely, restraining himself. Lost Valley was Jones's first Indian encounter as the commander of the Frontier Battalion, and it had gone poorly, left a Ranger dead, mutilated, and several others wounded—even though Jones boasted that it was a victory.

In many ways it *was* a public relations victory for the new Rangers, and they had needed that very much, at the time. Josiah had escaped with a knife wound, and the pain refused to go away, even now, months later. Jones escaped with his reputation intact, and the Kiowa, most notably Lone

Wolf, left on the run. The *Austin Statesman* had been kind in its depiction of the encounter, painting all of the Rangers as heroes. Now a fall from grace was much more interesting.

"Of course," Jones said to Steele. "We are not here to rehash my decisions that occurred in the past. We are here to discuss why Ranger Wolfe killed Captain Peter Feders."

"Very well," Steele said. "Ranger Wolfe, please tell us what happened after you suffered the loss of your family."

Jones crossed his arms heavily, rolled his eyes, and slammed his shoulders against the back of the chair.

"I was left to raise my son, alone, after I buried Lily," Josiah said. "After a couple of years of struggling, with the help of a midwife and wet nurse, I got word from Captain Fikes that he'd captured Charlie Langdon in San Antonio, and he offered me the chance to come down and escort Charlie to trial. And, if I was so inclined, the Frontier Battalion was forming, and the captain wanted me to ride with him again. He wanted me to be a fully employed Texas Ranger. He was offering me a new life, for which I will always be grateful."

"And you said yes, of course," Steele said.

"It was either that or die a very young man. I had lost my way, and Fikes knew it. He was more than a captain. He was a friend. When he was killed, it was my honor to escort his body home to Austin."

McNelly finally interjected. "This is when Feders took over as captain?"

"Not officially, at that point," Josiah answered, turning his attention to the captain. "But, yes, he was in charge. We made plans with Major Jones to capture Langdon, who had escaped after the captain was killed. He had gone back to Seerville and was holding my son hostage. Pete rode in at the end, and Ranger Elliot took the shot that put an end to the situation. Langdon eventually faced trial and was hanged, and I thought the bitterness of the past was behind me. I moved away from the farm, hoping city life in Austin wouldn't be so isolated for my boy when I was away."

"And you claim that's when the trouble with Feders started?"

Josiah nodded. "Pete told me, himself, that he stepped into the vacuum left by Langdon, protecting the gang and its chief operator, Liam O'Reilly. Pete directed the company of Rangers away from the crimes O'Reilly, eventually known to the world as the Badger, committed. It was a smart cover for Pete. I thought Liam O'Reilly was the worst outlaw on the loose, set on taking his place as one of Texas's most notorious, but I was mistaken once again. O'Reilly was only the brawn. Pete was the brain of the outfit."

"That's a tall accusation, Wolfe," McNelly said. "Accusing a captain of the Texas Rangers of being a traitor. A murderer, no less, especially when he is not alive to defend himself. You killed the man you're accusing, Wolfe, don't you think that's suspect?"

"I shot him straight on because I had no other choice."

Steele had settled back to let McNelly join the interrogation.

"It's only your word, Ranger, and I'm not convinced enough of the caliber of your character to know that you're telling me the truth," McNelly said.

"Ranger Elliot can back up my claim, Captain McNelly," Josiah said. "He heard Pete admit to it, too. I would also suggest that there's a bank account somewhere close in Pete Feders's name that contains a large sum of money. Money that came from the bank robbery in Comanche, along with others. That account will have more money than a captain of the Rangers would be able to accumulate on a simple salary that the man has carried over the years."

"Have no fear, we will look into all of Captain Feders's affairs. We will also be speaking to Ranger Elliot as soon as this meeting with you is concluded," Steele said.

Jones jumped into the fray next. "This makes no sense,

Wolfe. Why on earth would Peter Feders join up with an outlaw gang when he had achieved one of the highest, most honorable positions that a man of his stature could hope for? He was a Texas Ranger captain. The respect of the rank in itself was of a great value."

Josiah drew in a deep breath. "It was not enough, as you well know, Major Jones, for Pete. The prize Pete Feders was after was a grand gem. It is very expensive to even be in her presence. It is Pearl Fikes I speak of. Rank and position seem of little value to her."

"Ah, a fine beauty, that woman," Jones said.

"Exactly," Josiah said. "A beauty that rebuffed Pete's advances more than once."

"I, myself, have felt that sting," Jones admitted out loud.

"I may be speaking out of turn," Josiah said. "But, my life is at stake here. After the death of Captain Fikes, the financial status of his wife, the Widow Fikes, changed dramatically. I don't know the particulars, it may well be a result of poor investments, like many people suffered in the Panic of '73, but her need for money is said to be great. Very simply, Pete Feders was accumulating money and connections to be able to buy Pearl's presence and love from her mother. Robbing banks and rustling cattle was the quickest, easiest way for that to occur. Pete was running out of time, and he knew it."

"Why is that?" Steele asked.

"Because Pearl was becoming defiant. She rebuffed him publicly, embarrassing him and her mother. The papers carried it. You know of it."

"Why did that happen, Wolfe?" Major Jones asked in a tone that suggested that he knew the answer to his own question.

"Because Pearl didn't love Pete Feders, and she swore she would never let him touch her, regardless of her mother's intentions to marry her off. I don't know if she is aware of her mother's dire straits, her need to save the estate with the money Pete professed to possess and willingly infuse into her bank account."

"And that's the only reason?" Jones pushed forward, and stood up. "There was no other reason?" he demanded.

"I believe I am that other reason, Major Jones. Pearl Fikes has made no secret of her feelings for me."

"So, let me get this straight," Steele said. "You were a hundred miles from nowhere, and it was Pete Feders, you, and Ranger Elliot, and you, sir, have a motive yourself to kill Pete Feders, to get him out of your way . . . and Feders ends up dead? Can you see the problem we have here, Wolfe?"

The intensity of Steele's question and his change from friendly to angry took Josiah aback.

"Yes, sir, I can. But I promise you, I only fired my weapon when I feared for my own life, for Elliot's life."

William Steele stood up, joining Jones. McNelly remained seated, his attention solely focused on Josiah.

"That'll be all, Wolfe. I would suggest you wait until the crowd has dispersed before you leave. We will be in touch," Steele said, gathering up the papers in front of him. "Oh, one other thing, do not leave town under any circumstances. If you run, I will be under the assumption that you have lied to us all, that you are guilty, and I will have you hunted down like an animal. Is that clear?"

CHAPTER 4

———◆◆◆———

Fellow Ranger Scrap Elliot was standing in the hall, waiting to go in next to face the trio of men. Scrap was the only witness to the killing of Pete Feders, and Josiah had expected all along that they both would be called in to account for the incident.

"Wolfe." Scrap nodded sheepishly. "How'd it go in there?"

Josiah stopped, a slight smile crossing his face. Scrap, too, had dressed in his finest clothes: black pants, a white shirt similar to Steele's, in serious need of the touch of an iron, and a dark brown jacket that rode up his wrists about two inches.

"What are you smilin' at? These are the best britches I got since I spend most of my time on the trail. No need for nothin' fancy as far as I'm concerned," Scrap said.

"I appreciate the effort, Elliot, I'm not laughing at you."

"Oh." Scrap flashed a smile back, then let it fade away quickly. He was slightly shorter than Josiah, with a head full of solid black hair and eyes that never stopped searching. From a distance, Elliot could look bony, but his muscles were tight, and he was rangy, a quick-handed fighter, too, which was where his nickname most likely originated. He and Josiah had never discussed the origin of the name. Josiah thought it was fitting and had just accepted Scrap as being Scrap.

From the time Josiah joined up with the Frontier Battalion, it seemed as if the two of them were being paired together. Never by choice, but always by duty or fate. It was an unlikely partnership.

Scrap, whose real name was Robert Earl Elliot, was young—hardly twenty years old—impetuous, immature, and one of the best rifle shots Josiah had ever come across. The boy was a damn fine horseman, too.

Scrap's parents were killed in a Comanche raid when the boy was young. He and his younger sister, Myra Lynn, had survived the attack. Myra Lynn had joined a convent in Dallas and lived as an Ursuline nun. Scrap fueled his anger with the hope of becoming an Indian hunter with the Rangers. That same anger almost got Josiah killed in Lost Valley a few months back, when the Rangers had their first violent encounter with a band of Comanche and Kiowa—the same conflict Jones led and spoke of during the interrogation.

Trust and understanding were hard enough for Josiah to endow a stranger with—but especially a boy who had put Josiah's life at risk. He would carry the Lost Valley scar for the rest of his life. Still, Scrap had earned a bit of the treasure of friendship that Josiah doled out sparingly, and some respect, as well. But none of that meant that Josiah liked how Scrap acted sometimes, or agreed with the things that came unbidden out of the boy's mouth.

Josiah could barely hide the nervousness he felt, knowing Scrap was going to face a kind of pressure from the three men inside the small room like he'd never faced before.

"What you want me to tell them, Wolfe?"

"Just the truth, Elliot. You do that, and everything will turn out all right."

The door opened, and Captain McNelly glared at Josiah. "Ranger Elliot, we're ready for you."

Josiah nodded at Scrap, telling him silently to go on.

Scrap walked inside the room, pushing past McNelly as gently as he could.

"Remember what Steele said, Wolfe, don't plan on going anywhere until we've made our decision."

"I'll be waiting at my home, Captain, you can count on that," Josiah said, turning to walk down the long, empty hall, feeling more alone than he'd felt in a long time.

There was no easy way out of the building.

Josiah could barely stand the idea of sneaking around like an outlaw, but he'd seen, firsthand, the viciousness and rage that a group of vigilantes could impose on any man of their choosing.

When John Wesley Hardin killed a deputy, Charlie Webb, in Comanche, a gang had formed and dragged Hardin's kin, who'd been put in the jail for safekeeping, out into the dark night and hung three of them unmercifully, their toes dangling near the ground, their death slow and painful. Hardin escaped unharmed, but the destruction he left behind still haunted the town to this day.

Not that Josiah thought that he was in danger of being hanged, but the newspaper had been pretty hard on him. He was certain that the Widow Fikes was behind the stories, pushing for him to leave town, or be tried in a court of law for the killing of Pete Feders. She had promised to make Josiah's life miserable, promised that he would never see Pearl Fikes again, or be allowed on the Fikes' property. So far, the angry old woman had kept her promise.

The Widow Fikes had wanted nothing more than for Pete to marry Pearl and rescue her from the financial trouble that had befallen the estate. She blamed Josiah for her losses, her troubles, and the rift that now existed between her and her daughter.

It was difficult to take, knowing someone was out to destroy you. That was a position Josiah had never found himself in before. Hunted down, yes. The object of revenge, yes. But to experience the hate of a whole city, to be driven out of his own home, or at least to not feel comfortable, or welcome, well, that was a new experience, and not one that Josiah wanted to ever have again. He could become enraged if he let himself, but that would be a mistake, and he knew it. Losing control would result in terrible consequences, more than he was already standing in account for.

Josiah was certainly not going to walk out the front door and into the crowd of chanting demonstrators. It was hard telling what would happen if he did.

He made his way down the stairs to the back of the building.

There was no gun on his hip. There was no need to carry a weapon into the capitol building, or at least he hadn't thought so when he'd left the house.

The only weapon he carried now was a small knife in his boot, not that it would do him any good in the event of an attack.

The capitol building was quiet, with most people aware of what was happening. Still, once Josiah made it to the first floor, there were several people milling about in the hallway, waiting for something or someone to arrive.

One man he recognized right away was the reporter for the *Austin Statesman*, Paul Hoagland.

Hoagland, a short, mousy man, who wore a bowler, wire-frame glasses, and usually had an unlit cigar dangling from his pale lips, saw Josiah about the same time Josiah saw him.

"Wolfe!" Hoagland shouted, running toward him, drawing

a pad of paper from his hip pocket and grabbing a pencil from behind his ear at the same time. "Wait!"

Josiah picked up his pace, nearly breaking into a run. So far, he had been able to avoid meeting with the reporter face-to-face. But unless he could come up with a grand escape plan, it looked like his luck was about to run out.

Maybe, he thought, *it's time to face this nasty little man and make this all go away.*

Josiah planted his feet and spun around, coming to a sudden stop. "What?"

The look on the reporter's face was one of surprise, almost shock. He almost couldn't stop in time, almost ran straight into Josiah.

"I have a few questions for you," Hoagland said, taking the cigar out of his mouth, trying to catch his breath.

The man smelled of smoke and liquor, like he'd spent the better part of the day in the saloon across from the capitol building, which was probably the case.

"I've already answered all of the questions I'm going to, now why don't you leave me alone?"

Hoagland chuckled. "You're the big story, Ranger Wolfe. Until the next big story comes along, you might as well take some satisfaction from being the object of everybody's attention, if not their affection."

"I don't like that idea much," Josiah said, looking beyond the reporter as a crowd grew, coming into the building from outside.

Josiah felt a nervous twitch ride up his spine, and he regretted not carrying his gun.

A quick glance over his shoulder told him that the way out of the back of the building was still clear.

"Doesn't matter much what you want at this point, Wolfe. The people want their story, and they're making darn sure everyone on Congress Avenue hears those demands. This isn't going away anytime soon. You should have thought about that when you killed Captain Feders."

Josiah felt his anger rising. Hoagland was trying to provoke him. "I'm not answering your questions, sir."

"I won't give up."

"I'll tell you what, Hoagland. Let's wait and see what comes about after the meetings today, then you come to my house, and I'll sit down and talk with you. How's that?"

"An exclusive?"

"Call it what you want, but if I don't get out of here soon, you'll have your next big story. I'll be torn limb from limb."

"That sure would sell some newspapers, now, wouldn't it?"

The chants were growing louder, the crowd closer. Josiah could smell the anger in the air. It was like kerosene, ready to explode at any moment.

"Murderer! Killer!" was being repeated over and over again.

"I need to get out of here," Josiah said.

"I can have your word that you'll talk to me?"

Josiah nodded yes. "My word is all I have left."

"All right, then," Hoagland said. "I'd run if I were you."

CHAPTER 5

A shiny black coach sat waiting outside the back door of the capitol building. The polish gleamed in the midday sun, making it look like the fancy rig was downright glowing. Two horses, both solid black and impeccably cared for, stood in wait, while the driver, dressed professionally in black, too, began swinging his arms wildly upon seeing Josiah exit the Old Stone Capitol in haste.

"Come, Señor Wolfe, in here. Hurry, you have very little time. It is safe, I promise you."

Josiah recognized the driver immediately. It was Pedro, the manservant and general overseer of the Fikes estate.

The door to the coach popped open, but the window panels were pulled closed, so it was impossible to tell who was inside.

The last thing Josiah wanted to do was jump into the fire from the frying pan, boarding the coach that looked more suited for a funeral parade than an escape and coming face-to-face with the Widow Fikes. He'd had enough grilling for one day, and if he never saw that woman again, it would be too soon.

Noise from the crowd grew louder from inside the building. Josiah only had a second to decide whether to make a run for it, leading the angry mob to the only safe place he had left, his home, or trying to ditch them in the nearby Mexican section of Austin, "Little Mexico," with which he was more familiar than most Anglos—or trying his luck with the coach. Either was a risk, but in the end, with the screams growing louder, and the crowd drawing ever closer, Josiah chose to trust Pedro.

The manservant had showed him no ill intent in the past, but the allegiance the tall, well-groomed Mexican had to the Widow Fikes was unmistakable—he was loyal to her commands and whims more than to any other person without exception. Except for one: Pearl.

Pedro was even more loyal to the widow's daughter than to the widow, and it was that thought that prompted Josiah to jump inside the waiting coach.

He slammed the door behind him as he dove into an empty bench seat.

Darkness surrounded him as an unknown arm pulled the door closed and locked it tight.

Chants came from outside as the crowd burst from the building in fervent chase. Someone threw a rock at the coach, and another angry pursuer hit it with a hand, struggling to open the locked door.

"Murderer! Killer! Traitor! Hang! Hang! Hang!"

Before Josiah could scream at Pedro to get a move on, the coach lurched forward and began to pull away from the crowd.

Still lost in darkness, Josiah could not see what was happening outside of the coach, if they were surrounded or being chased. Nor could he see who was sitting across from him, but he had a hint; the smell of spring filled his nose. It was a familiar fragrance, one that he immediately recognized and associated with Pearl and not her mother.

The coach was at full speed now, the inside still jarring and shaking as Pedro cut and turned every which way he could, obviously trying to escape the mob without causing any harm to anyone inside or outside, as he tried to shake the pursuers off his trail.

"Josiah." It was a whisper in the dark. It *was* Pearl. "I'm sorry, Josiah."

A shift of weight, then a rustle of clothes met Josiah ears, and he suddenly felt Pearl against him, burrowing her face into his chest.

His eyes were adjusting now, and the side panels cracked and pulled as the coach sped away, teetering at the turns, allowing bits of harsh sunlight inside the close quarters. Thankfully, Pearl was alone.

He was relieved to see her, but having her next to him, being alone with her, under no scrutiny at all, made him extremely uncomfortable—and happy at the same time.

Josiah tried to pull away, but there was nowhere to go, no escaping Pearl's embrace. He felt his chest grow moist and realized that Pearl was sobbing into it. Her tears were warm and heavy. Crying women were a mystery to him.

The loudness of the crowd had dissipated, but the ride in the coach was still thunderous and noisy.

"I thought I would never see you again," Pearl said, raising her face to Josiah's.

Even tearstained and full of emotion, there was no mistaking the striking beauty of the face of the woman Josiah found himself in the company of. He had to restrain every muscle in his body not to kiss her deeply.

Pearl Fikes had long blond hair that looked like it came straight out of a fairy tale and could have been spun into gold. Her eyes, when not full of tears, were a soft blue and were gentle, loving, and kind—unless she was cross; then there was no mistaking that Pearl was the daughter of

Captain Hiram Fikes, unyielding to fools and idiots, with a stubborn streak a mile long.

Josiah was glad to be near Pearl, regardless of the scrutiny, glad to take in the fragrance of her skin, to touch her, to hold her.

From the first moment he had seen her—standing on the balcony of the grand house on the estate in the falling evening light—Josiah was certain she was the most beautiful woman he had ever seen. Guilt, of course, had taken over his heart, because his love for Lily still lived deep in his soul. He had tried to ignore Pearl, tried to deny the attraction he felt for her . . . but he could not resist. Not when she obviously felt the same way about him.

"How did you know that I had a meeting in the capitol?" Josiah asked.

Pedro had slowed the coach, and Josiah pulled away from Pearl slightly, freeing his arm so he could peek outside. They were north of downtown Austin. It looked like they had outrun the mob.

"I know far more about what's been going on than you think I do, Josiah Wolfe."

Josiah opened the blind halfway, wishing he had a gun with him. "I don't need a rescuer."

"Obviously you do." The sunlight beamed off Pearl's wet face. She straightened herself up and produced a delicate lace handkerchief out of nowhere and began to dab her face dry. "What was your plan? Just to run as fast you could?"

"I was going to lead them into Little Mexico, a place very few Anglos go, even in the light of day."

"But you know your way around there?"

"Thanks to Juan Carlos, I do."

"Well, I suppose that was a good enough plan."

"I wasn't expecting a crowd."

"I'm sure you weren't," Pearl said, tucking the handkerchief away in the folds of her dress. It was not black like everything else Josiah was surrounded by. Her dress was off-white, perfect in every way, and looked like it had come straight off the shelf in Hadley's Lady's Shoppe, a fine and expensive store on Congress Avenue.

Josiah exhaled deeply and focused on Pearl's face. The last time he had seen her was after he returned from near Laredo, after he faced Pete Feders and pulled the trigger. Her mother was furious, but Pearl had made it clear that she was not distraught by the news, that she saw it as their chance to be together. Josiah wasn't so sure then that they could ever have a life together. He was even less sure now.

"Where is Pedro taking us?" Josiah asked.

"A spot on the river where we can be alone and talk."

Josiah settled back into the corner of the seat, as far away from Pearl as was physically possible. "You think that's a good idea?"

"You shouldn't let my mother scare you."

"Have you read the papers lately?"

"Every word. You think my mother is behind the headlines?"

"I have reason to believe she is, yes," Josiah said.

Pearl nodded, glanced out of the open window quickly, then turned back to Josiah. Her face was less than serene, but not angry, perhaps annoyed. "I cannot dispute the fact that Mother may be feeding the flames, but even without any intervention or prodding on her part, the papers would be making this a bigger story than it really is."

"And you think it's a good thing to be seen with me?"

"I couldn't go another minute without seeing you." Tears welled up quickly in Pearl's soft blue eyes.

"How can I court you properly with all of this happening? With your mother banishing me from your property forever? I just think we need time, Pearl. Let things quiet down a little bit. At least wait and see what General Steele and the others decide about my fate. If there is a trial, then all of this will just get worse. And where's that going to leave us?"

"I'll stand by your side proudly."

"I know you will, but I think that would just make things worse for you. So far, the papers have been kind to you, painting me as an interloper, a specter of greed, only after your inheritance. That's why I suspect that your mother is pulling some strings. Otherwise, we would be flayed together as conspirators in Pete's death."

Pearl drew in a breath, exhaled softly, and looked upward for a long second. "Mother has very few strings left to pull, Josiah. You are more than aware of that. I don't know how much longer she will be able to keep up the charade of wealth. The bankers visited yesterday. My life is about to change in a way I'm not sure I understand, Josiah, and you are the steadiest, most trusted person I have to count on. I know you didn't kill Peter to get him out of the way. You had no choice."

It was not exactly a question, but the look on Pearl's face seemed to demand an answer. Josiah let the words linger, did not respond right away. There would always be a moment to consider whether or not Josiah had any other choice than to shoot first—but there was no way Pete Feders was going to be taken in to face the crimes he'd committed, not without a fight. The choice of his life, or Pete's life, or Scrap's life, would have come quickly if Josiah had let the shot go. He might be dead now himself. There was no way to know. He only knew he couldn't live with the regret for the rest of his life, like he was at the moment.

"I had no choice, Pearl," he finally said. "I didn't want to kill Pete Feders."

"I know you didn't. I know your heart. I felt it beating against my very own."

"As much as I would love to spend every second from

now until eternity alone with you along the river, I think we need to have Pedro take me home."

"I need you," Pearl whispered.

Josiah stiffened. "When the time is right."

"What if that time never comes?"

"Then we'll just have to treasure what time we've had together."

CHAPTER 6

—◆━▸◀◆◀◆◀—

Night came earlier as the winter season drew nearer and nearer. If a norther blew south from the plains, then the temperatures could drop to the high twenties at night. But that was rare, just like the sight of ice or snow in the state capital. Josiah had only seen snow once or twice in Texas in his life, and those were just flakes spitting from the sky and melting before they hit the ground. Snow was more common in his memories of when he was away at war, but he tried to forget those times.

Most of the time, the breezes in winter blew up from the ocean in the south, keeping the afternoons nice and comfortable. The winter season was short, generally two months, and then spring colored the land with hope and opportunity. That season seemed pretty far off, out of reach. All of the hope had been drained from Josiah's will. He was just plumb wore out, so tired he was almost staggering.

As it was now, a norther *was* blowing straight down on Austin, dropping the temperatures to their lowest depths in recent memory. Once the sun dropped below the horizon, it was like everything that held any hint of warmth in the world had vanished.

Josiah had left Pearl and the coach about a mile from his house and walked home, staying in the shadows as much as possible.

He hugged his arms tight to his chest to stay as warm as he could and was glad to see a thin snake of smoke rising from the chimney of his house as it came into sight.

He breathed a sigh of relief, glad to be within a block of home.

It was still a struggle for Josiah to consider the city anything other than the place he lived, the place where he slept when he was riding with the Rangers. But Lyle waited inside the tiny house, and that made the city, and the house, as much the idea of a home as was possible for Josiah. Wherever his son was, then Josiah considered that place home. Period. He wasn't permanently attached to his first home place, Seerville or Tyler, by any means. Not anymore.

Walking slowly, Josiah could not get Pearl out of his mind. There was no question that he was attracted to her, longed to touch her, hold her, and found himself lucky to be in her presence. He felt even luckier that she acknowledged him, felt something for him in return, wanted him physically, too.

The worlds Pearl and Lily walked in were a million miles apart, and somehow, if Josiah was going to court Pearl, he needed to figure out how to bridge those miles. He had little money, little prospect for fame or wealth, and even less desire for a house as big and overwhelming as the place Pearl called home.

Josiah could never see himself as a gentleman, a politician, or a man of means. He couldn't see himself as anything other than a Texas Ranger, and now even that vision of himself was in extreme jeopardy. It took all he had just to provide for Lyle and Ofelia.

How then, he wondered, almost out loud, *is a man like me supposed to show a woman like Pearl Fikes his love*?

The thought stopped Josiah in his tracks about a half a block from his house.

A gust of wind whipped around his face, stinging his eyes, forcing them to tear up. He wasn't sure whether it was the weather, the cold slapping his bare eyes, or his heart that was causing the tears. He tried with all of his might to make them vanish immediately.

Did he really love Pearl? Truly? Madly? Like he had Lily? And what did that say of his love for his dead wife? Was that love over, gone, or lesser somehow? Was it ever real in the first place, if it could be replaced?

The questions were immense and not ones that Josiah liked to consider—ever—but the ruminations would not go away, would not leave his thoughts. It was as if they were caged like some vicious animal, unable to break free.

Life had gone on after the death of his family. Life with only Lyle, a little boy being raised by a wet nurse who loved him more than her own life, but a boy just the same, who deserved the same kind of family as other normal children. One with a mother, a father, brothers and sisters.

Josiah's mouth went dry at the consideration of more children to feed, clothe, and care for.

Did Pearl want a family? Was he rushing things to even consider such a thing? Pearl had led him to believe she wanted a future with him. Only him. How could he not let his mind focus in on those places and embrace the idea, the realities, or be frightened, scared to death of losing everything again? That is what life had shown him more than once: Love something and lose it. That's the way it is. Why should it be any different now with Pearl, especially when he was on the very edge of losing his livelihood?

Pearl was the only woman Josiah had allowed himself to feel anything for since burying Lily almost three years ago.

He had had a brief tryst with a woman, Fat Susie, nearly a year ago, but she was dead now, killed by her brother. That relationship could have never worked anyway, since Fat Susie ran a whorehouse. And then there was Billie Webb, a girl who'd helped him escape Liam O'Reilly's grasp not so long ago, but Josiah just wasn't sure how he felt about her. She seemed to want more than he could give. Besides, Pearl was always on his mind.

It was all crazy thinking, as far as Josiah was concerned. Regardless of what had happened and what was going to happen, courting Pearl was going to be difficult, if not nearly impossible. Especially when he considered the changes that might occur if the Widow Fikes lost her estate. What would happen then? It was hard to say, hard to even fathom, and not something Josiah felt any responsibility for, even though Pete Feders had.

Certain that he couldn't solve any of the problems bouncing around inside his head, Josiah pushed forward toward home, toward the warmth of the house he'd found some comfort in anyway.

It wasn't until he was two houses away that Josiah saw someone standing on his porch.

He thought about stopping, about turning the other way, but he didn't know if the person meant him or his family any harm, since he couldn't tell outright who the person was.

The only weapon Josiah carried was the knife in his boot, and that was just going to have to be enough if it was someone who had come to look for trouble. He'd had enough of fear and mobs for one day, and it wouldn't surprise him if somebody like that damned reporter was waiting for him, or a madman set on his revenge for the killing of a Ranger. It was not that hard to imagine, considering the viciousness of the crowd outside the state capitol earlier in the day.

He kept walking, and it only took Josiah a minute to

realize that the person waiting on the porch was Scrap Elliot, his head hung low, pacing back and forth like he had done something wrong. Josiah exhaled heavily, relieved there was no threat, if only for a second or two.

"Damn, am I glad to see you," Scrap said as Josiah walked up to the porch.

"What are you doing here?"

"Waitin' for you. What the Sam Hill does it look like I'm doin', sittin' here whittling away the time?"

Josiah could smell tobacco smoke as he stopped a few feet in front of Scrap, and he thought he could smell the hint of a beer, too. Scrap was not a big drinker, but he'd been known to spend a little time in some saloons, just like a lot of boys his age.

There was a soft light on in the house, and Josiah was certain that Ofelia was still up and about, just as he was sure that Lyle was asleep for the night. He motioned for Scrap to step off the porch and walk out to the street so their voices wouldn't disturb anybody. The last thing Scrap would think about on a good day was waking a sleeping child.

"What did you do?" Josiah asked.

"I didn't do nothin', I just got a bad feelin', that's all."

"About what?"

"What the hell do you think it's about, Wolfe? You shootin' Feders. Those three stuffed shirts grilled me pretty hard."

"I figured they would. As long as you told them the truth, then there's nothing to worry about. Now, go back to the boardinghouse you're staying at, get a good night's sleep, and maybe we'll find out tomorrow what's going to happen."

"I told them I thought you did the right thing," Scrap said, the words almost tripping out of his mouth.

"That ought to be good enough," Josiah said, eyeing Scrap warily.

"I couldn't be sure, Wolfe, don't you see. I told them I couldn't be sure that Captain Feders was goin' for his gun when you shot him, though. But with him bein' with O'Reilly, and the lighting in the dark sky, and all, well, I just couldn't be sure."

Josiah nodded. "It's all right, Scrap. Really. I've questioned that moment a million times over. If they've got reason to cast doubt on the right or wrong of my actions, then maybe it is best that I face a trial."

"You can't mean that," Scrap said.

"You saw that crowd outside the capitol today. This thing isn't going away anytime soon."

"You're no killer, Wolfe."

"I killed my first man when I was younger than you, Elliot. Pete Feders was not my first, you know that."

"You was in the war. You had no choice."

"I didn't. But I also had to learn how to live with killing a man over the years. It's not easy. Wasn't then, and sure isn't now, either."

"I don't like what you're sayin'."

"Maybe I'm not that much different from John Wesley Hardin, Liam O'Reilly, or Charlie Langdon. Maybe I can pull the trigger and walk away like I just killed a skunk and not think a thing about it. Maybe I meant to kill Pete Feders all along."

"That's crazy talk."

"Just a bit of my thinking coming off of the tip of my tongue, Elliot. I can't control what happens. I had a choice not to kill Pete. I could have wounded him and let him stand for his crimes. Now I have to stand for mine, whatever they are, in the eyes of the law."

"You aim a gun at a man, you best use it to kill. That's the first rule every shooter learns."

"True enough. Now, you go on, get back to the boardinghouse. No matter what you did or said, I know it was your own version of the truth. We're right as rain. No need

to worry none about me holding a grudge however things
turn out, you hear?"

Scrap nodded, then turned and started to walk away,
but stopped before he got a few steps. "I'm damn sorry,
Wolfe, I sure am," he said, then broke into a slow trot and
disappeared quickly down the dark street.

CHAPTER 7

———◆◆◆◆———

Ofelia sat in a rocking chair just inside the door. She wore a long brown skirt and a plain white blouse that bore a few stains on it, obviously from the day's work. Her skin was dark brown, and her face was starting to bear happy wrinkles. She was squat, nearly as wide as she was tall, with a few gray streaks beginning to show prominently in her thick black hair that was bound in a woven braid so it looked like a small wheel on the back of her head.

"I am glad to see you, señor. Señor Scrap was pacing back and forth on the porch for hours. I invited him in, but he would not hear of it," Ofelia said, standing up. Lyle was nowhere to be seen, obviously in bed just like Josiah had assumed.

"Did you offer him any food? That usually works to get him from one place to another."

Josiah stood in the center of the small living area, with the kitchen just adjacent. A pot of *menudo* sat atop the cooling stove. The smell of the spicy stew filled the house, but Josiah barely noticed it since his nose was accustomed to Ofelia's cooking.

"Señor Scrap said he didn't want to eat no damn Mexican food."

"I'm sorry, Ofelia, that's just how Scrap is."

"I know, señor. I just smiled at him and said, '*Usted no podia saber comida buena si dio una palmada en la cara*.'"

Josiah shrugged.

"I told him he wouldn't know good food if it slapped him in the face, but I didn't explain it to him. He just twisted up his lip and stalked off like a mad donkey and started pacing on the porch."

Josiah laughed out loud, surprising himself. Ofelia laughed, too, watching Josiah's every move. There was no question that she was concerned about him but was obviously glad to see he could still laugh.

After the brief laugh, Josiah walked over to the stove, opened the pot, and took a big whiff of the stew. "I've really made a mess of things, Ofelia," he said.

Now it was Ofelia's turn to shrug. "You'll work this out, señor. You always do."

"I'm not so sure this time."

Josiah's stomach roared to life, reminding him that he hadn't eaten since early in the day. He grabbed his bowl that sat on the counter next to the stove, ladled out a generous helping of the *menudo,* and sat down to eat.

"Lyle is okay?" Josiah asked in between bites.

Ofelia was busying herself stowing away the day's dishes in a small cupboard that sat next to the stool she usually occupied when she watched after Lyle. Most days it was as if Ofelia lived in the small house, too, but she didn't sleep there, choosing instead to sleep at a small place of her own in Little Mexico, not too far away. She appeared before the sun came up and did not leave until Josiah came home and was in for the night. When Josiah was on the trail with the Rangers, she stayed in the house and often took Lyle to Little Mexico with her, which explained why, at three years old, the boy could speak and understand Mexican far better than Josiah could.

Scrap gave Josiah a hard time about the upbringing the boy was receiving, but Josiah ignored him. Mostly. Maybe not so much lately, as he considered the long-term effects of his absences on Lyle. There was no question it would be better for the boy if Josiah had a job in Austin that didn't require him to be away for long stretches at a time—as a tailor, or a blacksmith, a trade that involved less danger than being a Ranger. But that was not the life that Josiah had been born into, nor was it the life he had chosen. A Peacemaker on his side, a Winchester in his hand, on the back of Clipper, making a difference in the world, whether it was hunting down outlaws or facing down Comanche, was the only life that Josiah knew—or wanted, as far as that went. But want and need were two different things. Especially when there was a child to consider.

The time was drawing near when Josiah knew he would have to make a decision about his life: whether it was time to court another woman again—or not. But, with his own freedom, and future, up in the air, that was a hard decision to make. He didn't like it, but his fate was in the hands of three men, who, rightly or not, had to consider their own futures, political and otherwise, when they considered whether Josiah should stand trial for the killing of Pete Feders, or had just been doing what was right and necessary.

"*Sí*, señor. Lyle is fine," Ofelia said, drawing Josiah back to the question he'd asked about his son's welfare.

"Good." Josiah shoveled the stew into his mouth as quickly as he could swallow.

"A lady came here today looking for you, señor."

Josiah stopped chewing. "A lady? Pearl Fikes?"

"No, no, señor. I have never met this lady. She had a *bebé pequeño*, um, a small baby, with her. She was very direct and said I should tell you right away that she was here. She said to tell you that Billie Webb had moved to Austin if you cared to know."

"Billie Webb," Josiah repeated, "you're sure?"

"*Sí,* señor, I am sure that is what the lady said. She said she is staying down the street from the St. Charles House, in Mary Morgan's boardinghouse, and had seen the newspaper with your name in it, about all of the troubles, and she was very concerned for you. If you need her to tell the *alguacil,* the sheriff, how you helped her in Comanche, she would be glad to, she said."

"Thanks, Ofelia. I'll try to get by and see her tomorrow."

"I got the feeling, señor, that she will be back if she doesn't see you soon."

"That would be Billie," Josiah said, pushing the half-eaten bowl of *menudo* to the other side of the table.

"I'll go home now, señor," Ofelia said.

Josiah nodded and watched as Ofelia went and checked on Lyle, then gathered up her belongings—a shawl, and a canvas bag that held her own plate and eating utensils among other things that Josiah had no idea about—then walked out the door without saying another word.

The morning train woke Josiah up. Even though the rails were a block away, the house shook, and the noise was like thunder rumbling up from the ground instead of clapping down angrily from the sky. It was chilly, but Josiah was sweating, his dreams too dark and too far away to grasp and hold on to. Something told him that he didn't want to remember them anyway—they were most likely nightmares, born in loss and pain, the future foreboding instead of happy and trouble-free.

The smell of fresh coffee hit his nose, and when he looked over to see the empty little bed that Lyle occupied in the small bedroom they shared, he jumped up, hopped into his pants, and hurried out to see where Lyle was.

The boy was sitting in the middle of the floor while Ofelia puttered around the kitchen, trying to be as quiet as she could.

Josiah stopped, letting his panic subside, glad to see Lyle, and Ofelia, too. She was as consistent as the rising sun and just as dependable. Guilt struck him upon seeing the two of them, then he pushed it away, assured by Ofelia's own admittance, more than once, that she was only there because she wanted to be.

Still, he didn't know how much longer he could expect the Mexican to be the sole woman in his life, responsible for raising Lyle and tending to Josiah when he was home.

"Papa!" Lyle said, running to Josiah, tackling him at the knees and hugging him tightly.

Josiah had never been the kind of man who was openly affectionate to his children, but he had grown to be more so with Lyle. After the loss of his three girls, and nearly losing Lyle himself to the despicable outlaw Charlie Langdon, Josiah had found the value of a hug to be far greater than he'd ever thought it would be.

He reached down and hoisted the boy upward, settling him comfortably on his hip. Lyle favored Lily, had her eyes and facial features, and some days it was like looking at a ghost, seeing a glimpse of the woman he'd loved so dearly. Other days, there was no question that Lyle was a Wolfe and then he reminded Josiah of his father with his stubbornness, or his mother with his gentleness.

All in all, the boy was a fine mix of everyone Josiah had ever loved, and that in itself was more than enough reason to treasure every moment they shared—and why every moment away was becoming harder and harder to take as the boy grew older, into his own person.

"How's my boy this fine morning?" Josiah asked. The

train had passed, and the rumbling had ceased, leaving the house calm and peaceful.

"*Bueno, Bueno*," Lyle said.

"Lyle, *hablan Inglés*," Ofelia ordered, her back turned to Josiah and Lyle.

Lyle sighed. "I like to speak Spanish, 'Felia."

"Not here, not to your papa, we have talked about this."

Josiah did not interfere. He had mixed emotions about Lyle speaking Spanish. On one hand, it would be a great benefit to the boy when he grew up.

There was no question that any Anglo who could speak both languages had an upper hand, wasn't cajoled or lied to by translators, or left to sign language. But there was also the need for Lyle to mix with Anglos as easily as he mixed with Mexicans. If he got too used to speaking Spanish, the boy could be an outcast when it was time for school.

Ofelia knew more than anybody that Josiah himself did not speak Spanish, and had never taken an inclination to learn, though they had never spoken about it.

"Okay," Lyle said. "I'm good, Papa. Happy to see you."

"That makes two of us," Josiah said, hugging Lyle a little closer and a little tighter than he had the day before. "That makes two of us."

CHAPTER 8

The cool air carried the smell of freshly cut lumber, but the sound of hammers was yet to be constant, like an invasion of angry woodpeckers in an unseen forest. It wouldn't be long though, before the carpenters and laborers began their daily work.

At almost every glance there was a building in Austin under construction. Some of the buildings neared completion and others were stalled due to the current financial collapse, but mostly there was still a sense of reasonable prosperity up and down Congress Avenue, thanks to the arrival of the Houston and Central Texas Railway three years earlier, in 1871, and the demand for cattle north, and then, ultimately, in the east.

Josiah had hoped the early morning would be easier to navigate, offer less chance that he would be recognized and accosted. It was a risk stepping out into the world when you were the lead story in the newspaper, but he didn't want Billie Webb to get caught up in the shenanigans of the day, pulled into his troubles, when she had plenty of her own.

Billie hailed from Comanche, a small town north of Austin. A few months back, John Wesley Hardin, the outlaw and gunfighter, had visited some kinfolk of his in Comanche and was celebrating his birthday at the local saloon when a deputy recognized him. The deputy was Billie Webb's husband, Charlie.

John Wesley Hardin killed Charlie Webb in cold blood. Shot him in the back and left town in a hurry, ran like the coward he was, as far as Josiah was concerned. Billie was left a widow, at nearly nine months pregnant, in a sorrowful spot in her life.

Josiah had met Billie purely by accident, taking refuge in her barn, running from two Indians who had captured him, intent on getting a bounty from Liam O'Reilly. The bounty was a ploy to get Josiah out of the way early, so Pete Feders and O'Reilly could carry out their bank robbing and cattle rustling plans.

Billie had put Josiah up after finding him hiding in her barn, and in the end, he helped deliver her baby, a healthy little girl, then he borrowed Charlie's clothes, gun, and horse, so he could take care of what needed to be done. It was from there that Josiah tracked O'Reilly and Feders and ended up in the mess he was in now.

The last time Josiah had seen Billie was when he returned Charlie's horse and gear. By that time, she had recuperated from the birth of her baby, and had hinted that she was interested in Josiah in more than a friendly way, which Josiah had ignored, then rebuffed, saying he was interested in a woman back in Austin. Which, was true, but when Billie asked Josiah if he loved this woman—Pearl, of course—he couldn't answer her. Still couldn't as far as that was concerned. When he left Comanche, he figured that was the end of his relationship with Billie.

It wasn't that Billie was not attractive. She was not classically beautiful, not like Josiah thought Pearl was, but Billie was pretty in an earthy sort of way, and she was younger

than both he and Pearl by about ten years. Billie already
had a hard edge to her, one that Josiah understood and recognized immediately.

Loss shatters some people, and they never figure out
how to put themselves back together. Billie looked to be
the kind that was ready to pick herself up and dust herself
off and get back to living life—though with some hesitation when it came to trusting people. That in itself made
Josiah curious as to why Billie Webb was in Austin and
why she had sought *him* out.

The offer to talk to the sheriff and serve as a character
witness would do little to help Josiah's situation, as it was.
He feared the newspaper would draw Billie into the story,
and that's the last place she needed to be. He intended to
thank her for her offer, then ask that she stay as far away
from him as possible until everything was settled.

Josiah passed by the Jacoby-Pope Building, a brand-new
structure that had gone up at the same time as the building
next door to it, the Hannig. The two buildings looked to be
from two different worlds. The Jacoby-Pope was a simple
building, just a regular storefront, stick-built from the ground
up to serve a simple purpose: sell dry goods and add another
mercantile to Congress Avenue. The Hannig Building, on the
other hand, was an architectural marvel, an expensive proposition with a facade carved intricately from Texas limestone
and fitted with ornate wood-framed doors and windows. It
smelled new, just walking by, the stain on the trim not completely dry.

The difference in the two buildings was a perfect re-
flection of the growth in Austin, one Josiah had a hard
time not noticing. All of the movement in the city was
new to him, and honestly, since he'd spent very little of
the time he had lived in Austin actually in Austin, he still
felt more like a visitor than a resident. Maybe, someday,
he would feel like an Austinite, but he didn't expect that
to happen anytime soon. He wasn't sure he wanted it to.

He hurried past the Hannig Building and pulled his wool Stetson down to cover half his face. There were law offices on the top floor of the building, and the last thing he wanted was to cause a spectacle there, meeting face–to-face with an attorney set on making a name for himself, or anywhere else as far as that went.

The morning was still young, the sun barely poking up over the horizon, but there were horses on the street, and a few people on the boardwalks heading from one place to another. Sometimes, Josiah wondered if there was ever a time when there wasn't somebody coming and going on the streets of Austin.

He hurried down East Sixth Street, not running, but walking as fast as he could. He could easily have been mistaken for a bank robber or a criminal of some other sort on the run if he picked up his pace, acting as nervous as he was. Still, he wanted this chore over with.

It didn't take long to come up on the St. Charles House. It was more of a building than a house, built to service the passengers from the railroad, three storeys tall with a flat roof, and a fine restaurant on the main floor. Josiah could never afford such an extravagance, but he knew Pearl had visited the restaurant often. She had raved about the salads, steaks, and fine dishes in a way he could never understand. Food was food to him. Beans and biscuits, on the trail, were more suitable to him than the fanciness of a real restaurant where you had to act formal and wonder what fork to use. Manners were just another gulf that existed between Josiah and Pearl.

Mary Morgan's boardinghouse was a block off Sixth Street, and for a brief moment, Josiah thought about turning around and going home.

He liked Billie Webb, was grateful to her, and maybe at another time, in another circumstance, he would have been attracted to her, thought about courting her in a proper way, if she was receptive to the idea. They had similar problems, raising their children on their own and losing their spouses in tragic ways. Both of them were alone. Billie more so than Josiah, as far as he knew.

The boardinghouse was two storeys, about ten years old, simple in structure, but painted recently, a fresh white with black trim. A little flower garden fronted the street, but all of the flowers were dead now, the bushes void of any leaves.

The smell of fresh baking bread emanated from the rear of the house, so instead of knocking at the front door and risking waking up any residents who were still sleeping, Josiah went to the back door that led into the kitchen. He didn't have to knock. A woman, surely the owner, Mary Morgan, met him at the door.

Josiah tilted his hat back, exposing his face.

"What do I owe the pleasure of a visitor this early in the morning?" Mary Morgan looked to be in her mid-fifties, with hair the color of a rising sun; red as red could be. Her skin was pale white, like a statue, and her eyes were emerald green, as shiny as the jewels they reminded Josiah of. She looked happy, curious, and demanding. "The house is full, you know, so if'n it's a room you're seekin', then you might check on down the street at the Riverts' house. They got more rooms than they know what to do with."

"I'm here to see one of your boarders, ma'am," Josiah said.

Mary Morgan wiped a bit of flour from her hands on the apron she wore. "And which one would that be?"

"Billie Webb, ma'am. A girl and a baby."

"I know, I know. What you want with them this early on in the day? You look familiar. Do I know you?"

Josiah lowered his head. "No, I don't think we've ever had the pleasure of meeting."

Mary Morgan squinted at Josiah, drew her head closer to him, but blocked the door solidly with her body, so he couldn't see beyond her. "I've seen you somewhere, now, but I can't place you. I sure do know I've seen that face of yours, though. You ain't been in trouble, have ya?"

Josiah hesitated. "Not with the law, ma'am." It was true. No charges had been filed against him for shooting Pete Feders, and he'd never been in enough trouble to have his likeness printed on a wanted poster.

"All right, then. You wait here and let me get Missy Webb. Nice girl, that one. She sure could use a man in her life."

"I'm a friend, ma'am."

Mary Morgan trailed off with heavy footsteps echoing behind her. Josiah sighed, relieved that she hadn't recognized his face from the newspaper. He began pacing back and forth behind the back door.

The smell of the day's bread baking was almost overwhelming. Nothing smelled better than that to Josiah. It reminded him of his mother, of his life on the little farm he grew up on, that now seemed so far away, so distant.

He didn't know why he was nervous, but he was. A few minutes must have passed with him going to the street, then back, trying to figure out what he was going to say to Billie. Finally, he felt a pair of eyes on the back of his neck, and he turned around and met Billie Webb's gaze.

She was standing in the doorway. Mary Morgan wasn't that far behind, making noise in the kitchen, loud enough to let Josiah know she was keeping an eye on him. He liked that, was glad somebody was looking out for Billie.

"Well, there you are," Billie said. She smiled, and for a brief moment she looked young and happy, dressed in a simple fresh white linen dress, her hair still damp, but combed out. Once the smile faded, the pain Billie carried was obvious. Her lips pursed together, and she looked hard as a rock as she waited for Josiah to come to her.

Josiah nodded. He didn't know whether to hug her,

shake her hand, or kiss her on the cheek. What they were to each other was confusing. "It's good to see you, Billie. A big surprise."

Billie shook her head. "You are the most foolish man I have ever met, Josiah Wolfe. Ain't you got a proper greetin' for me, or are you just gonna stand there like a silly schoolboy unsure of what to do with your hands?"

"Stand here, I 'spect," Josiah said.

"Suit yourself." Billie walked out the door, then padded in her bare feet straight to Josiah. She slipped her arms around his waist and hugged him close to her. She was nearly a head shorter than he was. The scent of cottonseed oil touched Josiah's nose, not the scent of spring, like Pearl. It wasn't an unpleasant fragrance, just different, not as expensive, not as flowery as Pearl's, but still feminine and just as attractive, if not more.

Josiah stood stiff, then pulled away when he felt the hug had lingered too long. "What're you doing here, Billie?"

"Well, that's a fine howdy-do to you, too, Josiah. I figured once you helped deliver the baby we weren't strangers no more."

"We're friends, Billie. I'm glad to know you."

Billie stood back from Josiah and looked him up and down. "This trouble's got you all wound up. You look ten years older than the last time I saw you, and that wasn't that long ago."

"I suppose it's taken a toll, Billie. But it's trouble you don't need to be involved in."

"You saved me, Josiah. I could have never delivered that baby on my own."

"You don't owe me anything. I was there because I was running. We've talked about this before."

Billie drew in a deep breath and exhaled. "That woman you care about makin' things any easier for you?"

Josiah shook his head no. "Let's not discuss that."

"You still haven't told her you love her yet, have you?"

The best thing Josiah thought he could do was ignore the question. "I want you to stay out of this, Billie. It won't matter to the sheriff, or anybody else, what you think of me."

"I moved here to be closer to you, Josiah. There ain't nothin' for me in Comanche no more. Just bad memories. I need a fresh start, and I figured this here place would be the best place to give it a shot. I know you, and it won't take me long to know other folks, too."

The air went out of Josiah's lungs. He didn't know what to say, so he turned and walked away from Billie.

"Come back. Josiah Wolfe, come back here right now. I didn't mean to scare you off. I need you, damn it. This city of Austin is bigger than I thought it was, and I'm not sure how to set one foot in front of the other."

Josiah couldn't stop. Once he reached the street, he broke into a flat-out run. This time, he willed himself not to look back. He never wanted to see Billie Webb again. He was afraid if he did, he'd scoop her up and take her home with him.

Then he'd really have problems—if he didn't already.

CHAPTER 9

There was a horse tied up in front of Josiah's house that he didn't recognize. It was a big gray gelding, the muscles hard and well formed, its coat shiny and un-marred, with big flecks of black in the mane. The empty saddle was black and glossy, shining in the bright, rising sun like it was brand-new.

The day had drawn nearer to noon, and the sky was bright and clear, free of clouds, a fragile blue that went on and on forever. On a better day, the weather would have suggested a bit of optimism and a mild winter, but it wasn't a better day, and it might as well have been dark and gloomy as far as Josiah was concerned.

He hadn't stopped running until he was a block from his house. His heart was racing, and he was covered with per-spiration, even though the morning air was cool, bordering on chilly. He hadn't cared what kind of attention he gained as he made his way home, all he wanted to do was get as far away from Mary Morgan's boardinghouse as possible.

Billie Webb's presence in Austin complicated things for

Josiah in a way he had never considered possible. Courting Pearl would have its tribulations, even if it was possible at the moment, but having Billie near made Josiah reconsider if he even had the desire to court Pearl.

In reality, he didn't know either woman very well at all— just enough to leave him feeling confused and lonely. If it wasn't for the fact that Lyle needed a mother figure, then, at the moment, the only female company Josiah would consider would be the kind he could pay for. At least he could leave all of the emotion in the bed, and not carry it with him everywhere he went.

Upon seeing the gelding, Josiah picked his pace up, panting, curious at what, and who, was waiting for him at the house now.

He half-expected it to be the reporter from the paper, Paul Hoagland, come to collect his exclusive. If that were the case, Josiah was prepared to shoo him off. The last thing he wanted to do was add to the story at the moment, even though having his own say about what happened with Pete Feders was tempting. Still, he felt it was better to wait and hear from Steele before spouting off about the Feders incident. Not that he would say anything derogatory, but in his present state, Josiah had little trust in his own heart and mind, or what would come out of his mouth.

Josiah stopped at the porch and gathered himself, then walked into the house without an ounce of hesitation.

He was surprised to find Captain Leander McNelly sitting at the small table in the kitchen, drinking a cup of coffee and having a discussion with Ofelia.

Lyle was sitting on Ofelia's lap. "Papa!" he shouted, then jumped to the floor and ran to Josiah, wrapping his arms around his legs. It was a common greeting.

"Hey there, son." Josiah patted the top of Lyle's head and eyed McNelly curiously.

The captain stood up. "That was a fine cup of coffee, ma'am."

"*Gracias, capitán*," Ofelia said, remaining seated at the table. A look of concern crossed her face when she took in the sight of Josiah, but she said nothing.

"I'm surprised to see you here, Captain McNelly." Josiah lifted Lyle up, hugged him, then set him down on his feet just as quickly as he had picked him up.

"We need to talk, Wolfe. Privately," McNelly said.

Josiah nodded, and motioned to the door that led out onto the porch. McNelly returned the nod and made his way outside.

"You stay here with Ofelia, Lyle."

"I want to go."

"No. You have to stay here."

Lyle frowned, and before Josiah could say another word, Ofelia was out of her chair, her hand grasping Lyle's. Josiah and Ofelia made eye contact, a silent thank-you passed between them, then Josiah headed outside to face McNelly and whatever news he brought.

Josiah closed the door behind him. "I take it you're not here on a social visit."

"Hardly, Wolfe. We all felt it was better I speak with you here rather than drag you back up to the capitol building and cause another uncomfortable mob scene."

"I appreciate that, Captain."

Josiah was numb on the inside. McNelly was hard to read. He was dressed similar to the day before—formal, in all black, with the exception of his heavily starched white shirt. As with all Rangers, there was not a uniform requirement for the captain, but every time Josiah had seen the man, he was dressed nearly the same. The fact that McNelly was standing on Josiah's porch was an unusual event in itself, one that on any other day would have been considered a rarity and an honor. Overall, McNelly was a hero to most Texans.

"We've made a decision, Wolfe," McNelly said, his voice even, without emotion.

Josiah drew in a deep breath and waited to hear his fate. It was like time had stopped. All of the noises of Austin, wide awake now and in full motion, were amplified. Hammers sounded like giant mallets hitting a thousand gongs. The morning train, sitting at the station, hissing and spewing steam, sounded like it was right next to Josiah's ear instead of a block away. Even Lyle's footsteps inside the house sounded heavy, like drumbeats.

There was no need to plead his case any further, he had done that yesterday. From what he knew of the trio, once a decision was made by any one of the men, then it might as well be etched in stone.

"We believe," McNelly continued, "that you acted well within your duty and had no choice but to shoot first. More investigation into the activities of Peter Feders has shown that he was connected to a bad strain, as you suggested, and his intentions and actions were beyond the law. He was an outlaw, Wolfe. There will be no trial for the killing."

Josiah's legs suddenly felt like jelly. He couldn't believe what he was hearing. He had been sure he would have to go to trial, that he was in the midst of losing everything that he had worked so hard to hold on to.

"I'm relieved and grateful, Captain McNelly. Thank you."

"You may not be so grateful once you hear the rest of what I have to say."

"Why's that?"

"Do you really think this will go away, Wolfe, because two Texas Rangers and the adjunct general decided you were well within your rights to kill Pete Feders?"

Josiah shrugged. The numbness had vanished, and it felt like a ton of bricks had been removed from his shoulders. "I don't know, sir. It seems to me . . ."

"You have made some serious enemies, Wolfe. You know that?"

Josiah nodded. "I have."

"The *Austin Statesman* being one of them."

"I suppose so. I think the Widow Fikes is behind that."

"There is no thinking about it, Wolfe. It is true. Our decision will enrage a certain segment of the population, and I fear you will not be allowed to return to your normal life as easily and quickly as you think."

"I can take care of myself and my family, sir."

"I'm not saying you can't. I just don't think you understand the severity of the situation you're in."

"Maybe I don't," Josiah said.

"I have a plan for you, Wolfe. A new assignment if you like. I'm returning to my ranch in Burton, resting over the winter after that trouble in Dewitt County. The company will be on furlough, and our time will be portrayed as another budget cut by Governor Coke. I think it's best if I retreat, pull myself out of the public eye. I think it would be wise for you to do the same thing. I think you need to get out of Austin until this blows over and another story takes precedence."

"That could take some time, if you are right, sir, about the severity of the population's rage."

"Time is what I have in mind. I want you to go to Corpus Christi. There is a serious matter of cattle rustling going on in that part of the state, as you well know. I want you to assume another identity and develop a network of information for me concerning the movement of cattle and Juan Cortina's plans."

"Cortina? O'Reilly and Feders were going to do business with him."

"You can see the importance when it comes to us, then?" McNelly asked.

Both men stood facing each other, talking in hushed tones.

"You want me to be a spy," Josiah said, his words almost a whisper.

"Yes."

"For how long?"

"For however long it takes, Wolfe, for you to get us the information we need and for the situation in Austin to blow over. Could be six months."

"I have a son, sir."

"I know. And a fine one at that. Your wet nurse cares a great deal for him and for you. She is willing to take care of him while you are away."

"You've already asked her?"

"All of the arrangements have been made, Wolfe. Telling me no is not an option. Do you understand?"

"Six months," Josiah whispered.

"It might not take that long. It might take longer. We will make arrangements, over time, if necessary, for you to see your son."

"I've never been away from him that long, sir."

"We—the general, the major, and I—think this will be best for you, and, ultimately, for the reputation of the Rangers. It is not just you the paper is haranguing, you realize that, don't you, Wolfe? The organization is young, and though we've had our successes, there are many who still remember the days of the State Police and trust us very little, if at all. The Rangers need to be thought of as an institution founded on integrity, and this recent development has caused a great deal of questioning that is, at the very least, uncomfortable for all of us. Including Governor Coke."

"I understand."

"I'll be sending Ranger Elliot with you, in the same capacity."

"Elliot as a spy? Are you sure that's a good idea, sir?"

"I think it's best that Ranger Elliot is out of Austin, too, Wolfe. Surely, you understand my concerns? He is young and untried in the ways of politics and battle, as far as that goes. He seems very loyal to you and you to him. Your relationship is a great example of what we're trying to accomplish as Rangers, but unfortunately, that will be unseen by most people. You see my point?"

"I suppose I do. When do you want us to leave?" From McNelly's tone, Josiah knew any objection would go unheard. He knew when not to fight a losing battle.

"I think you've made the right decision, Wolfe. You need to leave as soon as possible. Within the hour. Sooner would be better. We do not want the newspaper to get wind of this plan, or of our decision. You will take the name of Zeb Teter and work as a hide trader. Here are your orders and your contact information. Guard them with your life. You are jumping out of the frying pan into the fire, Wolfe. Caution must be utmost in your mind. Cortina is a worthy adversary, and he surely is none too happy that the union with Feders and O'Reilly was stopped. He may want revenge, or he may be in the process of setting up another deal with unknown parties. You need to keep an eye out for everything, and trust no one."

Josiah took an envelope from McNelly and stuffed it in his pocket. "I suppose you're right. Cortina will be on the lookout for another business partner."

McNelly shook Josiah's hand, then turned to leave, but stopped before he stepped off the porch. "Elliot will be here soon. Be prepared to leave when he arrives, and under no circumstance should you make contact with anyone in the Fikes household. Do I make myself clear, Wolfe?"

"Yes, sir, you do," Josiah answered, knowing full well the captain was speaking about Pearl. He would not get a chance to tell her good-bye.

With that, Captain Leander McNelly departed, mounting his gray gelding without saying another word, leaving Josiah to stand there, feeling very much like he had just been sentenced to six months hard labor without the benefit of ever having a trial.

CHAPTER 10

———◆◆◆◆———

March 1875

"You better tell me what you're doing here, Ranger," or you're a dead man," the guitar player repeated.

There was no way Josiah could recount all of the actions that had led him to that very moment. Anger coursed through his veins at the realization that he had failed as a spy and ended up with a gun to his head, surviving four months without anyone so much as suspecting that he was a Ranger.

The time had flown, but he ached every day to see his son Lyle, to be home again. But that was not to be, not until he got orders from McNelly, or never, depending on what happened in the next few minutes.

Maria Villareal stood behind the guitar player, her position making it clear that she was in cahoots with the man on some level. Josiah was not sure whether he'd been double-crossed or not, but it sure looked and felt that way.

"I'm not a Ranger," he said. "My name is Zeb Teter. I hail from Austin, originally. Been a hide trader most all my life. Do I look like a Ranger?"

"All Rangers smell like you do." The guitar player chuckled. "Please do not treat me as a stupid man, Señor Wolfe. I
know exactly who you are. What I don't know is why you
are here pretending to be another man, a hide trader at that.
The role does not suit you well."

"My name is Zeb Teter," Josiah insisted, through clenched
teeth.

The Mexican rolled his eyes. He had not wavered with
the gun's position. It was difficult for most men to keep a
nine-inch barrel steady, but this man seemed to have no
problem holding his aim directly at Josiah's forehead.

Sweat beaded on Josiah's lip. He had always been a
bad liar. Which was one of the reasons why taking on spy
duty had greatly concerned him when it was assigned to
him. Still, when Captain McNelly handed him the assignment, Josiah could hardly have turned down the offer.
He'd had no choice but to leave Austin and everything he
knew and loved behind.

"Let's take this upstairs, Miguel," Maria Villareal said.
"There are too many ears and eyes about. The cantina is
close." She stared at Josiah, her eyes penetrating his so
deeply that he felt naked.

Miguel nodded and pulled the Walker Colt away from
Josiah's forehead, but did not holster it. "Do not do anything foolish, *amigo*, or you will die a quick death. I will
be a hero to many for killing a Ranger, no less one who
lies about who he is."

Josiah was glad to have a name for the guitar player.
Miguel. He still knew nothing of the man's association,
but he took his warning seriously. Being a bad liar didn't
make him a fool.

"Do as he says, Josiah Wolfe, and you will not suffer,"
Maria Villareal said. "I promise you that much."

"Suffering is the last thing on my mind at the moment."

"It shouldn't be," she said. "If you wish to continue this charade, you will do exactly as Miguel says and nothing more."

"This is no charade."

"At its core," Maria said, "I do not imagine it is. You were expecting me, and here I am."

"I've been double-crossed before," Josiah said.

Miguel raised his bushy eyebrow. "In a hide deal, no less?"

"How else?"

"You have conviction, I will give you that, Ranger Wolfe," Maria said.

Miguel waved the Colt upward. "To the stairs. Now!"

The second-floor room overlooked the back of the cantina and another building. It held no view of the ocean, not that it mattered for its intended purpose—brief encounters with the doves who worked the cantina.

The room had a bed, a dresser, and a walk-out balcony furnished with two café chairs and a small wooden table.

A cigar smoldered in a glass ashtray on top of the table, and the thick aroma of tobacco hung inside the room, overpowering any other smell that may have existed there. Josiah immediately wondered if there was someone else waiting for them, but he saw no one.

Miguel pushed Josiah inside the door and immediately lowered the Walker Colt from his head. The guitar player stuffed the long-barreled revolver into his belt, as a smirk settled on his face.

Maria hurried to the balcony doors and closed them softly, like she was trying to avoid notice of any kind. "We are safe now. Do not try to escape, Ranger Wolfe, or do anything stupid. We are here to help you."

Confused, Josiah stood in the middle of the room. He

still had a full bounty of weapons on his person and could easily use them if he felt he needed to. "How do you know who am I?"

"A friend sent us," Miguel said.

"I don't have any friends here," Josiah said.

Maria sat on the edge of the bed and smiled. "Juan Carlos would be disappointed to hear that."

That was the last name Josiah had expected to come out of the woman's mouth. The last he knew, Juan Carlos was still recuperating from being shot on the way to stop O'Reilly and Feders. "How do I know I can trust you just because you use Juan Carlos's name?"

"If we had no reason to keep you alive, señor, you would already be a dead man, and the name Zeb Teter would be written on your gravestone," Miguel said. He eased past Josiah and peered out through the curtains. "We haven't much time, and getting you out of here will be difficult the way it is. We have both put our lives at risk to save yours. The least you could do is be grateful."

Josiah shook his head. "You're not making any sense to me. The last time I saw Juan Carlos he was gut-shot in Brackett, Texas. I sent word for him, but have heard nothing in return."

"And that surprises you?" Maria said. The room was getting warm with the doors and windows closed. Sweat began to glisten under her throat and in between her breasts. There was a nervousness in her deep brown eyes that Josiah hadn't noticed before.

"No, it doesn't," he said.

Josiah could still smell the cigar smoke, but now it was mixed with perspiration. The room smelled old and used up and was filling quickly with fear.

"It shouldn't be a surprise to you," Maria said. "I have known Juan Carlos longer than I care to admit, given him parts of myself that I would like to have back, but it is much too late for those kind of regrets. A man like Juan

Carlos knows nothing of love or the fragility of a woman's heart. But, still, here I am doing his bidding. What does that say about his strength and power?"

Josiah felt his face flush. "Juan Carlos has always been more like a wraith than a human being. I'm happy to hear he is still alive, though I did not really fear he was dead. I would've come to know, somehow. Was he here?"

"The cigarillo is mine," Maria said. "Sorry to disappoint you."

"I'm not disappointed."

Maria nodded. "That is good. You must be important to Juan Carlos."

"Why do you say that?"

"Because my allegiance does not come cheap."

Miguel shot Maria an angry look. "You are sworn to gold and nothing else. Don't let her fool you, Ranger Wolfe."

The woman shrugged, obviously accepting Miguel's words as the truth. She pushed a wrinkle out of her long black skirt, then looked away from both men.

"Would either of you mind telling me what's going on?" Josiah asked. "You pull a gun on me, escort me upstairs, and now I am to understand that you're on a mission from Juan Carlos, to what, protect me? I am in no danger. At least no danger that I can't handle on my own."

"Don't be so sure of that," Miguel said. "You do not stink enough to be a real hide trader. No man worth his salt was going to tell you anything that is about to happen, even though Agusto was trying to warn you."

Josiah looked at Miguel curiously.

"He said the sky would change before the fall of night, and he was correct about that. Clouds are gathering."

"You have played in the cantina for days," Josiah said.

"Watching after you when your own Rangers would not. That and waiting for the beautiful Maria to appear." Miguel smiled. "Has it ever occurred to you that you were sent here to die?"

"I was sent here on orders from Captain Leander McNelly to serve the state of Texas. If I die in that service, then so be it."

"You are cavalier and stupid at the same time, Josiah Wolfe. Your life has no value to Leander McNelly or his battery of politicians that pose to protect us all. You are a mere pawn, easily disposed of for the purposes of commerce."

Josiah forced his rising anger deeper down. Miguel was trying to convince him of something that was not, could not, be true. "I don't need watching after. Where is Juan Carlos?"

"Close," Maria said. "He will not be able to restrain himself to stay away."

"Make no mistake, Juan Carlos is nothing more than a messenger," Miguel said with an angry tone of his own. "There are those who know his past and trust him less than you trust us."

Josiah stood firm, said nothing.

He was completely aware of Juan Carlos's past, that he himself was, and had, acted in the capacity of a spy for the government of Texas. It had been that way since the beginning, since Josiah had come to know the Mexican—who really was only half-Mexican. The man was actually the half brother of the late Captain Hiram Fikes, a man Josiah had fought next to in the War Between the States and ridden with as a Texas Ranger, an original member of the Frontier Battalion. But only a select few knew the two were actual brothers. Josiah hadn't discovered that information until after Captain Fikes had been killed.

Juan Carlos had saved Josiah's life in San Antonio, when he began his duty with the Texas Rangers the previous year, and that act had created a bond between the two men. One that had grown into a deep and sincere friendship. As much as that was possible with a man like Juan Carlos.

"You are a known spy, Josiah Wolfe," Miguel said. "And you have made a serious enemy of Cortina. Surely, you must know that? I will not stand by and watch this town fall into his hands. My allegiance is to freedom, not tyranny, do you understand that, Josiah Wolfe?"

Josiah nodded.

"We have been asked to get you out of Corpus Christi," Miguel continued, "to make sure you are safely on your way back to Austin, but I fear it may be too late." The guitar player peeked out the curtains again, this time a little more cautiously. He struggled not to shake the curtain and make their presence known to the outside world.

"Why is that?" Josiah asked.

Before Miguel could answer, Josiah heard gunshots in the distance, faint at first, then joined by others, like a battle breaking out and drawing closer. He instinctively reached for his own gun, a Colt Peacemaker.

"Because Cortina is already here," Miguel said. "The battle for Corpus Christi has already started."

CHAPTER 11

Josiah stood next to Miguel, his Peacemaker cocked, a bullet chambered. "Are you going to tell me what's going on? Or am I just supposed to shoot and ask questions later?"

"If what I have learned is correct, Cortina is planning to take Corpus Christi as his own. There was a rendezvous this morning outside of town. I have no idea how many men have joined his cause," Miguel said. "But I believe it to be a powerful army, attacking now a population unaware of its full intention."

An invasion by Juan "The Red Robber of the Rio Grande" Cortina did not take a lot of imagination to envision. He had tried to invade and take back parts of Texas before—most notably Brownsville, in 1859, when he swept into town and held firm control of it for the better part of two months. There were other incidents over the years, incursions by Cortina and his followers, that led all of those in power—government, military, and law enforcement, including the Rangers—to take any threat by him very seriously.

Maria slid a rifle out from under the bed, a Winchester Model '73 like the one Josiah normally carried. She loaded and cocked the gun like she knew what she was doing, then went to the window, just to the left of the bed, and slid it open only enough to prop the rifle barrel on the sill. She had a clear shot straight down the street. "There will be a team of men coming here for you, Josiah Wolfe. I believe there is a debt to repay," she said.

"I don't owe Juan Cortina a thing."

"From what I understand," Miguel said, "two of his men are dead because of you. Important men with strong and powerful ties that reached all the way to Austin and beyond, even to Abilene. You owe Cortina the money he has lost because of your actions. He will want something for payment. Either your allegiance or your scalp."

"He'll get neither."

"Just so you know," Miguel said. "Who were the men?"

"That would be Liam O'Reilly, a low-life outlaw who was true to no cause but his own. I did not kill him. Feders did."

"The Texas Ranger captain who betrayed you?" Maria asked.

Josiah took a deep breath, listened to the distant shots grow in number, grow closer. An explosion echoed from about six or seven blocks away. Cortina's men were coming in from the outlying districts and working their way to the center of town. There was nothing to shoot at. Yet.

"Pete Feders was a tortured soul," Josiah answered softly. "He rode with Juan Carlos, Captain Fikes, and myself for many a year. I thought I could trust him, until the captain was killed, then he became unpredictable. It seems Feders had taken a shine to the captain's daughter, and the money that was bequeathed her—all lost in the Panic of '73. He wanted her hand in marriage, but the daughter, Pearl, would have nothing of it, even though her mother was desperate for the marriage to happen. Feders and his stolen money were going to save everything she had to lose."

"Why would the daughter have nothing of it?" Maria asked with a wry smile.

"She did not love him," Josiah answered.

There was more to that story, but Josiah was not going to tell Maria Villareal that he had his own tangled feelings for Pearl Fikes, that the two of them had been intimate the night Pete Feders proposed to Pearl publicly and was turned down just as publicly. The embarrassment Feders must have felt had to have been immense, and Josiah had felt sorry for him at the time, regardless of his own feelings for Pearl.

"Pete was desperate to prove himself to Pearl's mother," Josiah continued. "He made a deal with the devil—Cortina in this case—to enrich both of their pockets from the proceeds of stolen cattle driven north, and in the end, it cost him his life."

"You killed him."

"I did."

It was a hard thing for Josiah to admit out loud to strangers, killing Pete Feders, a man he'd once considered a friend, but there was no way around admitting the truth.

Even though he had been cleared of any wrongdoing by General Steele, Captain McNelly, and Major Jones, Josiah had replayed the event over and over in his mind a million times. The killing still haunted his dreams, and his waking hours as well.

"Your face shows regret," Maria said.

Josiah did not answer her, did not acknowledge her observation as true, even though she had read his emotions correctly. "Feders and O'Reilly were on their way to seal the deal with Cortina. I had to stop them."

"And you do not think it is a coincidence that your new

captain, this tubercular man, McNelly, has sent you here, only miles away from Cortina's lair?" Miguel asked. "What do you know of his connections? *His* political desires, Josiah Wolfe?"

"McNelly has more spies than just me placed here in Corpus. There is pressure coming directly from the governor's office. It's important for all of Texas to end the thievery and uncertainty that Cortina is set on inflicting on our citizens," Josiah said.

He was not accustomed to spewing political hyperbole, but Miguel's accusations against Captain McNelly and the Texas Rangers had caught him completely off guard.

At the moment, he wasn't sure what was going on— except that he was in more danger than he'd previously realized—and the political machinations of Corpus Christi were as foreign to him as the jittery seagull perched on the rooftop across the street.

"If you are loyal to Juan Carlos, how can you question the intentions of any Texas Ranger?" Josiah asked.

"Do not be so blind, Josiah Wolfe," Miguel demanded angrily. "You must know that Juan Carlos operates as much outside of the law as inside it. He is no stranger to the halls of power, either. You have never been safe here in Corpus Christi. Not as Zeb Teter or as Josiah Wolfe. You must leave at once. There are two horses tied up behind the livery waiting for you. Maria will keep you safe."

"Shouldn't that be the other way around?"

Miguel's face twisted into a smile, but his eyes were cold as ice. "If only that were true. Now go. Before it is too late."

Maria Villareal insisted on taking the lead out of the door. Josiah followed close behind, his Peacemaker raised and ready to fire.

The late afternoon sun had tilted west, creating pockets

of deep gray shadows in the alleyway that separated the buildings that were packed into the district Josiah had taken up residence in. Shouting and gunfire were drawing closer. There was a smell in the air, smoke mixed with dust and gunpowder, that betrayed any idea that a natural storm was coming. Any thunder to be heard was man-made, and any rain that fell to the ground would be droplets of blood. The only thing that could cleanse a rebel uprising was a direct battle. Josiah hoped that those who wielded power in Corpus Christi were ready for the fight that had come to their city.

Maria stopped at the bottom of the stairs. "The livery is two blocks to the south."

Josiah shook his head no. "I know that livery, but my horse is in a stall near the boardinghouse I was staying at."

"Where?"

"The Hassit-Lee Boardinghouse."

"Are you a fool? That is right in the midst of the shooting," Maria said.

"I can hear that."

"And you insist on walking straight into this battle, knowing full well that there are men who are seeking you out to kill you?"

"I've been in that position before."

"Why does that not surprise me?"

"You are welcome to stay here," Josiah said. "I'd just as soon that you would, but I'm not leaving my horse."

"You are willing to die for a horse?"

"Yes."

"You are a strange, stubborn, man, Josiah Wolfe," Maria Villareal said, stepping away from him, easing alongside the building, and heading north toward the Hassit-Lee Boardinghouse instead of south to the preappointed livery.

"I've been called worse," Josiah said, pushing past her, giving her no time to protest, as he took the lead.

CHAPTER 12

A dead man lay in the street, his hand out-stretched, a fairly new Colt Single-Action Army, much like Josiah's Peacemaker, just inches from his grasp.

The man lay squarely in the middle of the intersection of Artesian and Antelope streets, blood still oozing out of the deadly wound in his chest. Black smoke filled the air as a small wood-frame house sat blazing half a block to the south.

The day was hot already, but with the fire and the tension, Josiah could feel sweat breaking out all over his body. The smells of the battle were bitter enough to overwhelm all of his senses, including the common sense he'd used time after time when he was faced with making decisions in a dangerous, or warlike, situation. He wasn't proud of the killing experience he carried, hardly ever gave it a thought these days, but was glad the skills were there when he needed to call on them.

Shots tore into the corner of the building he had stopped at, a two-storey affair made of shellcrete, concrete made of oyster shells fished out of the bay, crushed and used as a building material. The walls were two feet thick, and the bullets were fully embedded, a puff of dust exiting with each shot.

Josiah was not afraid for his own life, but he was unsure of who was doing the shooting, and which side they belonged to: Cortina's or the defenders of Corpus. Either way, it appeared he and Maria Villareal were targets. He'd expected that, from what Miguel had told him, but still, he would've liked to have known for sure that the shooters were Cortina's men. He didn't want to kill a man who was mistaken in his shooting, just doing his job, and fighting on the right side of the law.

The shots appeared to be coming from a window on the second floor, across the street.

"We did not have to face this," Maria said, with a sneer. "I think we are pinned in between both factions."

"I expected more men, an army," Josiah said.

"Cortina talks big, you must know that by now. If the town trembles in fear, he could take it over with thirty men or a thousand. It does not matter."

"Why?"

Maria smirked. "Not only is Corpus a trade center for cattle, but for sheep as well. Imagine the power a man would have if he controlled beef, wool, *and* the harbor. If he is not rich already, he will be *muy potente*."

"I'm sorry, I don't speak your language."

Maria stared at Josiah, incredulous, about to say something, when a bullet struck the building about six inches from her head. Dust exploded outward, raining into her hair and onto her shoulder.

"Very powerful," Maria said, spitting, cleaning her lips, and pushing the dust off her shoulder. "While we end up dead because of a horse."

"He's a good horse."

Maria rolled her eyes, angled the Winchester up at the window, and fired off two shots before Josiah could protest.

"What are you shooting at?" he demanded.

"Those who shoot at us." Maria fired off three more rounds, then waited.

"I hope they're Cortina's men."

"It does not matter to me. They can see us plainly. How many decent men do you know that would shoot at a woman with no questions asked?"

Josiah was impressed with Maria's rationale and how she handled the rifle, but said nothing. Instead, he fired off a succession of shots with his six-shooter, then joined Maria, waiting to see what would happen next. Blind shots had their pitfalls and consequences.

The shooting in the distance continued, up the street and over a couple of blocks. The house still continued to burn unattended. Smoke roiled angrily into the sky like a rising signal set to summon some unseen general.

Across the street, in the building where the shooters had taken their perch, thin lace curtains flittered in the second-floor window, void of any shadows or other movement that would suggest an ongoing menacing presence. Either Maria had gotten a lucky shot, or the men were waiting for a better chance to take aim.

"I think we should go back," Maria said.

"I think you should wait here." Josiah didn't give her a chance to answer. He sprinted across the street, dipping low enough in his run to pick up the dead man's Colt. There was no sense in letting the gun lie there.

Maria did not have time to be angry, or show it if she was. Her instinct must have kicked in, and she started firing automatically to cover Josiah's run. Bullets whizzed over his head, and he was glad that Maria Villareal was behind him, looking out for his best interest, instead of on the other side of the fight.

Josiah picked up speed and ran as fast as he could half a block down to the Hassit-Lee Boardinghouse, without looking back. He drew no fire, but continued to hear Maria shooting her rifle in an effort to draw the attention to her.

Miguel had been right. She looked after him and kept him safe. *She was something else*, that was for sure, Josiah thought, as he eased his run and turned the corner onto the property of the boardinghouse. He just wasn't sure what that something was, and he didn't think a thing about leaving a woman behind to defend herself—which surprised him even more than he'd have thought it would.

There was a four-stall barn behind the house. The boardinghouse was of recent construction—within the last year or so—barely showing any weathering at all. It was a grand house, with a multitude of rooms. Josiah had spent very little time there, preferring to become a regular face at the cantina, and knew very little about the layout or the history of the house. The breakfasts were good and hearty, and the beds were clean and comfortable. That's all he cared about.

He didn't rush into the barn. Instead, Josiah slid in the back door, hoping to take advantage of the late-afternoon shadows.

A thirty-foot retama tree stood just outside the barn door, offering a graceful helping of shade. The leaves looked like long flowing fern fronds, dotted with small yellow flowers with orange throats. Thorns also lined the branches of the tree, and the first time Josiah had exited the barn, in a hurry, not paying any attention, he'd pushed through the branches, scratching his face so severely it looked like he had taken on a wildcat and lost, hands-down. He didn't make the same mistake twice.

The barn was quiet, with the exception of the normal rustling around of the horses inside. Josiah quickly made his way to his horse—Clipper, a tall Appaloosa that had been his mount for more years than he cared to count. The two were trusted friends, rarely separated, and had the kind of relationship where a nudge could mean run or trot, depending on the situation.

Josiah set about saddling Clipper, conscious of every sound inside and outside of the barn. The gunfights in the distance could still be heard, and Clipper danced around a bit, nodding back and forth, until Josiah was able to calm him down with a bite of an apple he had left behind a few days ago.

"Shush, boy, it'll be all right," Josiah said. The horse snorted, finished chewing the apple, then stood still as a statue until Josiah had completely saddled him.

Josiah led Clipper to the doors, peered out, and decided it was safe before climbing into the saddle. There wasn't time to go up to his room and retrieve his belongings. They amounted only to a few pair of underclothes, a change of pants, and a fresh shirt. Any mementos of any value were carried along every day, not left behind to tempt a thief in a boardinghouse.

Besides, Josiah had kept a bedroll and his gear stocked and ready to go in the tack room, just in case he had to flee in a hurry. He might have been new at being a spy for the Texas Rangers, but he'd had enough similar experience in the War Between the States, and since, to last a lifetime. The last thing he wanted to do was find himself in a situation unprepared.

He half-expected to be ambushed coming out of the barn, but as it was, the air was clean, and the bushes didn't contain a threat of any kind that he could see, so Josiah hustled Clipper out onto the street and headed toward the intersection where he'd left Maria.

The sweet fragrance of the retama tree was just a memory now that Josiah was back out in the open, taking in the smoke from the burning house and the gunpowder that lingered in the air. He cut to the right, turning down an alley alongside a café that had shuttered its windows and barred the doors. Hopefully, he could come up behind Maria, scoop her up, and get on to wherever they were going.

It was difficult to push Clipper any harder through the narrow alley. There were empty crates, barrels, and rotting vegetables to avoid. A rat looked up, seemingly surprised to see a galloping horse heading toward it, but unconcerned to be out in the daylight, not far from an ongoing gunfight. The rat scampered away, still chewing on a wilted green leaf as it disappeared into a maze of crates.

Josiah could see the smoke growing thicker ahead, so he pulled his Winchester out of the scabbard, readying himself for anything that came his way. The dead man's Colt had been packed in the saddlebag.

He pushed through the smoke, pulling up his kerchief over his nose so he wouldn't have to breathe in too much of it. Clipper didn't complain at all, just ran as fast as he could, exiting the cloud of smoke in a matter of seconds. They were so close to the burning house, Josiah could feel the heat of it through his shirt.

Close now to the intersection, he reined Clipper to an easy stop. He had seen no one, had been accosted by no one, or confronted in any way, which he found extremely unlikely considering Cortina was supposed to have an army swarming about, taking over Corpus with ease. For some reason, that didn't seem to be happening. The attack seemed small in scale, more like a gang of outlaws had stormed into town on a looting expedition, instead of a foreign army invading, set on conquering a harbor and then a state.

With the Winchester in one hand and his Peacemaker in the other, Josiah eased along the cool shellcrete wall of a building and made his way to Maria.

She was exactly where he had left her, still shooting, then waiting, then shooting. He whistled softly, but loud enough to get her attention.

Maria forced a smile when she saw him.

Before Josiah could take another breath, before he could move to cover her, a bullet hit Maria squarely in the shoulder. She screamed and stumbled backward, away from the spray of blood, losing the grip on her rifle as another bullet exploded into her body, sending her spiraling quickly to the ground in a dusty, motionless heap.

CHAPTER 13

Josiah let loose and emptied the bullets in his Peacemaker, shooting upward, to the roof. Not drawing any return fire, he stooped down and rolled Maria over to face him. He wasn't sure if she was dead or alive.

"I hope you got your damned horse," Maria said weakly, her eyes flittering open with obvious pain.

"You're hurt bad," Josiah said. "I've got to get you to a doctor."

Maria nodded in between deep gasps. "Ride north out of town on Chipito. There's a row of fishermen's shacks not far off the bay. Look for the blue roof."

A shot rang out, hitting the dirt inches from Maria's boot.

Josiah turned from her quickly to see a man duck back down on the roof. He aimed the Winchester and waited until the man popped back up to see if he'd finished the job and killed Maria, or needed to fire again.

It was a mistake that cost the man his life.

Josiah fired the rifle, catching the man just at the base of the throat. The shooter stumbled backward, then staggered sideways, tripping on something that brought him forward again. He fell headfirst off the roof. The man landed with a thud in a cloud of dust, with no weapon, or sign of life, apparent.

Satisfied that the unknown man was dead, Josiah turned his attention back to Maria. There was no time to think about the right or wrong of the shooting, like there had been with Pete Feders. The burden of another death at his hands would come later, in the middle of the night, when wondering and regret would roil his stomach and test his heart.

It looked like Maria had been hit twice in the right shoulder. Blood was flowing freely, a large puddle forming in the street. Surprisingly, Maria was still conscious. She was every bit as tough as he'd been led to believe.

"We need to get some pressure on that wound," Josiah said.

Maria nodded, but said nothing. Her face was growing pale. She licked her lips. Life was starting to drain from her body.

Josiah groaned, kicked the dirt nervously, then whistled for Clipper. The Appaloosa responded right away, trotting to him out of the alley. "I need to get you on the horse. I'm going to lift you up, I'm sorry if it hurts too much."

"Do what you need to. I will help as much as I can," Maria whispered, as she pressed her bloody fingers as hard as she could on the wound.

Josiah took a deep breath and lifted Maria to her feet.

She bit her lip, forced back a scream that would surely have drawn more attention to their location. The sound was like a garbled plea, but Josiah was not going to stop until the woman was securely on Clipper's back.

"Are you all right?" he asked, guiding Maria to Clipper.

There was a hustle of noise behind Josiah. Horses running in the opposite direction. Somewhere in the distance, a church bell rang frantically. The smoke was fading; the wind had changed, sending the charred smell in the opposite direction. None of that activity captured Josiah's attention more than Maria's condition.

He gripped Maria's body as gently as he could and, with all his might, hoisted her, face-first, over Clipper's broad shoulders.

Without thinking of another thing, Josiah quickly slid the Winchester back into its scabbard, then climbed up on the horse.

Clipper remained steady as Josiah balanced himself in the stirrups, pulling Maria up so she could sit in the saddle with him. It was a tight fit, but once he got settled, Josiah could handle the reins in one hand, and put pressure on Maria's shoulder wounds with his other hand.

"Are you ready?" Josiah asked.

Maria didn't answer. She pressed back against Josiah, her body hard, heavy, and unresponsive.

Chipito was pretty easy to find—all Josiah had to do was head east, away from the incursion of Cortina and his men. He was leery of every new building that came into sight, sure that a man on the roof would rain a volley of bullets their way, but so far, not one person had showed them any concern. Mostly, the streets of Corpus Christi were vacant. The population was either hiding or engaged in the battle in one way or another.

Josiah had gathered Maria up against him as tightly as he could. He didn't run Clipper full out, even though he felt the need to. Close though. Fast enough to control the horse, hold on to Maria, and keep an eye out for any possible threat.

He could feel Maria's heartbeat against his chest. It was weak, but steady. His hand was thick with her blood, and he could smell nothing but life draining out of Maria, mixed with his own sweat and fear.

If she were not a woman, a woman whose life Josiah

himself had put in harm's way, then his thoughts would have been forced to return to his memories of the war, to the battles of his past. But the past was overcome by the present, by guilt and responsibility. He had to get Maria the help she needed, find the blue-roofed shack, and hope like hell she had the strength to survive the trip. He didn't know what he was going to do if the woman died.

He was heading east out of Corpus Christi proper. Multistorey buildings quickly gave way to simple houses and then to open, marshy fields. The street quickly turned into a wellused trail, visible on a steady rise as far as the eye could see. Knee-high grass swayed gently on the ocean breeze, and a seabird hung in the air like a child's kite over the water, effortlessly, just floating for the joy of it, it seemed.

The waves from Nueces Bay crashed ashore off to Josiah's right. It was high tide. The air was salty and sweet, a refreshing change from the city and conflict he'd just fled.

The blood from Maria's wound had begun to congeal, the flow slowing. At least it felt like it was slowing. Josiah knew the perception might have been nothing more than hope on his part, but he could still feel her heartbeat, feel her weak breath on his wrist as she exhaled and fought to live.

He said nothing; any words were lost in his sole desire to move forward. Once he crested the rise, he saw a line of fishermen's shacks in the distance, less than a mile away.

Josiah urged Clipper on, pushing the horse to run fast. Maria's breathing was becoming halting, more difficult.

It didn't take long to see a shack with a blue roof.

Josiah gave Clipper his head, stuck the reins in his teeth, and pulled his Peacemaker from the holster, firing off three quick shots, hoping to alert someone that trouble was close—and he was in need of help in the worst way.

At first Josiah didn't see anyone, not one living creature other than the seabird, who took umbrage at the gunshots and flew away quickly. But after a few seconds, he saw a man walk out of the shack—a man that Josiah would have recognized from half a mile away.

His old friend, Juan Carlos, hurried out of the shack as best he could, his hand cupped over his eyes, looking in Josiah's direction.

Josiah jumped off Clipper, not bothering to say hello to Juan Carlos. "She's been shot."

"Get her inside," Juan Carlos said. "Most of the men are out to sea for the day's catch, but Molly Flanagan will be able to help her."

"I hope so." As glad as Josiah was to see Juan Carlos, his response sounded clipped, harsh. Without wasting another step or breath, he pulled Maria Villareal off Clipper and carried her into the shack, cradling her like a groom carrying a bride over the threshold. Juan Carlos followed him inside.

The inside of the shack was sparse, but Josiah immediately spied a cot set against the back wall, and eased Maria down onto it as gently as he could.

"Here's some water," Juan Carlos said, handing Josiah a pitcher with a ladle in it.

Josiah took the pitcher and nodded. "Get her help, now!"

The only response Josiah heard was the quick run of bare feet on the sand as Juan Carlos exited the shack.

He filled the ladle half-full and put it to Maria's lips. Her eyes were closed. Sweat rolled off her brow, and her entire chest was covered in blood. From his experience in the war, Josiah knew if the bullets had severed an artery in her shoulder there were few options to heal the wound.

With a bit of insistence, he pressed the ladle harder against Maria's lips. "Take it," Josiah said, unsure if she could hear him.

After a couple of more tries, Maria moved her lips,

opening them so thinly that all Josiah could do was drib-
ble a bit of water onto them and down her throat.

"Where is Juan Carlos?" Maria whispered.

"Off to get help."

"If I die . . ." She stopped mid-sentence and began to
cough, her eyes opening for the first time since they'd
entered the shack. After the cough subsided, she continued, ". . . tell him that I have always loved him."

CHAPTER 14

The sun was diving toward the horizon, a half-red orb shooting long, shimmering fingers of soft light into the cloudless sky. The day was trying desperately to hold on for as long as it could. Night was racing upward in the east, and darkness dressed all in gray and depression, it seemed to Josiah, was always the victor, regardless of any effort by the sun to fend off the black void. He felt empty and demoralized.

From a stash of driftwood Juan Carlos had built a fire that was now nothing more than a bed of orange, pulsating embers. The coals looked like they were breathing, fanned as they were by the gentle breeze pushing in off the waves, less than twenty feet away. There was little smoke, and it differed in volume and smell from the violent smoke in town that Josiah had experienced earlier in the day.

"We need to catch dinner," Juan Carlos said. He handed Josiah a large bundle of netting that felt light on one end and heavy on the other.

Juan Carlos was quite a bit older than Josiah, probably

nearing seventy. His hair was completely white, most likely bleached completely by time and the sun, and his skin was deep brown, leathery. Wrinkles cut deep rivers of age into his face, and the only thing that belied the notion of his heritage being true Mexican was his intense blue European eyes, which were very similar to those of his white half brother, Captain Hiram Fikes.

But there was something new in Juan Carlos's face and actions that Josiah noticed now that he never had before— his friend seemed weaker than he ever was, perhaps not completely recovered from the gut shot he had taken four months prior. Still, Juan Carlos seemed more than capable of doing whatever needed to be done. He had always possessed an inner strength that Josiah admired.

"What's this?" Josiah asked, taking the netting.

"A casting net for bait fish. Do you know nothing of fishing, *mi amigo*?"

It was hard for Josiah to answer. His mind was still in turmoil over Maria's condition, worrying about her wounds, whether he was truly responsible for her being shot. There was no way he could have left Clipper behind, but now that he knew the outcome of his decision, it was hard not to reconsider leaving his trusted steed. A horse was not worth the loss of a human life.

"I spent most of my time in the woods. Any fishing I did was in the creek not far from our house in Seerville," Josiah finally said.

Juan Carlos nodded. "This will occupy your mind— trust me—while we await word of Maria."

Juan Carlos had returned with Molly Flanagan and another woman, who remained unnamed. Both women wore a look of concern when they'd arrived to look after Maria Villareal and had left Josiah and Juan Carlos outside to hurry inside the shack. The doors had remained closed, even now. Every once in a while a moan would escape, muffled voices, but not much else.

"Whatever you say," Josiah said.

"I say we have to catch bait fish, or there will be no dinner, and leave the fate of Maria in better hands than ours." With that, Juan Carlos walked straight into the surf and didn't stop until he was knee-deep in the water, the waves occasionally crashing against him waist-high.

Josiah wanted to protest, scream that he wasn't hungry, but he didn't. Instead, he pulled off his boots and socks, rolled up his pant legs to his knees, and waded cautiously into the water.

The light was soft, rays from the sun still reaching up over the western horizon to see out into the distance, where the water met the sky, a colorless line that divided the world.

"Hand me the net," Juan Carlos instructed Josiah, "and watch."

The Mexican wrapped a cord around his right wrist, then grabbed the net about six inches from the top. Small, round, smooth rocks were tied into it at even increments, providing weight. Juan Carlos grabbed a rock, about four down, pulled it up, then took the bottom of the net with his other hand, reared back, and launched it into the air. The net burst open like a white blooming flower, fell to the sea in a perfect circle, and sank out of sight. Juan Carlos quickly jerked back and began to pull the net closer to him.

Three slender silvery fish bounced about in the bottom of the net, which had closed together. "*Salmonete*," Juan Carlos said. "Anglos call them mullet. Bait for fishing. *Dale a un hombre un pescado y lo alimentarás por un día. Enseñe a un hombre a pescar y lo alimentarás para toda la vida.* Give a man a fish and you feed him for a day. Teach a man to fish and you feed him for a lifetime."

Josiah shrugged his shoulders as he watched Juan Carlos walk out of the surf and empty the net into a bucket filled with seawater. *I have no interest in learning how to feed myself at the moment*, he thought, but didn't say.

When the Mexican returned, he handed Josiah the net. "You try. Watch the waves for the flash of silver, watch for the schools to run. I will spot them for you. Then throw the net into the water as gently as you can."

Josiah turned the net over in his hands, untangled it, and situated the weight in his hand just like Juan Carlos had. He watched the man, glad to be with his friend, though he would have preferred better circumstances. There was no way he could take his mind off Maria—or what might be happening in that shack.

"There!" Juan Carlos shouted, pointing to a wave.

At first, Josiah could barely see the fish in the fading light. He squinted, focused on the rolling water, and finally saw the school of fish swimming right under the surface. He tossed the net toward the fish. It hit the water with a thump, and the fish scattered.

It took five tries before Josiah actually netted a mullet, and in all that time, he had no other thoughts . . . or regrets.

"Here," Juan Carlos said, offering a stick to Josiah with a freshly cooked fish on it. "*Caballa* are plentiful here, Señor Josiah."

After the sun had gone down, by the light of a torch, they had fished with the bait they both caught, with Juan Carlos proving to be a knowledgeable fisherman.

Josiah knew little about the fish of the ocean, what their names were or even what most tasted like. His tongue knew the taste of squirrel meat and the different flavors of beef. Fish were caught out of the streams and creeks. Redear and catfish, nothing with teeth. And eating even those was rare— usually out of desperation.

"You would call this fish mackerel," Juan Carlos said, urging Josiah to take the stick again.

The fish was long and slender, silver, and looked very angry to Josiah. Even dead, the fish did not look or smell appetizing. "I'm not hungry," he said, still ignoring his needs, keeping his eyes, instead, on the shack Maria Villareal had been taken to.

Juan Carlos pulled the stick away. "As you wish."

It had been several hours since Maria had been taken away. Mostly, the two men had sat in silence, staring off into the darkness. The moon had not shown itself yet, so the sky and the water, beyond the firelight, were all one sheet of blackness. Josiah questioned silently whether the moon would show itself or not. Any possibility of light on a night like this seemed remote to him.

"It is good to spend some time with you," Josiah finally said. "It has been a while."

"Since we rode together to stop Cortina and Liam O'Reilly's bond," Juan Carlos said.

"I stopped that."

"I heard."

"I should have kept riding into Laredo and put an end to Cortina, as well."

"It would not have been as easy as you think, señor."

"I don't imagine so, but I had Elliot with me, and that Negro Seminole scout until we found our lead, then he disappeared. Still, Elliot's a fine shot. I regret not finishing the job."

Juan Carlos chuckled. "Dixie Jim is a good man, too."

"The scout helped us find O'Reilly. I'll always be grateful for that."

"And your captain."

"Yes, sadly, we found Pete Feders ready to join a nest of men no better than snakes."

"I never did trust that *gringo*," Juan Carlos said, taking a bite of the mackerel and spitting a bone into the fire.

"Feders rode with us all for a long time," Josiah said. "I thought he was a good soldier, a man I could trust with my life. I thought I knew his intentions."

"Money and love came in between you and him, between the right and wrong of his heart—and it cost him his life. *Diós lo bendiga su alma.* God rest his soul."

The breeze rose up over Josiah's back, then dropped down, swirling around his feet, fueling the embers in the fire enough to flame up along a thin piece of remaining driftwood. He still had not settled within himself what had happened between him and Pete Feders, and the final confrontation continued to haunt his dreams and sometimes his waking hours, as well. The whiskey and beer he'd tasted daily, pretending to be another man, Zeb Teter, in the cantina, had the potential to be the tonic to his ills—though he constantly resisted the pull. Many more days away from himself, from his true identity, and those that he really loved and cared about, could have been even more dangerous than facing Cortina's men. The liquor was becoming a habit that Josiah was losing the desire to control. It numbed his fears and his nightmares. He could use a taste right now.

Juan Carlos nibbled on the piece of fish, then looked over his shoulder to the shack. "Regret is not something you should carry around for the rest of your life. Especially for this action. It was not your fault, *amigo*. You should not feel responsible about anything that has happened."

"You mean Feders or Maria?"

"Both."

"I wish it were that easy," Josiah said.

"You are an honorable man, Josiah Wolfe. Doubt does not suit you. Do you love my niece? Do you love Pearl enough to tell her the truth?"

Josiah shrugged. "I tried to avoid her when I was in Austin. But she is persistent. She knows enough of the details to understand the situation as I saw it. Still, I have a hard time being in her presence."

"Which is why you took this assignment from McNelly. To flee Austin."

"I had no choice but to take this assignment. The newspaper was ready to see me hanged. Once the higher-ups were certain that I was innocent of any wrongdoing, they felt it best that I leave town until things calmed down for everybody involved. But with Pearl's mother fanning the flames, I think that will take a while." Josiah could not lie to Juan Carlos even if he wanted to.

"There are other reasons why you avoid my niece?"

"I cannot support her in the way she is accustomed, you know that."

"You would make a wonderful gentleman. I fear my brother's estate will vanish from Pearl's grasp. Her mother is a *criatura codiciosos*, a greedy creature. I do not know what my brother saw in her."

"I'm sorry to hear that, but I don't think I am suited for that kind of life," Josiah said. He looked out to the sea, to the blackness that was making it one with the sky, so he wouldn't have to look his friend in the eye.

"Is there someone else, another woman that you care about?"

Josiah took a deep breath, then faced Juan Carlos. "I never thought I would care about the welfare of another woman after my Lily died."

"But your son needs a *mamá*."

"One day Ofelia will need a life of her own."

"She has a life with you. With Lyle."

"Maybe." Josiah could feel a tremble in his voice, in his chest

"But now you think you are *listo para el amor*, ready for love?" Juan Carlos asked.

"I don't know that anyone is ever ready for that," Josiah answered. "I just know what I am not ready for."

Juan Carlos nodded, then glanced over to the shack. "I understand, señor. I will not fault your heart if you cannot love my niece. It is a selfish desire of my own that you do. I see how she looks at you—and you her. Time will tell for each of you."

Silence fell between them, the waves crashing gently on the shore.

"Where is the little gnat, Elliot?" Juan Carlos finally asked, changing the subject.

Josiah was relieved and chuckled silently at Juan Carlos's description of Scrap. There was no love lost between the two men. "In Corpus, too. On the other side of town. His assignment was the same as mine, be a spy and report back to Captain McNelly. It seems we both failed to detect an attack. McNelly will not be pleased with either of us, I'm sure."

Juan Carlos chuckled. "Scrap Elliot has a difficult enough time being himself. Where is he now?"

"I don't know. If things got bad, we were supposed to meet up north of town. That was until this man, Miguel, that you sent, found me."

"Ah, Miguel, what has become of him?"

"We left him at the cantina."

A distressed look crossed Juan Carlos's face, but he said nothing further about Miguel. "I can send a man to find Elliot, at least, and make sure he made it out of the attacks alive."

Josiah nodded. "He needs to know where I am. McNelly will need to be informed of the incursion by Cortina's men."

"Trust me, señor, he will know soon enough."

Josiah was curious about the information Miguel had given him. "Do you think I was sent here to be killed?"

"Who would make you think such a thing?"

"Miguel."

"Do not trust a guitar player with a hunger for power of his own. He did not tell you everything he knew. He was just satisfying a debt."

"A debt to who?"

"To me," Juan Carlos said. "I saved his life once."

CHAPTER 15

———◆━✦━◆———

Molly Flanagan exited the shack with a grave look on her face. The woman was large, shaped like a top-heavy whiskey barrel, and wore a simple linen sack dress. Her feet were bare, and in the light cast off by a rise in the flames of the fire, there was little left to the imagination about what lay underneath the dress. Josiah looked away and craned an ear to listen to the hushed conversation she started with Juan Carlos.

"'Tis not good, she has lost a lot of blood," Molly Flanagan said. Her accent was unmistakably Irish, her tongue thick and lilting, hard for Josiah to understand even under the best circumstances.

"Will she live?" Juan Carlos asked.

"Hard to say. 'Tis in the Lord's hands, now, 'tis. We dug the bullets out of her shoulder, cleaned dem the best we could, and sewed her up. I ain't no doctor, but I've seen enough blood and wounds in this life to know what's in me hands and what's not."

"What do we do now?"

"Wait," Molly Flanagan said. "Wait and pray. Matilda will stay the night, keep her comfortable. Nothin' else but that can be done."

"Can I see her?" Juan Carlos asked.

"She's a-sleepin' now. Best wait till mornin', or if Matilda hollers out for you."

"I'll just look in on her then." Juan Carlos pushed by Molly and, without an ounce of hesitation, stepped inside the shack, closing the door softly behind him.

"That man will be the death of us all," the woman said. She was staring directly at Josiah. "Who are you?"

"Josiah Wolfe. I'm a friend of Juan Carlos."

"Don't be thinkin' that'll impress me none."

Josiah stepped around the fire, so that he could face the woman. "He's a good man."

Molly shrugged. "Been a blight on the happiness of this here community, if'n you ask me. Walked in here like he belonged, and here you are, bringin' us trouble and a fine lady, double shot and nearly dead. How'd that happen, anyway?"

"Cortina's men attacked the city."

"Likely story, that is."

"It's true."

"Makes no difference to me. We just want left alone. Who's who and who's in charge ain't nothin' to us. The bounty of the ocean is our landlord, and our dear, sweet Lord Jesus continues to be the hand that guides us through our daily troubles."

Josiah took a deep breath, and noticed the waves crashing into the shore with more force. He felt compelled to remain silent. Molly Flanagan unnerved him.

The moon was showing itself after all, rising on the horizon. It was almost full, just a sliver of a fingernail from being completely round. Night was going to be bright.

Whether that was a help or a hindrance to what came next was hard to say. The presence of the moon did nothing to lighten Josiah's mood.

"It's been a pleasure talking with you, ma'am. I appreciate everything you've done for Maria. And if you're worried about Juan Carlos bringing you trouble, don't. He's like a possum. He never stays in one place too long."

"That's what you say."

Josiah shrugged his shoulders. "Thank you for being here to help. I'm in your debt."

"'Tis the thing to do. Now, where are you going?" Molly asked as Josiah turned to walk away.

"Tell Juan Carlos I went back into Corpus to look for an old friend. He'll understand."

Josiah eased back into town on the same trail he had left on, only this time there was no dire sense of urgency, no life at stake but his own—and now that concern seemed distant.

His shirt still carried the stain of Maria's blood; he did not have the luxury of a change of clothes, having departed his post in the cantina as hurriedly as he had.

The blood had dried, but he could still smell the metallic stink of the senseless injury. It was a smell that he was certain he would never get accustomed to, but one he had experienced far too many times in his life. War, it seemed, was going to be a companion, in one form or another, for the rest of Josiah's life.

The ride was short. The streets were quiet now that night had fully taken its hold, though the moon was casting a good deal of light onto the street, emanating down from the cloudless sky. Time and reality seemed all twisted around, and Josiah was feeling the weight of uncertain emotions, as well as the uncertainty of what had happened since the start of the day.

He had barely seen one man on the streets since reentering Corpus.

Either Cortina's incursion was over, short-lived and fizzled out, or the citizens of the seaside community were arming themselves and planning for battle again tomorrow. For some reason, Josiah doubted that—there wasn't that recognizable feeling in the air that usually accompanied a long, dug-in battle. Maybe Cortina had been routed out of town and the fighting was over with.

Victory would be a surprise, just as the attack had been, but Josiah knew that nothing was settled, at least as long as Cortina still lived to rise up another day. If the past was a predictor of the future, Cortina would continue the assaults on Texas until he was unable to do so any longer. It seemed the man was focused, persistent, and totally intent on claiming ground that he still believed was owned by the country of his birth and blood: Mexico.

Either way, no matter how things had turned out since the raid, Josiah needed to locate his fellow Ranger and fellow spy Scrap Elliot and find out what was really going on. It had been nearly a week since the two of them had met discreetly and traded information . . . at that time neither of them had stumbled on plans of any kind for incursion by Cortina.

There was no reason to believe that McNelly would send Josiah to Corpus for punishment, to be killed or captured by Cortina, or for revenge, as Miguel had suggested in the room above the cantina. It made no sense to Josiah—and the fact that Miguel had now, essentially, disappeared, his debt repaid to Juan Carlos, didn't add to the story's believability—but he wanted to find out if Scrap had heard anything similar.

McNelly had returned home after the meeting in Austin and was operating now from his ranch in Burton, directing his league of spies to keep track of the cattle rustlers in south Texas. The relationship Josiah held with

McNelly, especially after their face-to-face meeting, was less than accommodating, but still Josiah was having a hard time even considering the idea that the man meant him harm.

Somewhere in the distance, Josiah heard a gunshot. South, near the shore.

He turned down the nearest street—Lawrence, he thought it was. He was certain that the street ended at a long pier that stretched pretty far out into the water, the horizon and whatever lay beyond a mystery that he could not imagine.

Josiah urged on Clipper, who gladly responded, nearing a full run but holding back until the reins were let loose.

Beyond the gunshot, Josiah started to hear the murmur of what he thought was a crowd.

As he rushed down the street, even from the distance away that he still was, the growing ruckus sounded like a gathering swarm of insects, bees maybe, with the hive under threat. The rumble of anger was rising into the night air like a familiar song.

The thing was, though, Josiah didn't know what he was riding into—and still the street was vacant, like all of the town's inhabitants had fled. Or worse, like he had ridden into a ghost town, anybody living having been plucked from the beds, barber chairs, and saloons a long time ago.

He eased back on Clipper, and the Appaloosa came to a steady, decisive stop.

The stallion stood waiting for its next instruction, next command. The loyalty of the horse was a great comfort to Josiah, even when he didn't recognize, or express, the feeling consciously.

He did now, though, knowing full well that he had left Maria Villareal in harm's way because of Clipper, because he refused to leave the horse behind. How could anyone know why he had done such a thing? Even Josiah couldn't fully explain his action, leaving a woman behind to defend herself, no matter how capable she appeared to be.

But he had lost Clipper once before, had been stripped of everything he owned, and it wasn't going to happen to him again. Josiah had made that promise to himself when he had been lucky enough to get the horse back, along with nearly everything else he'd lost.

Josiah was surprised that he had acted almost as impetuously as Scrap Elliot. Perhaps he had come under the spell of his own guise, acting as he thought Zeb Teter would. Still, that thought did not absolve Josiah of any wrongs, and he knew he would have to face the consequences of his actions sooner or later. Hopefully, all that would amount to would be a grand apology to a healing and healthy Maria Villareal.

He was close enough to the buzzing crowd to see the glow of a large fire shimmering over a few of the single-storey buildings that stood along the shore.

The smell of wood smoke was different than that of the burning house earlier in the day. This smelled like pure wood—very similar to the driftwood fire he had shared with Juan Carlos outside of the fishing shacks.

Josiah dismounted, pulled his Winchester out of the scabbard, then grabbed Clipper's reins and made his way toward the noise and light.

Just across an intersection, Josiah could see the silhouette of a deep crowd, gray images transforming into a mass of well-dressed and stricken people alike, pushing and gouging to move forward, to get a better view of . . . something.

He picked up his pace, tightening his grip on Clipper's reins, until he was close enough to see clearly over the heads of hundreds of people. The street sloped down toward the bay, providing a wide view as the buildings fell away and the road ended at the pier.

A gallows had been erected—or stood permanently, Josiah didn't know which—at the point on the land before sand completely took over the beach. A large bonfire burned brightly behind the simple stand of wood, and only one hangman's noose dangled in the breeze.

Three men stood on the gallows. One was a lawman of some note, since he wore a silver star on his chest, probably the marshal or county sheriff. Josiah had met neither man, deciding to keep his identity as much a secret as possible.

The man next to the lawman was a short Mexican, hands bound behind him, feet shackled. Most likely the cause of the gathering.

Josiah wondered if the man was Cortina himself, since he had no earthly idea what the Mexican outlaw and cattle rustler looked like.

He would find out quickly enough, as it were, since the man standing on the other side of the doomed Mexican was Scrap Elliot himself, egging on the crowd, enjoying being the center of attention, getting the population of Corpus Christi all lathered up for the impending hanging.

CHAPTER 16

———◆◆◆◆———

Josiah could not reach Scrap Elliot before the noose was slipped around the Mexican's quivering neck. Pushing through the crowd was proving to be nearly an impossible feat. Every inch of ground had been claimed by a man, woman, or child, pulled from the comfort of his or her home to view a spectacle that obviously could not wait until morning.

Clipper had been tied to a hitching post just beyond the start of the pier, along with a collection of other mounts, hosted by a young boy eager to take a bit to keep an eye on the horses. Josiah was leery of trusting the boy, a shag-haired waif of no more than ten, but felt like he had little choice.

Standing now, unable to move much farther forward, Josiah asked a man next to him what he knew of the hanging.

The man, tall and hefty, with thick blond hair poking out from under a floppy brown felt work hat, spoke with an accent that Josiah did not know the origin of. He spoke with a squeak and pronounced his r's really long, like he was growling all the time. The accent wasn't German or Irish, the most common foreign tongue Josiah had encountered.

"One of Cortina's men that lived," the man said.

Josiah nodded. "The attack failed then?"

"It did," the man said, nodding, too, not taking his eyes off the Mexican. A priest was saying a prayer over the man. Josiah looked away. "None too many of them lived," the man continued. "Cortina will try again, but we need more help from the north, from the powers in Austin, to stop the villains that strive to take what is ours and not theirs."

Still uncertain how much longer to keep his spy identity a secret, Josiah groaned in agreement. "Maybe someday they will send the Rangers down here."

"Someday may be too late. There's a gatherin' of men goin' after Cortina."

"Into Mexico?" Josiah asked.

"Wherever the trail leads. Blood was spilled. The deed must be paid in full. Cortina's head on a stick would end it all—for a day or two until another outlaw steps up to take his place. Thievery abounds when there's so much money to be made in the north country."

Josiah took a deep breath and restrained himself from saying anything further. Even he knew that a vigilante raid into Mexico was a recipe for more trouble than the people of Corpus Christi were bargaining for. They certainly had a right to want revenge against Cortina for the raid, but there were more civilized ways of ending the violence, as far as he was concerned. Ways that would not lead to a larger war. There was no question that Josiah now knew he had to communicate with his superiors—Captain McNelly and the commander of all the Frontier Battalion, Major Jones, and maybe even the adjunct general himself,

William Steele, as soon as possible—before things got out of hand. Before a war started. There were channels set up to do just that—but first, he needed to retrieve Scrap Elliot, and see what damage had been done to their cover.

"I'd be careful out there," Josiah said, taking leave of the man with a nod, pushing forward.

"Won't be me. I got a wife and six children to feed. Work's my only revenge, as long as I am alive," the man said.

"Excuse me," Josiah said, trying to ease past two women looking up briefly to the gallows.

The priest had finished his business with the doomed man. Maybe all of the Mexican's sins had been absolved, his path to heaven open and free—if that were possible, or to be believed. Religion was not a concern of Josiah's. Not since the preacher man in Tyler had objected to coming to the side of his dying wife, Lily, who had asked to be prayed across the river of death. The man was afraid of catching her sickness, afraid his own journey to see his Maker would be hastened.

Josiah had never been much of a believer in the first place; seeing too much war and suffering made sure of that. He could never agree that a higher being was making all of the plans, guiding every man's actions. Such thoughts brought about nothing but pain and sadness. Once he'd lost his own family, a church to him was nothing more than a building full of sheep, eager to accept an order of nothing but chaos and greed. All a man had to do was look around to see the truth as far as Josiah was concerned. Still, he held little contempt for a man that believed; sometimes he wished he could imagine a day when he would be reunited with those that he had lost, living side by side with them for eternity. It all sounded too good to be true to him.

"Excuse me," Josiah said again. The women who were

blocking his way complained with disdainful moans, almost in unison, but finally squeezed together and allowed Josiah by.

It took a concerted effort, but Josiah made his way to the front line of viewers, to the foot of the gallows, pushing out of the crowd, coming to a stop just at the steps that led upward.

The hangman had slipped the rope around the Mexican's neck, then placed a black hood over the man's head.

Josiah stood and watched. There was nothing else to do. It was not the first time he had been witness to a hanging.

The crowd grew quiet, and Scrap, upon seeing Josiah, stepped back into the shadows, behind the priest.

Scrap Elliot was about a head shorter than the padre, lacking any facial hair, his skin soft. He was a scrawny boy, still coming into manhood, with not an ounce of fat on his bones anywhere to be seen. He was all muscle. Which was a good thing—except for the muscles that operated his mouth, as far as Josiah was concerned.

Watching a man hang was never an easy thing, but like every citizen that had staked a claim to be witness to justice, Josiah could not, or would not, look away.

The hangman tightened the knot on the left side of the man's neck, just under the jaw.

The drop would dislocate the neck bone, then sever the spinal cord—if everything worked as it should—bringing a swift and sudden death to the outlaw. But most of the time, hangings didn't go as planned—for whatever reason, intent or lack of experience by the hangman. In some cases, the rope was too long, so the victim's feet would drag the ground, the death slow and suffocating. Intention was obvious if that happened; if hanging wasn't enough, a slow death was its own revenge in some men's minds.

Josiah had never seen such a thing, hoped he never would, but he'd heard of it—recently, when the kin of John Wesley Hardin had been hanged in Comanche. Josiah's own neck had been intended for the noose more than once, and it was only by good luck and good fortune that he wasn't a dead man himself.

Before Josiah could take another breath, the lever was pulled, and the trapdoor flew open beneath the Mexican's bound feet.

If there was a plan to save the man, it was too late. He had been abandoned, left to the fate of the rope—which stretched out like it should, snapping the appropriate bone.

But something went wrong.

The man bounced upward too high. Maybe the rope was too new or chosen poorly by type. Whatever the reason, there was give in it, and on the halting descent, the man's hooded head popped off at the neck, severed like the cap of a mushroom with a sharp knife.

The head went flying through the moonlit night like a cannonball, shot into the air by a silent weapon. It landed with a thud at the foot of a proper lady dressed in scarlet velvet and white satin that was now drenched with the blood of an invader.

The silence of the deed was broken by a constant high-pitched and heightening scream, then a thud as the woman wilted to the ground in a faint.

CHAPTER 17

———◆◈◆———

Scrap Elliot made his way down the stairs, looking more like a cat caught with a canary in his mouth than a fellow spy glad to see his compatriot. "I figured I'd see your snarlin' face sooner or later," Scrap said to Josiah.

Josiah didn't acknowledge Scrap. Instead, he watched the hangman carry the Mexican's head out of sight, leaving a trail of blood all of the way behind the gallows.

The woman who had fainted was lost in a crowd, her tightly laced boots the only part of her body showing. Someone, a man, yelled at the crowd to stand back and give the woman room to breathe, but no one moved.

"That was some spectacle," Josiah answered, turning his attention to the young Ranger. "How'd you come to be in the thick of it?"

"Was right near the shootin' when the fight broke out." Scrap looked down and kicked the sand with the toe of his well-worn boot.

The ocean was not far off, less than fifty feet, and now that the larger crowd, beyond the fainted woman, had begun to disperse, the sound of the waves lapping up to the shore made its way to Josiah's ears. He found no comfort in the persistent cadence of the crashing tide.

"And you just happened upon this Mexican and his fellow bandits, and you couldn't resist lettin' folks know you're a Texas Ranger."

"Somethin' like that." Scrap still hadn't looked Josiah in the eye.

Every muscle in Josiah's body was tight and tense. "Under no circumstance—"

"I know," Scrap snapped, cutting off Josiah, midsentence. "Don't tell no one I'm a Ranger. I'm a spy, but heck, if somebody calls me by my real name, Robert Earl, I'd just walk on by. I don't answer to the name of Hank Sutton. I ain't Hank nobody, Wolfe. I'm me. People been callin' me Scrap so long I don't know nothin' else."

"You took the assignment." Josiah looked over his shoulder and watched the crowd part as the woman, and perhaps her husband, were guided away from the gallows. Several girls followed after the couple like they were maidservants or ladies in waiting, like the woman was a queen or something. The sight did not amuse Josiah. Decapitation was a horrible thing for a woman or a child to witness. Hangings of any kind where never pleasant, and Josiah was most certainly glad the spectacle of this night was coming to an end.

"I know I took it, but what else was I supposed to do? We lost our place in the company because of Feders and the budget cuts in the Frontier Battalion. McNelly didn't need us since he was off restin' up after endin' that feud in Dewitt County. I want to keep bein' a Ranger, Wolfe. Punchin' cattle ain't no life for me. I came here to keep what I had, to do what McNelly wanted, and with all the troubles goin' on in Austin 'cause of the killin', I thought it was the best place for me."

Silence settled between the two men for a long minute. Josiah still carried the rank of sergeant, giving him authority over Scrap, but he was prone not to flaunt any kind of power. Still, he felt the boy needed to learn a solid lesson—that there were greater things than yourself, and by running your mouth, you put more at risk than you realized. Like other people's lives.

"That's no reason to tell somebody the truth. McNelly said to trust no one," Josiah said. His tone was strict and cold, and he stared hard into Scrap's young, inexperienced eyes.

Scrap looked down again, nodded, then looked up. "What are we gonna do now? This is a new war, Wolfe, you know it. The Mexican banditti and the state of Texas are at full-out war, but no one seems to give a damn."

"We need to get word to Austin and make our way back there as quickly as we can."

Josiah looked up at the gallows. The priest had disappeared. The rope dangled in the slight breeze. A wagon pulled away from behind the structure, carrying the Mexican's body—and head—to its final resting place. Only the lawman remained, and he was glaring down at Scrap and Josiah with an odd, angry look on his face.

"Besides," Josiah continued, "I don't think we're going to be safe here for very much longer."

Josiah was glad to find Clipper where he'd left the horse, that he and the rest of the population hadn't been tricked by an eager, unsavory boy set on capitalizing on acting as a watchman over the horses. He'd seen it happen before.

Scrap's horse, a blue roan mare named Missy, was hitched in with a bunch of other horses, too.

"You got your gear with you?" Josiah asked.

"Yup, everything I own."

"Good, let's go." Josiah rounded to the left side of Clipper and easily mounted the Appaloosa.

"Where we goin'?"

"As far away from here as we can get. We need a company of men or more to handle this madness."

Scrap shrugged, obviously realizing that he had no choice but to follow after Josiah. He was not as quick to saddle up on Missy, and in the time that it took the boy to settle in, the lawman who had been standing on the gallows appeared in front of both horses, with his boots firmly planted and his big rancher's hands solidly anchored on his hips.

"You men aren't going anywhere just yet," the man said.

"Wolfe, this here is Sheriff John McLane," Scrap said. "Sheriff, this is Josiah Wolfe, the other Ranger I was tellin' you about."

McLane was of medium height, his face almost indiscernible because of the flickering light from the fire and the darkness of night fighting each other with a battle of shadows. But Josiah could see that the man had piercing eyes, and hands and feet that looked like they belonged on a bigger boned man.

"I'm not fond of having spies in my midst that don't make their presence known to me," McLane said.

"Kind of defeats the purpose, doesn't it, Sheriff?" Josiah made no move to dismount and introduce himself properly to McLane. He sat statue-like, staring down at the man with the same dissatisfaction and tension that he was receiving.

"There isn't a law that makes it necessary, just common decency," McLane said. His voice was strong and carried on the breeze blowing in off the ocean. "Man's got a right to know what's going on in his town, at least set on from the outside world."

"Well," Josiah answered, "that's what we were trying to figure out. Looks like we both failed."

"I'm none too happy about that."

Scrap eased back on Missy, letting Josiah do all the talking.

"I suppose you aren't," Josiah said.

McLane stepped closer to Clipper and lowered his voice. "Word's been sent up to Austin already if you're plannin' on doing such a thing. I've requested a company of Rangers. The whole Frontier Battalion would be more than appreciated since there's more than one of the men here pushing for their own militia. Minute groups they call them. I don't favor them. Revenge is an ugly business, and killing a man just because of the color of his skin or the accent on his tongue is no way to live. The Union war should have proven that to all men, but it is a dim memory, lost to those that didn't walk the battlefields. You look of age, Wolfe, you certainly must understand what I mean. The employment of blood is an uncertain business, the promise of bankruptcy almost a guarantee, wouldn't you say?"

Josiah nodded yes, but said nothing. His service to the state of Texas and the Confederacy was as much a nightmare as a memory. He did not carry his experience serving in the First Texas Brigade in an external, prideful way like some men did. There was no shame involved, and he was as proud as any man should be. He had been a ready volunteer at the start of the war—as much to please his ex-soldier father as for any other reason. But mostly Josiah wanted to leave the battles of the North and South, the politics and blood of it, behind him. Yet it seemed at every turn in his life that the War Between the States was not only a constant shadow but a motivator of men to hate, kill, and pull him further into the deeds of their own nightmares.

"So you have vigilante groups that can't be stopped, and raiders under Cortina's command clashing. No Mexican is safe in this town. Is that what you're saying, Sheriff?" Josiah asked.

"It is. A Mexican with a new saddle will be shot on sight. No questions asked. The governor has got to send a message to everyone involved. This isn't just a rancher's squabble or a hide-skinner's revolt. Richard King is demanding protection from the government for all of his acres and assets, and I'm asking for the same in kind. I know the flavor of war in the air, and this, sir, has a familiar taste," Sheriff McLane said, spitting to the ground.

"I will send word right away to meet the request you have already sent, Sheriff McLane," Josiah said. "I have a channel that'll promise results of some kind, though I can't speak to the arrival of the battalion anytime soon."

He fidgeted with Clipper's reins, eager to get on with the ride. Concern about Juan Carlos returned to the forefront of his mind. Only now, Josiah was not just worried about Maria Villareal's fate, but that of his friend, too.

"Be gone then," the sheriff said, calling out as Josiah turned Clipper and set the horse to run. "But if you come back, Wolfe, make damn sure I know it!"

Josiah didn't answer. He looked over his shoulder to see that Scrap was following him and headed straight for the saloon where Josiah had taken up residence upon arriving in Corpus Christi. The place where he had become—and left behind—the hide trader known as Zeb Teter.

Agusto, the barkeep, would be waiting for him and any news he had for Austin.

CHAPTER 18

The fire was gone, but smoke was still rising off the timbers of the house that had burned earlier in the day. A steady breeze carried the acrid smell of destruction and loss in all directions. Josiah's nose stung.

The moon was fully in its place, high in the black sky, bright enough to swallow up any sight of stars close by and to create more shadows along the streets and alleyways than normal. It was eerily quiet on the way to the cantina. There was not an owl or any other night bird to be heard.

Josiah knew the threat of violence in Corpus Christi was not over by any means.

Every man in town was keeping his trigger finger warm and his gun cocked and ready for the next outbreak of violence or incursion by Cortina's banditos. Any sight of a Mexican, known or unknown, friend or not, would be enough reason to pull that trigger, no questions asked—Sheriff McLane had validated that notion.

A huge chunk of the population of Corpus Christi was now on the side of a war that was not of their choosing.

But they would suffer the consequences nonetheless. The mechanisms of war never changed as far as Josiah was concerned. Innocents were dragged in the mud and into the line of fire.

The street was vacant. No music filled the air, no laughter or rowdy play of hardworking men blowing off steam after a long day spent laboring out in the bay, or on the trail moving cattle or sheep from one place to the next.

Riding up to Agusto's cantina was like tying up in a ghost town, a place devoid of any life due to disease or the bad draw by a railroad planner, taking the trains and all their commerce to another town.

Josiah had seen it happen to the small town where he grew up, just outside of Tyler. He knew all too well how the roll of dice affected the lives of the many and enriched the lives of the few. Corpus was not in danger of dying a slow, painful death because of a lack of money or a bad location—the economy was thriving due to the demand for cattle and wool. The citizens of Corpus were afraid, angry, and plum tired of being attacked, and that was a dangerous combination as far as Josiah was concerned.

Scrap dismounted first, his six-shooter, a Colt Army .45, a Peacemaker similar to Josiah's but newer, already out of his holster.

The boy had changed guns recently, since they had been in Corpus on spy duty, but Scrap had offered no reason about the switch from his old gun to the new one. Josiah smiled inwardly, happy that Scrap had chosen well.

"No need to be jumpy, Elliot." Josiah slid off Clipper. He wore a swivel holster, had for as long as he could remember. He was always ready . . . or at least he thought he was. Scrap, on the other hand, had an itchy finger, always ready to shoot first and ask questions later—if then. Some formal military training would aid the boy, mature his anxiousness to shoot, but the experience was unlikely, at least on a volunteer basis. Scrap was dead set on staying a Texas Ranger, and for the most part, Josiah couldn't blame him.

He grabbed Scrap's shoulder gently and stopped him from walking inside the dark saloon. "These folks know me as Zeb Teter. I'd like to keep it that way," Josiah said, his voice hushed.

"Don't look like nobody's in for a round tonight, Wolfe, so it won't matter much what I call you, will it?"

"It's not a request. These are cautious people, and from what Sheriff McLane told us, they have a right to be."

Scrap scowled at Josiah. "Whatever you say, Sergeant Zeb."

Josiah pushed by Scrap and eased inside the saloon, his own Peacemaker drawn and in hand, at the ready.

Moonlight lit the way into the saloon, but pure darkness took over about three feet inside. Josiah stopped to let his eyes adjust. Scrap bumped into him.

"Pay attention, you fool," Josiah said as quietly as he could through gritted teeth.

Scrap exhaled loudly but didn't say anything.

It only took a second for Josiah to start making out shapes in the darkness: chairs overturned, tables strewn about in chaos, not organized like they usually were every day. The smell of whiskey was thick, like a barrel had been opened and spilled. Beyond all that, Josiah was certain that he saw a body lying on the floor just beyond the bar, facedown.

Without saying a word, Josiah rushed over to the body and found that his greatest fear had quickly proven true. It was Agusto, his skin cold as ice, his head lying in a pool of blood that looked shiny black in the darkness.

"Damn, Wolfe, looks like the battle came inside," Scrap said.

Josiah closed the Mexican barkeep's eyes. "In one way or another."

"Was he your contact?"

Josiah nodded. "Could have been killed for that if somebody found out."

"Seems to me there's a number of reasons for him to be dead," Scrap said, looking over his shoulder, out into the dark street. "He been there for a while? Or you think someone is still around."

"He's not stiff yet. Been a little while, but not long," Josiah said.

"Don't mean nobody's upstairs."

Josiah stood up. "We're not going to find out. This isn't our fight. We need to go." He was out the door before the boy could say another word or raise a question why Josiah was in such a hurry and willing to leave a man lying in his own blood.

There was no question that Josiah was concerned about the fate of another man there, the guitar player, Miguel, who had filled his head with doubt about McNelly's cause to use him as a spy . . . but now was not the time to track the man down. For all Josiah knew, Miguel was dead, too. Shot after they had left each other's company.

It didn't matter to Josiah if Scrap followed him or not; all he could think about was Juan Carlos, whether he was safe, or if he had already suffered the same fate as Agusto.

The shacks came into sight only because of the brightness of the moon and the lack of any thick clouds in the night sky. Any fires that had been used for cooking during the day had long since withered away into orange beds of hot embers. High tide was pushing out, and the roll of waves was softer, gentler, a sound Josiah wasn't sure he could ever get used to. The cadence of waves was foreign to him, the ticktock of it, hypnotic and annoying at the same time because he could not ignore it.

Scrap had indeed followed Josiah out of the saloon and through the streets of Corpus, the distance between them far enough not to afford any contact.

The last thing Josiah wanted to deal with was Scrap Elliot's dislike and distrust of Juan Carlos, so he had pushed Clipper as hard as he could. It would come soon enough, once Scrap caught sight of the old Mexican.

There was no question that Scrap carried his own saddlebag full of prejudices. His lack of respect for Mexicans was as obvious as the new Peacemaker on his hip. But there was something about Juan Carlos in particular that plagued Scrap, caused him to react harsher even than he did around other Mexicans.

Scrap knew that Juan Carlos was Captain Hiram Fikes's half brother and a half uncle to Pearl, who Scrap seemed to like well enough, but none of those relations seemed to matter to the boy, or to deter his anger. Whatever the problem, Josiah didn't care as long as it didn't affect him too much.

The last time Scrap had seen Juan Carlos was after the Mexican had been shot outside of Fort Clark and left to recover. He had made no mention of Juan Carlos since.

Josiah brought Clipper to a halting stop, sand flying forward as the big Appaloosa snorted and turned, avoiding any debris that might fly into his eyes.

"Juan Carlos," Josiah called out, as he slid off the horse, his gun out of the holster in a flash.

Scrap came to a stop just behind Clipper. Both horses were accustomed to each other, seemed to be on friendlier terms than their riders. Missy, the roan mare, nudged Clipper immediately, as if to say hello.

"So that's what this is about," Scrap said, dismounting. "I should've figured as much—what with you takin' out of that cantina like lightnin' had struck your forehead, Wolfe."

Josiah ignored Scrap and headed for the shack where Maria Villareal had been taken. He had no idea what time of the night it was, only that it was late. It didn't matter to him at the moment whether he woke up the entire camp or not.

The door opened, and Juan Carlos pushed outside, a rifle in his hands. "You need to leave, Señor Wolfe." The Mexican's face was drawn tight, his brown leathery skin almost completely free of wrinkles. Veins were protruding on his forehead, and even from a distance, Josiah was almost certain the man's eyes were red, like he'd been crying.

Josiah stopped and stared at Juan Carlos. The rifle was cradled in his arms, but the man had not dropped the weapon or lowered its aim at Josiah upon recognizing him. Nor had the anger on his face vanished, as Josiah suspected it would.

"I will repeat myself only one more time, señor. You need to leave."

"You are not safe here, Juan Carlos," Josiah said. "We all need to leave as soon as we can . . . while the moon offers us passage into the night."

"I am not going anywhere, now or ever."

"You heard him, Wolfe," Scrap said. "He ain't leavin', now let's get out of here before one of them minute groups shows up and starts a gunfight we don't want to be a part of. 'Cause I sure ain't takin' the side of this here Mexican. You sure as hell knew that when you led me here."

Josiah glanced over his shoulder, offering Scrap a look that he should have been able to decipher by now: It meant shut up.

"You should listen to the wily one this time. Scrap Elliot knows of what he speaks, Señor Wolfe." Juan Carlos said. He stepped forward and raised the rifle, aiming it directly at Josiah's chest. "Maria is dead."

"I'm sorry," Josiah said. The air had left his chest. He felt like he had been gut-shot himself. "I only left her for a minute," he whispered.

"Sorry is no offer of remorse," Juan Carlos said, his face twisting with so much grief that Josiah barely recognized him. "You are responsible for her death, Josiah Wolfe. You left a woman to defend herself in the streets. It does not matter how capable you think she was. I shall never forgive you for putting the only woman I have ever loved in such danger that it cost her her life. Now leave. Or I will kill you myself."

CHAPTER 19

There was nothing to do but leave.

Josiah felt like he was walking through quicksand as he trudged slowly toward Clipper. His mind was numb, posing objections to Juan Carlos silently, not daring to speak another word, rewinding the events of the day, seeing the reality of blame in the angry eyes of his friend.

If anybody knew the depths of grief, it was Josiah. He had lost his wife, Lily, and three daughters, in the matter of a year, to a silent killer, a sickness that was slow and the suffering long. Watching a child soaked in fevers, struggling to live, raising her arms up in need, begging for relief, for help when there was none to be had, was the worst kind of pain a man like Josiah could imagine. To watch three children fall to the same fate, then his pregnant wife, too weak to give birth to their son, too, was a journey to madness that always ended at the cemetery.

His son was three years old now, a survivor of the grip of death only because of the courage of the midwife, Ofelia, who would become the baby's wet nurse and caretaker. A woman who Josiah was glad to call friend, Mexican or not, and one that watched over his son at this very moment in Austin so he could continue to serve with the Texas Rangers and rebuild his life. One more time.

It was to Josiah's surprise, then, that Juan Carlos had a relationship with anyone as close as that he claimed with Maria Villareal. That he loved her as he stated, and claimed her as the only woman in the world who had a deed of any kind to his heart, was news. Josiah had never seen Juan Carlos give any woman a hint of affection—either with a look or an act—other than Pearl Fikes, his niece, and then it was a different kind of affection.

Whether Juan Carlos had reason to live, to fight through the grief that was surely hanging hard on the old Mexican's heart now, was beyond telling. All Josiah knew was that he had lost a good friend. Lost one of the few men he trusted his back to and would willingly die for without a second thought. He still felt that way, would gladly take a bullet for Juan Carlos if it came to that.

There was no way Josiah could give Juan Carlos the message Maria had given him, that she, too, had loved the man who claimed to love her. There was no way to know the story, why the two of them could never get their love together, but it felt all too familiar to Josiah. He could see loving Pearl Fikes from a distance, just like Juan Carlos had loved Maria Villareal.

Losing his friend, on top of everything else, was too much to swallow. It would have been easier if Juan Carlos were dead, killed in a great battle of some kind—offering his life for a valiant cause. But that was not the case. Juan Carlos still walked the earth, carrying a grudge, a matter of deep hatred for Josiah that did not appear able to be settled. It was a sad turn of events, one that Josiah could have never predicted.

There was no hope of forgiveness in Juan Carlos's eyes or in his actions.

Knowing that would be the hardest note to take. Josiah was not sure how to handle any of it, other than to do as he was told and leave his friend behind. Perhaps forever.

He stopped and looked over his shoulder at Juan Carlos one last time before mounting his Appaloosa.

The Mexican stood solidly, the rifle aimed at Josiah, with no offer to change anything that had happened or been said.

Scrap was already situated on Missy, ready to go. "Come on, Wolfe, let's get out of here before that old fool goes and does somethin' stupid. If he shoots, I'll shoot. And you know I'll be glad to take an extra shot just to make sure the devil is dead."

"Careful with your tongue, Elliot."

"Ain't my tongue you should be worried about. I never trusted that man in the first place, always showin' up and disappearin' at the moment of the worst consequences. What you see now is the reason why. Given the chance, he'll turn on you like a snake—bite you in the back of the ankle and scurry off to Lord knows where. Some place like this, a row of shacks left off by somebody else for him to take up in. He's a bad streak just waitin' to show himself."

"I'll never believe that."

"Don't matter to me much what you believe, Wolfe. I know what my gut says, and that's about the only thing I trust at the moment." Scrap hesitated a second. "Come on, Missy, let's go," he said, urging the roan mare forward, scowling at Josiah as he went off slowly, his finger still on the trigger of his Peacemaker.

Josiah settled into his saddle but was in no hurry to follow anyone.

His skin felt like it was being stung by a million bees, each one stabbing its stinger into every open pore it could find. His mouth was dry, and he could hear his heart beating. If he'd been a crying man, tears would have already busted through the dam in his eyes. Josiah had lost his ability to cry a long, long time ago—burying everything you love in the family cemetery will do that to a man. Still, inside, Josiah's own gut was shredded to pieces.

The waves continued to beat against the shore and then retreat. The moon reflected off the water like a giant light hung over a mirror. Corpus Christi was behind him, south, and if Josiah had it his way, he'd never, ever, set foot in that city again.

"Giddy up, Clipper. Let's go now," Josiah said, catching up with Scrap, forcing himself not to look back.

The luck of the weather and the cycle of the moon were on Josiah and Scrap's side, making it easy for them to navigate the trail in the thick of night. For once, Josiah was more than glad to let Scrap take the lead.

The boy seemed to know where he was going, and that was just fine. All Josiah wanted to do was ride, let Clipper run without worry or caution. Which, of course, was something Josiah would never do at night under normal circumstances. But this had not been a normal day, or an ordinary night that called for discipline and common sense—even though he was putting himself and his horse at risk. The irony of that decision was not lost on Josiah, but any other structure of normalcy *was* lost to him. He could barely think and, in reality, had no desire to think or feel anything.

It was like the moment when he realized that Lily was dead, that all he had built after surviving everything he had in the War Between the States was gone. Just gone. He'd cursed God then. Wanted to die himself. Could not feel anything but rage.

Now the rage was directed at himself . . . for making a bad decision, a choice that had resulted in the death of a fine woman. He wanted time to stop or to be able to turn back time, but he knew that was impossible. Even now, in his current state, Josiah knew he could not undo what had been done.

Clipper rode directly behind Scrap and Missy, keeping a steady and consistent horse length between them. The horse seemed to sense that Josiah had lost the ability to control anything in the present moment, but Clipper continued to handle himself with surety and confidence. That was one of the reasons Josiah had refused to leave the Appaloosa behind; they knew how to communicate, how to survive with each other. He trusted the horse with his life, and Clipper in return obviously felt the same way. At least there was still that.

Josiah and Scrap skirted the ocean, never straying from it. The moon hung over them, finally reaching its apex, continuing to light the way as they rode hard, farther and farther away from the village of shacks and the unstable city of Corpus Christi.

The salt air had lost its ability to soothe Josiah like a tonic; now it stung his nose, smelled putrid and dead. The night had cooled dramatically, and the steady breeze blowing in off the water was turning cold—a sensation Josiah was not accustomed to. He ignored the discomfort, instead focusing on the darkness that lay ahead, pushing off nightmares of the past as quickly as they popped into his head. This was no time to revisit the war, his loss of Lily and the girls, or any other tragedy, and he knew it. Still, it was difficult not to get caught up in the pain he felt.

Clipper pushed on, trailing after Scrap and Missy. The creak of the saddle was familiar and much more calming than the crash of the ocean waves rising up out of the darkness.

They drew close to a town, mostly dark, but a few bonfires still blazed on the shore, reflecting back on a main street lined with several single-storey buildings. Distant music met Josiah's ears, a sudden, but dim, distraction from the silent conversation he was having with himself.

Somewhere in the town there was a saloon, still alive into the night, drawing wayward men like himself to the light. For a moment, Josiah thought about protesting, about rushing up to Scrap and taking the lead. The last thing he wanted to do was ride into another town and deal with strangers.

But . . . there was still duty to think about. If there was a saloon, there was a telegraph operator. The trick would be to rouse one at this time of night. Hopefully, the currency Josiah and Scrap carried by being Texas Rangers would serve the cause.

The need was not lost, just jumbled in with the emotional torment unleashed by Juan Carlos's actions and the death of Maria Villareal. Captain McNelly needed to be made aware of the seriousness of the situation in Corpus, that the state of war was real and not created by small groups of anxious cattlemen. The governor and General Steele needed to be made aware, too. It would take all of their powers jointly to put an end to Cortina and his raiders once and for all. And Josiah still wanted to be a part of that battle.

With a gentle push and a couple of loud clicks with his tongue, Josiah told Clipper to speed up, to catch up with Scrap and Missy. Just as he thought, the Appaloosa was holding back, waiting for him to tell him what to do.

"You know where we're going?" Josiah asked, riding up alongside Scrap.

Scrap nodded. "Ingleside. We can get word out to Austin, then ease in the rest of the way. I, for one, am darn glad to be free of Corpus and that spy business. I like bein' a Ranger with a company a heck of a lot more than I like playin' like I'm somebody else."

Josiah didn't respond, he just settled back, giving Scrap the lead again, and watched the little village come into full sight.

He wasn't so sure the spy business was over with . . . at least for him.

CHAPTER 20

———◆◆◆———

Ingleside was a much bigger town than it looked from the distance. It sat inland, not right on the shore, but close enough to enjoy the gentle night breeze off the water. Three wide streets, cut off with intermittent alleyways, made up the commercial district. Simple frame houses made up the rest of the town, situated under canopies of live oaks and the occasional palm tree. Most of the houses were dark, as were most of the businesses.

A dim lamp sat burning in the sheriff's window, a small white stone building with heavy bars on all of the windows.

Scrap pulled Missy up to the hitching post, tied her off, dismounted, and stood in wait. "You comin' in, Wolfe?"

Josiah sat solidly in the saddle, staring down the street at the brightly lit saloon. Music and laughter flooded out into the street, along with a good deal of light, cutting into the night like a flare set high in the sky. In an odd way, a way that was unusual for Josiah, he was drawn to the light, to the liveliness. He knew if there was one place to numb his mind and body, he was looking at it.

"No, I'll wait. Things didn't go so well with Sheriff McLane. You tell him what you need to. Maybe he can rustle up the telegraph operator and make the morning in Austin a lively one."

Scrap stared at Josiah with a curious look on his face. Innocence still showed on the boy's face, even at night, but there was a knowing consideration in his eyes that was surprising. "You're gonna wait for me, right, Wolfe?"

Josiah ignored the question. "Go on, now. Do what you came to do."

Scrap shrugged and loped inside the jail, checking over his shoulder twice before disappearing behind a closed door.

Josiah waited until he heard voices before easing Clipper down the street. The saloon was two blocks south.

Ingleside shared a lot of the same construction techniques as Corpus—most of the buildings were made of shellcrete or wood; the hard shell made the buildings more durable and able to withstand the massive storms that billowed ashore in the summer and fall of the year. There was only one two-storey building that Josiah could see, a hotel, welcoming even in the dark. It was whitewashed, and the sign over the double doors was gilded with gold lettering and fancy leaves, announcing that the Stratford House was a place of fine comfort. Most all of the windows were dark, but a few, the ones closest to the saloon, still burned.

The buildings in between the hotel and the saloon consisted of a hat maker, a mercantile, and a newspaper office. Josiah could see a clock on the wall in the newspaper office, from the light emitting out of the saloon. It was nearly midnight.

There had to be a livery close, but Josiah decided to wait to stable Clipper. He hitched up the Appaloosa and patted the horse's neck. "Don't go causing any trouble now, you hear."

Clipper didn't respond, just stood motionless, his nose pointed toward the batwings of the saloon.

The ground under Josiah's boots was soft, pliable, but not muddy. He'd had trouble getting his footing on sand from the day he arrived in Corpus Christi. It just seemed harder to walk on, to get where he was going.

He gladly made his way to the boardwalk, hopped up on it, then walked into the saloon without a second thought. Elliot would have no trouble figuring out where he'd gone— even though he didn't know Wolfe as a drinking man, or a man who partook in libations on a regular basis. Now that he thought of it, the boy had never seen him smoke, cuss, or take enough whiskey to his tongue to make him the least bit . . . drunk.

The noise and light were overwhelming, and it took Josiah a second to adjust his vision and get his bearings. He stopped just inside the door.

It was a long, narrow, single-level room, and every lamp was burning as brightly as possible. The bar took up a whole wall, a mirror reflecting the action on the floor. Bottles were heavily stocked, and there wasn't an empty stool to be had. Cowboys mixed with ranch hands. Gentlemen gamblers sat at the tables, which were jam-packed tight in the room so that it was difficult to navigate the floor without rubbing or bumping into someone. Women, brightly and provocatively dressed, flittered about, pouring beer, hanging on to men, hoping to bring some luck or a customer after the last faro card had been dealt.

Smoke hung in the air like storm clouds forming on a spring day, the bite of the tobacco stinging Josiah's nose. There were other smells—whiskey, perfume—mixed in with the smoke, the business of rowdiness and relief creating an aroma all its own.

Josiah pushed his way to the bar and stood patiently

behind a man already waiting his turn for a refill of beer.

"You're off da trail awful late. You pushin' in dem woollies?" The man was short, wore a grizzled beard that was gray, like his eyes, and was dressed in shepherd's clothes, a loose-fitting sack shirt, tied at the waist with a rope. He wore a black felt hat with a hawk feather stuck in the band.

Josiah shook his head no. "Just coming in for a drink, that's all."

"You see any of dem damn Meshicans?"

"No."

"Two fellas traded shots earlier. Won't be long and dat der trouble will make its way here, I tell you."

"Maybe."

Josiah watched the barkeep, a thin rail of a man, his black hair thick with pomade, move behind the bar with grace and purpose. There was not a wasted move to be witnessed. The pull of a draft with one hand brought the other hand around to an empty glass in anticipation of the next drink to fill. Obviously, the saloon was consistently busy. That or the man was a dancer of some kind; he orchestrated drinks for a thirsty crowd like a performer on a stage.

Josiah was leery of barkeeps. Had reason to be. He knew of their shooting skills firsthand. He was sure there was a cache of weapons under the bar, within quick reach of the talented barkeep.

A beer and an open hand appeared almost out of nowhere, taking the shepherd by surprise. The barkeep's demanding eyes were close behind. Time was being wasted.

"Der, der, you go . . ." the short man said, dropping his coins into the barkeep's outstretched hand. "You watch out for dem damn Meshicans, now."

The barkeep scowled at the shepherd, as the hand with the money in it disappeared behind a short apron. He pointed at Josiah with the other hand. "What is it for you, mister?"

The shepherd quickly disappeared into the crowd, leaving the smell of wet wool to linger a bit longer just behind him.

"Whiskey," Josiah said. "Rye whiskey. And make it two."

CHAPTER 21

A stool emptied at the opposite end of the bar, and Josiah made his way through the crowd of men. He'd downed the whiskeys one right after the other. His nostrils flared, his throat burned, but he didn't feel invigorated. The problem was, he still felt every bit of the guilt and anger that he'd tried to rid himself of in the first place. There was no immediate numbing of his heart or memory, and that unsettled him more than his inability to move through the saloon without bumping into someone or catching an elbow in the side himself.

He'd drunk more whiskey since arriving in Corpus than any other time in his life. Being young and away from home, when he'd first gone off to fight in the War Between the States, had presented many temptations. Drinking whiskey was one of them, and women, of course, was another. But the enjoyment of drunkenness had never taken hold with Josiah. Whiskey left him feeling sick, made his head hammer with pain even before the anguish of the next day set in. Losing all sense of his common faculties was not something that appealed to him, either, even at a young age.

Over time, as his life changed, and the reality of drinking whiskey made itself known to him, there would be months in between a swig of the alcohol, then years, especially after he married Lily. There was no desire to live a rowdy life then, if there ever had been before. There was no temptation to avoid because the desire was just not there.

His father had never taken a liking to whiskey, either, so Josiah supposed it was a family thing—maybe it didn't agree with them the way cabbage or milk disagreed with some people.

Life as a spy and Ranger seemed to be changing everything, and Josiah was growing accustomed to the taste of fire and ferment, though he still couldn't say he enjoyed it. Enough whiskey just eased certain parts of his mind to a quiet, or unrecognizable, place, made him forget for a brief moment that he still had responsibilities in the world, like a son waiting at home, growing up quickly without the presence of his father. That thought, missing out on Lyle's childhood, was harder to swallow most of the time than the burning whiskey. Add on the dizzying emotional torrent unleashed by the senseless death of Maria Villareal, and whiskey sure seemed like a quick cure for a haunting memory, even for a man like Josiah Wolfe.

He could still hear the woman's dying wish, *Tell Juan Carlos I have always loved him.* And that made him push harder to the bar, made him hunger for another drink of whiskey so he could rid himself of that ghostly voice.

The vacant stool faced toward the door, which was a good thing. Keeping an eye out for Scrap was not a priority, but never having his back to the door was. It was a mistake that he would not make, even in a nearly inebriated state. Josiah was also in direct sight of the barkeep and signaled his desire for another glass of whiskey as he settled onto the seat.

The barkeep nodded and, within a matter of seconds, produced the desired drink without asking how much, or what kind of whiskey.

Josiah had adjusted to the smoke in the large room and the loud noise, the laughter, and the ping and chink of the piano, which probably had metal taps installed on the keys, from the sound of things. It didn't matter; the louder the music the better as far as he was concerned. It was typical saloon fare—fast and wordless—the piano player an obvious professional who knew what he was doing.

The crowd in the saloon was a surprise so late, packed as it was, and through the week. Most men looked like cowboys, probably readying for a long ride north. Others were woollies—sheep men—fewer in number, wary of the cowboys, and all huddled together in a far corner, either keeping together by choice or maintaining their safety in numbers, much like the animals they served as guardians to.

The whiskey had taken its course and warmed Josiah from head to toe. As it was, he was sweating.

"Hey, there, brother, you look familiar," the thin, balding man sitting next to Josiah said. "You ever get up Fort Worth way?"

"I've been through there."

"We all been through there, brother. Have you spent any time there? Put your boots under the bed a time or two? Lived there, son, or just punched through?" A cigarette dangled from the man's lips. Scrap called them quirlies, and the man's cigarette smelled similar to what the boy hand-rolled and smoked, like a sheaf of useless weeds, all bound together and set afire.

"No, can't say that I have. That where you're heading?" Josiah asked.

The man drew hard on the cigarette, then exhaled, exposing a mouthful of yellow teeth. "What makes you think I'm heading anywhere?"

Josiah smirked. "We're all heading somewhere, brother," he said, mocking the man's original tone.

The man flashed a cockeyed look at Josiah. Anger rippled across his thin face, then disappeared as quickly as it had appeared, replaced by a look of knowing in his beady eyes. He nodded. "I suppose we are. Or coming from some place else, like Corpus. That your story? You take a fight to them Mexicans who sought to invade that peaceful city on the bay?"

"Could be. I'm just looking for relief, I guess," Josiah said.

"Well, it looks like all the doves are spoken for; you're gonna have a long wait if female comfort is what you're after, brother."

"That's fine. I'll take companionship with my drink, if you don't mind."

As with whiskey, Josiah had never taken a liking to rambling, searching out one woman and then on to the next. He understood Maria's claim of true love for Juan Carlos more than he could admit, but his one true love was dead, buried in the family plot on the little farm outside of Tyler. Now his temptation was to love again, whether it be Pearl Fikes, Billie Webb, or temporary female companionship. It wasn't like he'd never purchased time with a woman—his first time was like that, in the war. But that was different. That was a mountain to climb, a rite of passage. Now he was just lonely, unwilling to allow another woman to get close to him like he had Lily. At the very least, he could have his way with a dove, as the man had called the whores, and then leave. There would be no memory or requirement of emotion, the bill paid in full, left on the table after the deed was done. It was always an option for Josiah—but thinking about it was as far as he ever got these days.

The man shrugged off Josiah's comment. "Like I would care about your choice of companionship."

"I suppose you wouldn't."

The man motioned for the barkeep. "Two. One for me, and one for my new friend here."

"That's not necessary," Josiah said, but it was too late. Two whiskeys appeared in front of them, like they had been conjured in a magician's show.

"Too late now." The man picked up his glass and downed the whiskey in one hungry gulp. For a thin man, it looked like he could hold his drink.

Josiah followed suit, the whiskey traveling easier into his gullet this time around, the warm buzz growing, and the numbness that he was seeking when he first arrived in the saloon slowly taking over, but taking over nonetheless.

The man reached down and tapped out the cigarette on the well-worn heel of his boot, then stuffed the remainder of it in a pouch he pulled from his pants pocket. "My name's Edgar Leatherby, by the way."

Josiah nodded, extended his hand, and didn't miss a beat with his response. "Zeb. Zeb Teter. Nice to meet you, Edgar." They shook hands cautiously, then Josiah returned to staring at the bottom of the empty glass in front of him. His ears were starting to ring.

"My friends call me Leathers. Used to be Father Leatherby, but that was a lifetime or two ago."

"You don't look like a preacher man."

"I'm not now. But I was once. I spent the best years of my life in the New Melleray Abbey in Iowa. Trappist monks. You know about them?"

Josiah shook his head no. "I don't know much about religion. Can't say I ever met a monk. Wouldn't know one if I saw one."

"Perhaps you're better off," Leathers said, motioning for another drink. He poked his index finger in the air, ordering just one drink this time around, leaving Josiah to buy his own—which he was not inclined to do, at the moment.

"What are you now?" Josiah asked.

"Just a drover, setting off north like most of these fellas. Working the trail, making money, still wandering, but still seeking, too. 'For then are they monks, if they live by the work of their hands.' A Rule of St. Benedict. I guess I can't escape my past. How about you?"

"I've never been a monk," Josiah laughed. For some reason he found his own response funny. It had been ages since he'd cracked a smile and let out a laugh. It was a foreign sound to his ears, and there was no question that the laugh was provoked by the amount of alcohol he'd drunk.

Leathers laughed, too. But it was a short laugh. His face grew serious faster than Josiah's. "Well, Zeb Teter, you never did answer my question about Fort Worth. You ever spend much time there? I swear I've seen you somewhere before, brother."

Josiah shook his head no, again, and studied Leathers a little closer, looking to see if he looked familiar, too. He didn't like being called "brother" and was sure he would remember that if he'd met the man before.

Edgar Leatherby was as tall as Josiah, but thin as a hitching post. He smelled of tobacco and whiskey, and his clothes were worn, not quite rags but not store-bought and green with hard creases, either. A black felt hat lay on the bar. It looked like a surviving relic of the man's past life; a padre's hat to cover up his balding head. Josiah had seen men wearing the hats and black robes before, in and around the churches and missions of every town he had visited, but never paid them much attention, or wondered about the meaning or use of the attire.

"I grew up near Tyler," Josiah said. "Spent all my life there until I left out for the war. Came home to it, then moved on to Austin not so long ago. Been on the trail since, but I get back to the capital from time to time. I'm not sure I'm cut of the cloth that will allow enjoyment of city life. Was up Fort Worth way nearly a year ago, but that was for the matter of a day. Not much more than that prior, maybe passing through a few years back, too. I think you must be mistaking me for somebody else."

"What are you doing here?"

"Trading hides."

Leathers chuckled, took the drink from the barkeep, downed it, then looked Josiah square in the eye and said, "You're a terrible liar, Zeb Teter."

"Now, why would you go and say that?"

"I've known hide traders, been friends with them, and you don't have the fingers or the smell they did."

"Ever cross your mind I was new at it?"

"No. It crossed my mind that you're saying you're something you're not." Leathers put his hand on Josiah's shoulder and stared directly at him, a hard, penetrating look in his eyes. "It's all right, brother, you can be anything you want to be. I don't mind, but you're fooling yourself, not me."

Something stirred deep in Josiah's stomach; rage quick to rise, an uncontrollable feeling that was as alien as the taste of salt air on his tongue and his belly full of whiskey. "My name is Zeb Teter. I am what I say I am. Now, take your damn hand off me."

Just as Leathers retreated, taking his hand back, reacting to the strong tone in Josiah's voice, a chorus of anger and loud voices rose up behind the two men.

Josiah turned, cast a threatening glance toward the ex-monk, then saw the beginnings of a fight breaking out two tables beyond where they were sitting, nearly in the center of the saloon.

It was a faro table, and all four men were standing, hard and tense. Before Josiah could take another breath, a spunky young cowboy, outfitted in new and unused gear from head to toe, threw a punch. It landed squarely on the jaw of a man who could have passed as a banker but was probably a professional gambler, caught, or suspected of, taking the young cowboy's last dollar in a game that was likely crooked from the start. Another man, catching Josiah's eye, looked a lot like Miguel. But the fight began before Josiah could be sure that the man was who he thought he was—the Mexican disappeared in the crowd, looking over his shoulder warily at Josiah.

The piano music intensified. Chairs scooted. Tables toppled over. One swing turned into a dozen, and in the blink of an eye, the entire room had broken out into a fight among strangers and friends, a free-for-all that had just been waiting to happen.

CHAPTER 22

Josiah blocked the first swing that came his way; surprisingly it was not from Leathers. The tall man had stepped in front of Josiah and taken on a cowboy who was aiming to use a bar stool as a weapon on the first person he came to. Leathers ducked, swung, and pummeled the man with two quick fists to the nose, followed by an uppercut to the chin and then a punch in the gut, sending the cowboy slithering to the floor. The bar stool tumbled to the ground.

The favor was not lost on Josiah, no matter the state he was in. Leathers, who had fast hands for a one-time monk, had saved him a hard beating with the stool, and that was duly noted. But saved for later, other than a nod, a direct look in the eye. The attack quickly sobered Josiah, and it came as a great surprise to him that he was fighting in tandem with Leathers, as they made their way toward the door.

Leathers batted down a flying bottle, and Josiah pummeled a man blocking their way. Luckily, at least at this point there had been no gunfire.

The saloon was loud with shouts, music, and a few screams. Most of the girls had scattered behind the bar or out the front door. The barkeep kept working as if it were a typical day, until a man slid across the bar, causing him to duck and drop to the floor. When he reappeared he had a Parker Brothers eight-gauge shotgun in his hand and a scowl on his face. No one heard the barkeep load the shotgun, but they heard the thunder boom and saw the plaster shower from the ceiling once he pulled the trigger. It was a one-storey building, and now there were holes in the roof. It didn't look like it was the first time the shotgun had been fired into the ceiling; darkness poked through into the brightly lit room in an odd, distant way.

A sudden hush fell over the saloon. Not one man dared to breathe, including Josiah, who was about to throw a punch at a man who had appeared out of nowhere and punched him solidly in the mouth. The blow had dizzied Josiah, but left him standing on his feet with enough strength to muster a retaliation.

Blood drizzled out of the corner of Josiah's mouth, the taste salty and sour at the same time, mixed with the whiskey and the adrenaline from the riotous fight.

"Clean it up, and get the hell out of here," the barkeep yelled, lowering the barrel of the shotgun with a sudden sweep downward, fanning out to the center of the room, threatening to begin firing into the crowd at any second.

It was nothing short of a stampede as every man rushed for the door, all of them clearing out of the saloon as quickly as they could. Josiah was forced to keep up or get pushed to the floor. Everyone took the barkeep seriously.

It only took a minute to push through the doors of the saloon and be out of shotgun range and able to break free of the running mob.

Most men were laughing now, the aftermath of the fight transforming into a glow of satisfaction and relief from the pent-up rage that had started the whole thing in the first place. Rarely was a fight on that scale a personal matter. Months on a cattle drive can be maddening and lonely, and the same can be said for the shepherds, out with sheep, moving them from range to range, without seeing another human being for months.

Josiah got his bearings—to search for the Mexican, Miguel, and to look down the street and see Scrap riding toward him with another man trailing after him, not far behind.

"Lord have mercy, Wolfe, what in tarnation did you get yourself into?" Scrap asked, a half smile on his face as he slid off Missy and met Josiah face-to-face.

"Just a friendly fight," Josiah answered, his words slurring together slightly as he wiped the blood from the corner of his mouth.

"Are you drunk?"

"Have you ever seen me drunk?"

"Not until today."

Josiah rolled his eyes. He wasn't in the mood to argue with Scrap. All he wanted to do was find a place to bed down for the night, then get as far away from Ingleside as he could first thing in the morning.

"Marshal's gonna go wake up the telegraph operator, get him to send the news about Cortina's raid to Austin," Scrap said.

The other man that had been trailing after Scrap waltzed up and stood in between the men like he belonged there, like he had known the two of them all his life, even though Josiah had no clue who the man was. He was in his late thirties, with a droopy mustache that matched his droopy eyes, and clothes that hung on his skinny frame. "You must be Wolfe," the man said, sticking his hand out for a shake.

"Most people know me as Zeb Teter," Josiah said, casting a scowling glance at Scrap—who just shrugged and smiled in return.

"Your secret's safe with me, Ranger. Phil Harlan's my name. I'm the marshal here in Ingleside."

The man had a hearty handshake for looking so much like a weakling. Josiah assumed the eight-inch-barreled Colt on his hip was a warning as such, for the uninitiated to take him seriously.

"Safe or not, Marshal Harlan, I'd just as soon keep my name quiet. I spent a lot of time in Corpus trying to get people to believe in me."

"How'd that turn out for you?"

Josiah cocked his eyebrow. "What are you saying?"

"Not saying anything, just askin'. Don't matter much anyway, since I figure you won't be staying around long. Unless you'd like to give Bert Shoose a hand at patching his roof again."

"That eight-gauge was nearly as big as the barkeep," Josiah said with a chuckle, relaxing on the marshal's tone.

"Bert's a good man. Just ain't got much patience for a fight. That eight-gauge makes my job easier and keeps a few good men in work cleanin' up after the mess he makes with it."

Josiah relaxed a bit more, the pain from the fight subsiding. Leathers caught his attention, coming to a stop on the boardwalk, just outside the hotel entrance.

"We'll be leaving in the morning," Josiah said.

The marshal nodded. "I best get on. The sooner Austin knows of the war with Cortina, the sooner we'll get some help down here."

"I wouldn't count on that," Scrap said.

Marshal Harlan grimaced. "You might be right. I sure as heck hope not. There's a back room with a couple of cots down at the jail if you fellas need a place to flop for the night. Feel free to stable your horses there, too."

"That's kind of you, Marshal," Josiah said.

"Well, I'll tell you, if I didn't have a wife and three little girls waitin' for me at home, I'd join right up with you and be a Ranger myself," Marshal Harlan said. "But I'd be hard-pressed to convince my wife that ridin' roughshod on the trail with a bunch of boys is a way to make a living. Besides, that ain't no way to raise a family, is it?"

Scrap glanced over at Josiah and kept quiet.

Josiah's mouth had gone dry, and his stomach felt like he'd been punched solidly. "Thank you for your kindness, Marshal Harlan. We'll try not to be any more trouble before we leave." The tone was cold, all business, as was the look on Josiah's face.

The marshal turned and headed south, not so much in a hurry, but he seemed glad to be relieved of Josiah and Scrap's company.

"Some men don't know what they're sayin'," Scrap said.

"Doesn't matter," Josiah answered. "Why don't you go get the horses bedded down in the marshal's stable. I'll be there shortly."

"Where you goin'?"

"I need to thank a friend for saving me a bit of trouble."

Leathers was sitting on a bench just to the left of the hotel door, smoking a cigarette. "Didn't expect to see you again, Teter."

"Wanted to thank you for fighting along with me instead of against me."

"I have no quarrel with you."

"I was about to have one with you."

"That was the whiskey sitting on your tongue talking the devil's talk."

"Could be, but I appreciate the intention. So, thanks. It was good of you." Josiah turned to walk away.

"Are you lost, Zeb Teter?"

He stopped. "I know where I'm at. Why would you ask that?"

"You just seem like a man who's lost an arm, but acting like you're still carrying it with you."

Josiah squished his forehead. "Is that what monks do?"

"What's that?"

"Ask questions that don't make any sense?"

Leathers laughed out loud, exposing his yellow teeth and a twinkle in his eyes that made him look years younger. "Well, I suppose that's part of it, but I gave up being a monk a long time ago. The best I could, anyways. You just look like you could use a friend, Zeb, that's all."

"Problem is, I think I've lost one," Josiah said.

"Well, that's never easy, Zeb, but it's not the end of the world."

"I'm not so sure of that."

"You know what, me either," Leathers said, tapping the cigarette out on the bottom of his boot. "Me either."

CHAPTER 23

───────❖───────

The sun was barely peeking over the horizon, but Josiah had pulled himself out of a deep and restless sleep to spend some time brushing Clipper, readying the Appaloosa, and himself, for what came next.

His body ached and his head pounded, obvious ailments from the aftermath of drinking too much whiskey and being in a fight. Each time he drank too much, Josiah promised himself it would never happen again—especially once he returned home to Austin. But that was turning into a false promise, one that he continued to break the longer he was away from home, from the touchstones that told him who he was.

Marshal Harlan's words about family, and the demands of the Ranger life, had circled around in Josiah's head like a worm trapped in an apple, as he'd tried to sleep off the fight and whiskey of the prior night. The words were a nightmare within themselves, but like Scrap said, the sheriff didn't know what he was saying, didn't know that he had hit a nerve with Josiah, talking about the toll of Ranger life on a family.

In reality, Josiah doubted that he would be a Ranger, either, spending weeks and months away from home, if his own family were still alive.

Still, he loved the Rangering life, though the most recent spate of time spent as a spy was not a duty he cared to repeat. Josiah liked being in a company, liked the structure of the battalion. There were certainties, things were common. You knew what to expect, unlike the past few days and weeks.

As he continued to brush his horse, lost in his thoughts and glad for the silence, Josiah allowed himself a moment of grief, not only for the loss of Maria Villareal, but for the damage done to his friendship with Juan Carlos.

There was an empty spot inside him that he didn't know how to fill. It was like experiencing a sudden, unexpected death, the emotion too raw to know what to do. More whiskey was not the solution, as far as Josiah was concerned, but neither was sulking about things he could not change. That had never been his way, and he vowed silently that it wouldn't be now.

Regardless of his deep feelings, he had a lot of unanswered questions that were starting to nag at him about what he had been doing in Corpus Christi in the first place, what Miguel and Maria Villareal's motives really were, and whether Cortina had a real vendetta against him. Was he still a hunted man? Josiah had thought those days were past.

"Looks like you're fixin' to leave, Wolfe."

The voice startled Josiah out of his thoughts. He turned, his hand instinctively dropping quickly to his Peacemaker.

Once he saw Marshal Harlan standing there, holding two tin cups of steaming coffee, Josiah loosened his grip on the gun and relaxed his trigger finger. "Sorry, Marshal, I didn't hear you walk up," he said.

"Understandable, Wolfe, don't worry about it. Coffee?" Harlan offered Josiah a cup, his expression just as droopy and sad-looking as the night before.

Josiah nodded, gladly taking the coffee. He took a long, deep drink, pleased to rid his mouth of any whiskey residue. "That's damn fine coffee, Marshal."

"Thanks. Not much I can do around a stove but make a pot of coffee. It helps to ease the mornin' along with a swig of somethin' that don't stand your hair on end."

Josiah feigned a quick smile, then looked away from the marshal. He was wearing a clean set of clothes. A tear in his faded red shirt had been mended nicely. There was evidence of a woman's touch in the marshal's appearance that Josiah immediately recognized, and was sorely beginning to miss in his life. He found himself envying any man who enjoyed the comforts of a female presence in his life.

"Heard back from Austin," Harlan said, sipping his coffee, looking over the rim of the cup. His mustache was nearly fully immersed in the coffee. "They're mustering McNelly back into full service and sending him to Corpus Christi. You're to meet the company in Goliad, you *and* your friend Elliot, to settle on a plan."

"Goliad?"

Harlan nodded. "'Bout sixty miles to the north of here."

"I'd like to keep my cover as a hide trader as long as I can."

"Is that somethin' I should be worried about, Wolfe?"

Josiah shrugged. "Maybe. I'm not quite sure about any of the events of the last few days. They're all a jumble in my mind at the moment."

"Well, I'd say you'd be safe in Ingleside, but I sure can't guarantee you that. Besides, orders is orders."

"I appreciate your hospitality, Marshal," Josiah said, patting Clipper's neck. The horse stood comfortably, waiting.

"There's a cattle drive heading out this mornin', you might want to tag along with them until you get to Goliad.

Most of them fellas in the saloon last night were blowin' off steam before taking to the long trail to Abilene. Spring's like that in these parts. I've come not to pay any mind to the silliness of men getting ready for a long, hard journey."

"That might be a good idea," Josiah said. He thought back to the saloon, to thinking he saw Miguel—maybe, just maybe, the Mexican had endeared himself in a way to someone who would let him ride north, away from the certainty of violence in Corpus. He was one hell of a guitar player, and he seemed to know far more about Cortina and what was going on than he was willing to say.

"Well, it'll be about four days before McNelly lands there, and nobody would pay you any mind if you were with the crew."

"That's true."

"Beats bein' out there on your own, amongst the Apache, or the men ridin' with those minute groups, all in a rage to find and kill any Mexican they can. It's rough country, even for an experienced man on his own," Marshal Harlan said.

"I can handle myself," Josiah said, as he turned his attention to an open window and put his index finger up to his lips to quiet the marshal. He was certain he'd heard a twig snap, or something, like somebody was standing outside the window listening to them.

The marshal nodded. "I'm sure you can. Just a friendly suggestion, that's all," he said, acting like there was nothing wrong.

Josiah eased his Peacemaker back out of his holster and crept over to the window. He swept up, bringing the barrel of the gun out first, then looking up and down the alleyway behind the livery. There was no one there.

"I'll think on it, marshal," Josiah said, shaking his head. "But I expect you're right. The drive would be a good place for me and Elliot to fit in for the next few days, allow me to piece together what's happened."

"A little jumpy there aren't you, Wolfe?"

"Wouldn't you be?" Josiah asked, sliding the Peace-maker back to its rightful place.

Marshal Harlan forced a smile, then turned and walked back inside the jail, just as Scrap was coming out of the back door of it, wiping sleep out of his eyes, his shirt not buttoned up yet.

"I thought I heard y'all talkin'. What's going on, Wolfe?" Scrap asked.

"Marshal heard back from Austin," Josiah said. "They're sending McNelly down here to quiet things down. We're supposed to meet up with him in Goliad in four days."

"Hot damn!" Scrap jumped up and spun around, a smile glued to his face, ear to ear.

Josiah scratched his head. "You weren't standing outside just now listening, were you?"

"No. How come you're askin' me that?"

"Doesn't matter, was probably nothing. What're you so excited about anyway?"

"We're gonna go back into battle to settle this thing down with them damn Mexicans. They'll learn this ain't their country once and for all. We get to go back to fightin' with all the boys at our side. No offense, Wolfe, but this spy business is lonely work, and I just don't like it so much."

"I understand, Elliot," Josiah said, tossing the saddle blanket on Clipper's back. "On that note, I surely do agree with you."

CHAPTER 24

━━━◆━◈━◆━━━

The trail boss was easy enough to find. He was standing alone at the rear of the chuck wagon, staring out over a herd of at least two thousand longhorns that were grazing easily on fresh, spring grass.

The chuck wagon was fully loaded, sitting on the ridge of a shallow valley. A river cut thinly toward the ocean in the distance. The banks were lined with a smattering of tall trees, mostly oak. Wildflowers flourished everywhere the soil would allow, mixing in with the healthy grasses, dotting the landscape with deep reds, yellows, and blues. The ground looked like a rainbow had fallen from the sky, the vibrancy of the colors staining everything they touched. The air would have been fragrant and full of promise if not for the presence of the longhorns. As it was, the air smelled of cows, but it was not so stringent, or foul, just not as sweet as the air should be. Even the flies seemed intoxicated, glad for spring and the opportunities their hosts provided.

The boss was a tall, willowy man with grizzled gray

hair and a smooth, serious face. His eyes were deep blue, nearly akin to the color of the sky, and looked like they could be hard and mean if they had to be, but preferred not to. He stood stiffly, looking out over the field of long-horns, finishing off the morning's cup of coffee.

"Don Bowman?" Josiah asked, as he walked up to the man.

"That's me. Who's asking?" The trail boss had a no-nonsense way about him, not accustomed to being called on when he was deep in thought, probably plotting the journey in his head as he looked to the north.

Josiah glanced around to see if there were any other men within earshot. No one was except for Scrap, who had followed after him and stood impatiently on his heels. "I'm Josiah Wolfe. This here's Scrap Elliot. We're Rangers. Marshal Harlan suggested we might ride along with you to Goliad. Captain Leander McNelly and a company of Rangers are heading down to quell the violence Cortina started in Corpus, and we're to meet up with him there."

Bowman squinted his eyes, took in Josiah from head to toe. "Rangers you say? Both of you?"

"That's right," Josiah answered, curious as Bowman looked past him to size up Scrap, too.

Bowman nodded his head. "You got any experience ridin' with a cattle drive, there, Ranger Wolfe?"

Josiah looked down to the ground, then back up quickly, staring the boss in the eye. "Can't say I do, no sir. Never had the opportunity, or desire, until now."

Scrap stepped up next to Josiah. "I wrangled with an outfit that took me from Fort Worth to Kansas City a few years back before I joined up with the Rangers, Mr. Bowman. I sure would be glad to help out with the remuda. I'm a fair hand with horses, and I can work with just about any man."

"Elliot here is a fine horseman, that's true," Josiah interjected.

"I'll be the judge of that," Bowman said coldly.

Scrap smiled, obviously glad to accept the challenge to prove himself. "I suppose you will. You won't be disappointed, I'll guarantee you that."

"I got all the thirty-dollar men I can afford," Bowman said. "And we've signed on every man we need. You're a day late."

"We're not looking for a wage," Josiah said.

Scrap shot him a disdainful look but said nothing. He stepped back, out of range of Josiah and Bowman.

"You got trouble followin' you?" Bowman asked.

"Maybe," Josiah answered. "Elliot and I were both sent to Corpus on the order of the adjunct general, William Steele, and Captain McNelly to act as spies. Neither of us had any previous experience and most likely failed more than we succeeded. The attack on Corpus by Cortina's men was a complete surprise to us. We may have made our fair share of enemies before leaving town."

"Speak for yourself, Wolfe," Scrap said.

"I can't risk the herd for a favor to the marshal of Ingleside. I ain't got no orders." Bowman tossed what coffee remained in his cup to the ground, then spit right behind it.

"I'm not going to beg you, Mr. Bowman," Josiah said. "But there may be some men on your crew who are fleeing Corpus with blood on their hands."

"I don't hire outlaws."

"Didn't say you do—or have. Just that it might become necessary for a Ranger or two to show themselves if any trouble comes along," Josiah said.

Don Bowman drew a deep breath and furrowed his brow, glaring at Josiah. "I run a tight outfit, Wolfe. No drinkin', no gamblin', and no gallyboutin' while we're on the trail. What a man does in town is his own business as long as he don't bring it with him. If the need comes, I can handle any pup in this company on my own, you understand me, mister?"

"I understand," Josiah answered.

"All right then, I suppose you both can ride along. Elliot, you say you got horse skills?"

"Most folks call me Scrap, Mr. Bowman, but yes, sir, I surely do. Been on a horse before I could stand on my own two feet."

"I ain't gonna call you anything, if I don't have to. You ride up north about a quarter mile. Fella by the name of Peewee Wilson is gatherin' the rides. You tell him I said to try you out. Peewee's got a bad eye and he's as tall as a mountain. You'll know him when you see him. I wouldn't go boasting on about how good with horses you are to him. Just let him see for himself. He likes you, you'll ride with him to Goliad. He don't, come back here, and you'll work drag, you understand?"

Scrap smiled broadly again and started to push past Josiah, obviously anxious to get to work. Josiah put his arm out and stopped Scrap cold.

"What in tarnation now?" Scrap bellowed.

"No man on this trail needs to know we're Rangers. You give them your spy name, you understand?" Josiah said.

"Hank Sutton?" Scrap said. "I thought I was rid of that nonsense."

"Not until we meet up with McNelly in Goliad, you understand?"

There was no mistaking the order, the hard-as-steel tone in Josiah's voice. He turned his attention to Bowman. "I go by Zeb Teter. I'd appreciate it if you played along. We're still duty-bound to our original orders until we rejoin the company of Rangers. I don't mind giving you some free labor, but we're still on a mission. As you understand."

"I don't give a damn what you call yourselves as long as you don't cause me any grief. Now, get on there, Elliot, ur, I mean, Hank Sutton, or whatever your name is. Peewee could use the help you're so eager to offer, sooner rather than later."

Scrap nodded, glared at Josiah, then broke into a happy run to Missy, who was waiting about ten yards away.

"There's some fire in that boy's belly, that's for sure," Bowman said.

"Too much sometimes. But I've been glad for Elliot's company over the last few months. He's a fine shot. Just needs to calm down a bit," Josiah said, watching Scrap disappear into a cloud of dust over the ridge.

The cows groaned and their horns clattered in the distance, a foreign sound to Josiah's ears. It sounded like a thousand sticks battling against one another, except there was no anger in the air, no smell of blood, or fear, just shit and the smell of a thousand animals all packed into one small place. It would all take some getting used to.

"What do you have in mind for me, Bowman?" Josiah asked.

"Since you ain't got any experience with driving cattle, I'll have you ride the flank, and keep close here to the wagon. If the cookie needs you, you can help him with simple chores. But mostly, I just need you to lay low and keep yourself out of trouble until we reach Goliad. It'll take a long time just to get every man settled into the ride."

"I know less about food than I do about cattle," Josiah said, surprised at the assignment.

"My guess is you won't touch a bite of food unless it's on your spoon. Be a pot washer for a day or two, that'll be good for you, I suspect, if flank is too much for you to keep up with."

Josiah started to protest, then swallowed his words and just nodded. The cookie came walking around the corner of the chuck wagon and came to a full stop. Josiah knew the man. It was Leathers, the ex–Trappist monk he'd fought alongside at the saloon.

CHAPTER 25

◆━━━━◆✕◆━━━━◆

Don Bowman disappeared, off to a duty of his own, riding a sorrel mare that seemed to suit the man in stature and attitude; it was lean, proud, and sure-footed.

Leathers stood staring at Josiah. "Now, what exactly am I supposed to do with you, Zeb Teter?"

For some reason Josiah was not surprised to see Leathers. "Bowman said I was to ride flank."

"A greenhorn, aye?" Leathers's thin, hard, face was difficult to read. Josiah didn't know if the man was poking fun at him or if he was trying to antagonize him further. Their encounter at the bar had been a little contentious, but then again, Josiah knew he had been drinking whiskey, had been set on drowning his sorrows about Maria Villareal and Juan Carlos in a bottle, so the sour attitude might well have been all his own. For all he knew, Leathers was a good man, nothing more than a cook on a cattle drive, making a life for himself—just like Josiah. Still, there was something unsettling about the man, and Josiah didn't immediately trust him or put aside the contention he'd felt when he met him.

"There's not much left of me that's green," Josiah said. "I can ride flank easy enough. I'll be dropping off in Goliad anyway, so the stay will be short for me."

"Goliad? There isn't anything there."

"I think there is," Josiah said. "I didn't take you for a cook. You said you were a drover when we met at the saloon."

"Cook's in jail, friend. Bowman needed a man with skills who could do a little more with Pecos strawberries and chuck wagon chicken than the previous man. I suppose I'm that man since I spent time in the kitchen at the abbey in Iowa. We'll see how the boys like my biscuits in comparison to the last cookie's. I won't be burning any beans and bacon, I can tell you that."

"You got a good recipe for sourdough bullets and most of these fellas will follow you off a cliff."

Leathers laughed out loud. It was a tenuous laugh that lasted only a second or two. Then the man grew serious again, his face void of any expression, just hard like a statue. "You wouldn't follow a man over a cliff, would you, Zeb? Still Zeb, right?"

"What else would it be?"

"You tell me."

"No," Josiah answered, just as flat and cold as Leathers had responded to him. "I wouldn't follow many men over a cliff. There are a few. Were a few. But most of them are dead now."

"Ghosts of the war?"

Josiah nodded. "Of one war or another. There always seems to be one starting or ending, a chance given for bravery and fool's errands to change the world."

Thin wrinkles appeared in Leathers's brow. "I knew there was some wisdom inside that hard skull of yours."

"More experience than anything," Josiah said. "I don't know a whit about wisdom. Nor do I want to. I'm just saying there are very few men in this world who have the heart to lead, to sacrifice enough to make a man want to follow them into battle, or across the land for unknown reasons. Seems I've done that most all of my life, and look where it has brought me."

"Following another man, like the friend you were grieving back at the saloon?"

The air went out of Josiah's lungs. He didn't remember speaking about Juan Carlos to Leathers . . . but then he'd been drinking. Another reason to stay away from whiskey.

Josiah had to wonder what else he had said that he didn't recall. "My friend is not a captain, or a well-heeled officer, just a friend, and I'd just as soon leave it at that, thank you."

"Sorry to offend you," Leathers said. He started poking around the chuck wagon, stooped down and checked the security of the boot at the rear. "Maybe you should take the lead. Ever thought about that?"

Josiah glared at Leathers. "No need to lead if you're a hide trader."

"I expect not."

"Life on your own has its rewards," Josiah said. "Besides, if a battalion of men are going to follow you off a cliff, you got to be the first one to jump. I'm not so fond of heights myself."

"We're going to move soon, Zeb Teter, so you best find your place and start working for your wage, no matter how short the journey will be for you. But I'm glad to have a friend on the trail. You're a fine man to stand next to when the stools start flying." Leathers stuck his hand out, an offer to shake and, perhaps, put the past behind them.

Josiah shook the man's hand firmly but not heartily, then nodded. "You, too, Leathers. It's good to know you're all right after that melee in Ingleside. Even though you're a religious man, I had the sense you'd seen more than one bar fight in your life. You're pretty spry for your age, even if you are a bit wiry."

"Religion and I parted ways long ago, friend. That was man's doing more than anything else, but I have no regrets. My life is good. I'm fit as a fiddle and fine as a dandy man on a Sunday morning. You take care out there, and if things get troublesome, I could always use the help here at the wagon. You're welcome to help out here anytime."

"Thanks," Josiah said, walking away. He'd meant what he said, but he wasn't planning on washing pots anytime soon.

"There's a man out there by the name of Hughes. He's a good drover, knows more about moving cattle than any man I ever met," Leathers hollered after Josiah. "He'll set you straight, but he won't tolerate laziness."

Josiah stopped. "Why would you think I'm lazy?"

Leathers shrugged, tightened up the back door of the boot, the storage compartment at the rear of the wagon, and walked away, leaving Josiah feeling annoyed and angry all over again. He sure didn't understand Leathers at all. One minute he was a friend, then the next he was parsing words that drew dangerously close to starting a fight.

Josiah stalked off, unhitching Clipper, quickly hopping up into the saddle, and riding toward the herd as fast as he could, ready to find his spot and leave this part of Texas behind.

The herd of longhorns stretched out for almost two miles. There were at least two thousand of them, all in varying sizes and colors—some were nearly white or multiple shades of brown, while others were striped or brindled. The constant bawling of cattle, the horns clanking, the movement forward, bore little musicality, at least the kind a man like Josiah found comfort in.

He was a Ranger, not a cowboy, unaccustomed to the shouts of men, of whistling, of clapping after a stray cow. Riding in a cattle drive was a noisy, smelly proposition, and Josiah quickly found out he was much greener than he thought he was. It was like standing in the middle of one long clap of thunder, muted only by the softness of the ground his own horse was standing on.

He'd quickly found Hughes, a solid man the size of a good boulder, who'd told him to "keep the cows close, and don't cause me no trouble, or you'll be ridin' the long trail home on an empty belly." With that, Hughes had disappeared, shouting orders as he went, moving cattle seamlessly that parted at his coming—or going—depending on how you looked at it.

As far as Josiah could tell, other than Scrap and the wrangler he'd been sent after to help, there were twelve cowboys driving the longhorns north. They'd cover about ten to fifteen miles a day, making the sixty-mile journey to Goliad equitable for Josiah, the timing just about right to meet up with Captain McNelly.

Josiah's experience in riding flank was completely void of any true knowledge, and he was more than nervous about it, wondering why he'd let Marshal Harlan talk him into signing on with the cattle drive in the first place. But it was a simple task, or at least it appeared that way. All he had to do was keep the cattle close. He could watch the men in the distance chase after strays, whooping, hollering, and whistling, to get them back to the herd, and figure out the best way to get it accomplished.

The longhorns were so strung out that it seemed there was always something to chase.

Clipper was not accustomed to the demands of a cattle drive, either. The constancy of cutting in and out, back and forth, chasing after this cow or that, seemed to quickly annoy the Appaloosa. There was nothing that Clipper enjoyed more than a full-out run. Short jaunts and breaking this way or that was hard on his untrained legs. Still, the horse responded to Josiah's demands, though sometimes with a snarl of the lip, a whinny, or a disgusted snort.

Josiah noticed Clipper's difficulty keeping up, but they soon found a rhythm to moving the cows.

After an hour or so, Josiah's eyes were always searching the upper scrubs for a wanderer. Luckily, he'd yet to rope a cow. Not that he'd never done it; he had, growing up on a small farm in East Texas. But his roping skills were a thing of the past, barely remembered, and the farm was by no means a cattle ranch; his family never had more than three head of cattle at one time and never a longhorn. He looked at the rope with anxiety, knowing sooner or later he'd have to take it in hand and try to capture a running, live cow.

The fact that it was spring was not lost on Josiah. It was impossible to forget it, what with all of the wildflowers in bloom and with the bulging bellies of so many pregnant cows. He began to wonder how the cows could make the journey in such a state, but the thought quickly passed when a shadow on a ridge caught his eye.

At first he thought it was a smaller cow, way off the trail, out of the cut of the rest of the longhorns. But the ridge was high, and the way up too rocky for a wanderer to make its way up there . . . unless it had started there.

No, it was a horse, and even though he was looking almost directly into the sun, squinting, Josiah was almost certain he saw a man squatting behind a rock, sighting a rifle at the herd.

CHAPTER 26

———◆✦◆———

Josiah whistled at the drover, Hughes, but could not raise the man's attention. The noise of the moving cattle was almost deafening. Beginnings were always difficult, and this one seemed to be no exception—the cattle were all strung out, and the cowboys had yet to settle them down completely.

Still focused on the man with the rifle, Josiah swept out of an easy ride and up a trail of broken rocks, keeping the man clearly in sight. He wasn't sure of the intention, if the man was with the drive or not, but any man pointing a gun down at a moving herd of longhorns wasn't up to any good as far as Josiah was concerned.

Just as Josiah crested the top of the hill, the man fired his first shot into the herd. The gun was a Sharps Big Fifty, a long rifle mostly used for hunting buffalo, and the report echoed out over the shallow valley like thunder.

Josiah spurred Clipper to a full run, drawing his Peace-maker out of his holster to get a shot off at the unidentified man.

The shooter was about a hundred yards away. It didn't take a second shot to accomplish the goal of starting a stampede. The longhorns were already nervous. Before the echo of the Sharps was silent, the cattle were spooked and running at full speed.

In nearly the blink of an eye, the ground began to shake, and a dense cloud of brown dust began to rise fully into the air like a series of explosions a mile long had gone off all at once.

Josiah pushed Clipper harder, trying to get a clear shot at the man with the Sharps, who'd caught sight of Josiah. From a distance, they were staring each other in the eye, albeit for a brief second—but long enough for Josiah to recognize the man.

Miguel, the guitar player, had come to wreak havoc on the cattle drive for some unknown reason. Josiah was now certain that he'd seen the man in the saloon. It didn't take a great deal of deductive skill to figure out that Miguel was trailing him but had yet to show himself and do direct harm.

There wasn't time, at the moment, to question his motives or actions.

Josiah pulled the trigger and did something he rarely did; instead of taking a careful aim and assessing the shot so it counted, he fanned the hammer, and pulled the trigger six times as fast as he could, emptying all of the bullets from his gun in the direction he saw Miguel standing.

The cloud of dust from below rose into the sky as fast as it had started and swirled around Josiah, completely enveloping him, blinding him momentarily, causing him to pull back on Clipper as hard as he could, bringing the Appaloosa to a full stop. He had no idea whether or not he'd hit Miguel. He sure hoped he had.

There were men on the cattle drive now at serious risk because of the actions of the guitar player. There was no reason Josiah could think of, nothing that made any sense to him, why Miguel would do such a thing—unless it was to take advantage of the start of the drive, when the wranglers were green, uncertain, maybe a little lazy as things got moving.

What better time to break up the herd and scatter as many cattle as possible to waiting rustlers, Josiah thought to himself, lost in the dust cloud, still unable to move about freely. It was a ploy used before by Cortina and his ilk.

If the rustlers managed to run off with a hundred head of the two thousand that were heading north, then they'd add nearly four thousand dollars to their coffers. The coffers of Juan Cortina, most likely, if that was truly the case.

Which, of course, meant that Miguel had been working for Cortina all along, if Josiah's assumption was true.

The realization sent shivers up and down Josiah's spine. That would mean Maria Villareal had been taken in by Miguel, trusted him, let him know what she knew, that there were Texas Ranger spies in Corpus Christi. Not just one. At least two. Miguel had come looking, portraying himself as a friend, trying to alter Josiah's view of McNelly, when all along Josiah should have been more suspicious of Miguel. If he had been, then maybe, just maybe, Maria would still be alive, and Juan Carlos would not hate him—they would still be friends.

Trust no one, McNelly had ordered. An order that Josiah had examined over and over again, certain now more than ever that he had failed.

The rumble in the valley below grew more distant as the cattle ran north. The dust cloud began to thin, and Clipper pushed and pulled nervously, dancing a bit against Josiah's hold on the reins.

Particles of dust had made Josiah's eyes water, but as soon as he saw clearly, there was nothing before him. The spot where Miguel had stood on the ridge with the Sharps was vacant of anything—like the guitar player had never existed at all—but Josiah knew what he'd seen, and the results were obvious as the longhorns continued to stampede north.

Josiah heard a maddening whistle and looked below to see Hughes swinging up behind the running cows. He waved his arms angrily, the message clear: *What the hell are you doing up there? Get down here and help round up these cows!*

Another quick glance told Josiah for certain that Miguel was gone. There wasn't time to see if he had been wounded or was just gone; Hughes needed him and needed him now.

Josiah spun Clipper around and raced down the side of the hill to meet up with Hughes, who was riding on the right flank of the trailing cattle, keeping a sharp eye forward.

They were at the tail end of the herd as it rushed ahead. Josiah had never felt the earth rumble so violently, so distinctly. There was nothing but the smell of fear in the air.

He finally caught up with Hughes.

"We need to head to the front and help run the head of the herd into a tight circle. That's the only way they'll stop. Bowman will already be up there and need all of the help he can get," Hughes shouted.

Before Josiah could say anything, Hughes spurred his horse and tore away with an expected sense of urgency. Every man on the drive was facing a life-or-death situation, and no matter whether Josiah was being paid or volunteering his services, the truth was, he might be responsible for having led Miguel to the herd. Not that the rustlers wouldn't have found it anyway.

Hughes disappeared into the dust, dodging horns and wild-eyed bulls and cows.

Josiah followed suit, tapping Clipper with both heels of his boots, giving the horse his head and yelling, "Let's go, let's go."

The Appaloosa understood the command, sensed the urgent need to run, and followed after Hughes.

Josiah pulled the bandana on his neck up over his nose so he wasn't breathing in lungfuls of dust, gripped the reins, and let Clipper run as fast as he could.

Minutes seemed like hours, sweat poured out of Josiah's skin—a mixture of heat and anxiety. His eyes burned. Clipper's coat began to lather up. Running full out was becoming more and more normal, and under some circumstances, Josiah enjoyed the ride. But not under this circumstance. At every glance, he was dodging a longhorn or, at the very least, the points of horns, which could be deadly to Clipper. Add in the disappearance of Miguel and his Sharps Fifty, and the uncertainty of every second that the longhorns continued to stampede was one of the most dangerous situations he'd found himself in in recent memory.

It seemed like the herd went on forever, screaming, running at breakneck speeds. Somewhere in the distance behind him, Josiah heard another loud boom. It was hard to tell whether it was a gunshot or thunder, but the sound frightened the longhorns even more, making them run wildly and even more unpredictably.

The last time Josiah had seen the sky there was barely a cloud to be seen. It was highly unlikely that the boom was thunder. Most likely, it was a gunshot, set to keep the longhorns running as long as possible.

Josiah dodged a big bull with a tip span on his horns about six feet wide, probably weighing in at nine hundred pounds or more. It was a big longhorn, the biggest Josiah had ever seen, and barely missed gouging Clipper in the neck.

He pulled a hard right on the direct lead, just in time to keep the horse safe.

Hughes was completely out of sight, and the dust still rose up from the ground like smoke. They had ridden hard for nearly a mile, and there were still plenty of cattle running alongside him.

Silhouettes of men on horses began to appear, and it

didn't take Josiah long to be able to distinguish Scrap in the midst of the longhorns, riding tight in the lead like he was as experienced as any man on the drive. Seeing the boy in the middle of the herd didn't surprise Josiah. Scrap had never lacked for heart and was usually the first man to jump into the fray and put up a knuckle or gun with the least amount of prodding needed.

Josiah caught up to Hughes, who had slowed as the herd grew thick. Bowman was up ahead, as well, where he should be, where Josiah expected him to be, and was shouting out orders, but the words were muffled.

"Stay behind me," Hughes ordered. "Push all the cows in as close as possible."

The screaming and bawling had turned into a chorus of moos, annoyed at the growing close quarters the longhorns found themselves in.

Josiah did as he was told, kept an eye on Hughes for any further instructions, and was glad the running had slowed to a hearty trot.

The cattle were slowing, too, as the head of the heard rounded into a tighter circle, their trot slowing to a walk and then, finally, a stop, since there was nowhere to move, with nearly every available man winding the stampede down.

The threat was over, but not gone, as far as Josiah was concerned.

CHAPTER 27

———◆◆❈◆◆———

Evening was setting in under a calm sky. The herd of longhorns had settled into an easy graze, acting as if nothing had spooked them earlier in the day. The cowboys, too, seemed to be as forgetful as the cows. One of them played a harmonica softly, sitting next to the fire. Leathers's chuck wagon was not far off. A black kettle of beans and bacon was just starting to simmer, overcoming the smell of sweat and fear that had been created by the stampede.

Scrap was talking to a few of the other cowboys, all huddled together, out of earshot.

Josiah had yet to learn the names of the men riding with the drive. There would be time for that, or not, since he and Scrap were only going to be along for a four-day ride. Goliad loomed in the distance, and unlike Scrap, Josiah felt stuck in an uncomfortable spot.

Scrap almost always seemed comfortable and at ease in new situations. Now, with the cowboys, it was like he'd been riding with them all of his life. It was the same as when Scrap was riding at the peak of the stampede—there was no doubt that the boy had skills that went way beyond being a Texas Ranger, and Josiah had not failed to notice, even though he'd known Scrap had his own talents all along.

Josiah sat alone on a boulder, removed from the crew, staring out at the herd, wondering where Miguel was at and what exactly the guitar player was up to. He knew he was going to have to speak to Don Bowman sooner or later and tell the trail boss what he had seen. There was no question his presence, and Scrap's, had led the rustlers right to the herd. It was not a conversation he was looking forward to. The trail boss had been hesitant to take them on in the first place.

The smell of food in the air made Josiah's stomach rumble, and he suddenly felt tired and weak. He was in need of a bath and a nice shave. All things of a personal matter had been in short supply over the last few days. Mostly, the time since he'd met Maria Villareal in the cantina was a blur, the events too much to make sense of. Especially after her death, after being run off by Juan Carlos.

There'd been little chance to stop and regroup and get a grip on himself. He felt way off kilter. More so now than in previous days. The lines between Zeb and Josiah were melding together, and he barely recognized each man's separate motives or desires. Some days he wanted to be neither man, though there was no question that he was anxious to rid himself of Zeb Teter forever.

He was not looking forward to meeting up with Captain McNelly in Goliad, but at least then he'd be riding with the company again. That was a small thing to look forward to, but Josiah was, even though he wasn't anxious to return to Corpus Christi. What he wanted was to go home to Austin. There was no question that Josiah missed his life there. Not so much the city but those that he cared for. He longed to hear Lyle's laugh and feel the warmth of his hugs. The thought of Pearl did not lighten his heart, but rather the vision of her, the one stuffed deep in his memory when they had shared their most intimate moment together, along with a collection of the brief moments they had shared before and since, only made him feel even lonelier.

He wondered what had become of Billie Webb in the time he had been gone and if the newspapers had forgotten about him and gone on to another story. Surely, they had. It had been four months since he'd left, a lifetime in the cycle of news.

"Hughes said I should talk to you."

The words startled Josiah out of his thoughts. He turned to face Don Bowman. His gray hair was even more grizzled than the first time Josiah had seen him, and his blue eyes were hard and serious, like a storm was brewing inside the man's skull. Dirt was still caked on the trail boss's forehead, and his clothes were layered with dust and mud from the stampede.

Josiah stood up. "I saw the man who fired down into the herd. I tried to stop him, but I lost him, sir."

"A Mexican, no doubt."

"I'm afraid so."

"Why would you say that?" Bowman asked. Both of his hands were firmly on his hips. Bowman wore a gun on his right side, a Walker Colt, and a full battery of bullets. The pearl handle on the Colt glimmered in the setting sun.

His shadow fell long behind him, reaching almost back to the fire.

The harmonica player stopped the music, and silence suddenly entered the camp like an entity all its own.

Josiah could feel all of the eyes and attention of the cowboys on him and Bowman. He drew a deep breath. "I recognized the man from Corpus Christi. A man pretending to be a guitar player in a cantina. I cannot say for certain, but I'm almost sure he double-crossed us and is on the side of Cortina. I think he may have killed the barkeep once

Cortina attacked the city, preventing me from contacting Austin right away. The barkeep was my messenger."

It was the first time Josiah had spoken about the death of the barkeep out loud. Agusto was neither friend nor foe, just another man doing his job in service of the state of Texas, no matter how covertly. But the two of them had spent plenty of time together, alone in the cantina, talking, not talking, sharing silence and homesickness for their families. There was no way he could not grieve for the man's death. He had just chosen not to, had not found the right time, or place, until, perhaps . . . now.

"I saw him again in the saloon in Ingleside," Josiah continued. "I'm certain he was the man on the crest of the hill. There's no question he intended to start a stampede, and I think we may have led him to the herd."

"They would have found the herd anyway. I doubt the theft has much to do with you. But there's a bunch of madness about. Seems to me those minute groups will kill any Mexican they see. I should have been expecting them Mexicans to take advantage of the start."

"I hate to say it, but I hope you're right, Bowman. I surely do."

"I didn't think we'd have to worry much about rustlers because this is a smaller drive than what's coming up. I am at fault here."

"So you lost cattle?"

"Ninety-seven head. I'll have to answer for that loss, or get them back."

Silence fell between the two men for a long minute. Both stared out over the content longhorns.

"I figured that might be the ploy, rustling head at the beginning," Josiah said.

"I've got too few men to spare, the way it is," Bowman said, "now that we're under more of a threat than I thought we were. I want you and your man, there, Elliot . . ."

"Sutton. Hank Sutton," Josiah interjected tersely.

"Whatever his name is. Anyways, I want you and him to go after the thieves. You're Rangers, after all, it's your job. And since you seem to know this man who started the stampede, all the better to be rid of you in case he's following after you like a coyote in wait. I told you from the start I didn't want any trouble, but it sure looks like you brought it to me and my men here. I'm just glad no one got hurt."

"Me, too," Josiah answered. For a brief moment, he thought about protesting. He was tired and worn out. The last thing he wanted to do was hit the trail, tracking rustlers and Miguel. But he could offer no valid argument against the order. Bowman was right. It was his duty, his job, and more than anything else, going after the rustlers—Miguel—was the right thing to do.

Scrap loaded up a passel of warm biscuits in his saddlebag, then climbed up on Missy and readied himself to go. He had a broad smile on his face as he settled into his saddle. "Well come on, you ole slowpoke," he said, urging Josiah on.

Leathers handed Josiah a tin of cooling beans and bacon. "This ought to get you through the evening, brother," the cookie said.

"Thanks, I appreciate it. It's a little late to hunt down rabbit for stew."

"Good luck with that in this pitiful land."

"You don't like South Texas?"

"I like the green fields of Iowa. Spring stirs the poet in me there. This desolation does little for my constitution except darken my mood," Leathers said.

"Well, thanks again." Josiah extended his hand for a shake. "I 'spect we'll see you farther north."

"God willing." Leathers shook Josiah's hand and smiled

as warmly as he could, exposing his mouth full of rotting teeth a little more than normal.

"I suppose." Josiah retreated, pulled his hand away, walked over to Clipper, and packed away the tin of food. He could smell the beans and still hadn't eaten, but the prospect of leaving the drive so soon and chasing after a bunch of rustlers had caused him to lose his appetite.

"It's about gall dern time," Scrap said. "We barely got any light left at all."

"The trail isn't going to be that hard to find," Josiah snapped back.

And he was right. Once he settled into his own saddle and headed away from the cowboy camp, up over the hill where Miguel had fired the shot from, Josiah picked up a trail of hooves and beaten-down vegetation heading west, back toward Corpus Christi.

CHAPTER 28

The rising full moon cast enough light onto the trail for Josiah and Scrap to keep traveling at an easy pace. It was hard to tell how much time had passed, maybe an hour, maybe two, since they'd left the camp. Once they had settled into the ride and were able to identify the tracks left by the stolen longhorns, Scrap had gone silent, riding behind Josiah, keeping a decent distance between the two horses.

Traveling at night had its risks. The horses could step into a badger hole or onto an unseen rattlesnake, and both prospects could cause harm, or even death, to either of the men's trusted steeds. Still, with the moonlight providing clear passage, Josiah felt it necessary to keep going.

No man, no matter how skilled, was going to keep a herd of nearly a hundred longhorns moving into the night. They would have to stop, and that made the risk all that much easier to take. The sooner they found the herd, the better.

Josiah wanted nothing more at that moment than to find Miguel and the rustlers and put an end to whatever scheme the guitar player was involved in. It was a turn from his sobering mood back at the cowboy camp, where he felt responsible for the stampede. One more thing gone wrong, at his hand, to weigh him down.

Guilt was not an emotion that Josiah was accustomed to experiencing, much less carrying around like this, but lately, that was about all he could feel. Guilt and regret. But he agreed with Don Bowman. The rustlers would have found the herd anyway and taken advantage of a green and anxious crew. The theft really had nothing to do with his presence among longhorns.

Miguel was the only card in that deck that didn't make sense, and Josiah was focused on finding the man, now, so he could toss off the guilt about the stampede and get on to Goliad.

Somewhere in the distance, a coyote yipped, then started barking at the moon.

Josiah slowed Clipper down to barely a trot. The coyote was north of them, not too far away, less than a mile. There was nothing unusual about the yipping. The coyote didn't sound alarmed or on the hunt, but something made Josiah take notice—a chill ran up and down his spine, and then it was gone as soon as the coyote went silent.

Scrap eased up alongside Josiah. "What's the matter, Wolfe?"

"Don't know."

"Whoa," Scrap said, softly, stopping Missy.

Josiah quickly followed suit, and looked at Scrap curiously. "You see something?"

"There." Scrap pointed to a dark lump, ahead about ten feet, just on the side of the trail.

"I knew something was wrong. What is it?"

"Don't know, but I'm going to find out." Scrap slid off

Missy and pulled his gun from his holster at the same time.

Josiah followed suit and in the blink of an eye was a step behind Scrap.

"It's a calf. A newborn," Scrap said, squatting. "Afterbirth's about half licked off, and the legs are still not stiff. It ain't been dead long."

"Coyote smells a free dinner."

"Probably so. Happens a lot on cattle drives. Mommas drop calves, and they're forced to leave 'em behind, or a cowboy gets the bad luck of havin' to put it out of its misery. Shoot it, leave it for whatever comes along. Seems like a waste to me, but a nursin' mother slows down the travel. I heard some drives scoop up the calves and put them in a wagon, then let 'em loose to find their mothers at night."

"A calf always knows its mother," Josiah whispered.

"And a mother always knows her calf. They find each other, and the owner has more head at the end of the drive than he started with." Scrap stood up. "Nothin' we can do now. Them thieves weren't gonna slow down for a cow birth. They got money on their mind and nothin' else."

Josiah turned his back on the calf and walked slowly back to Clipper. He could smell the dead calf, the sourness of the afterbirth, and almost taste the death that was lingering in the night air. It was a recipe that could weaken the strongest stomach if a man let his mind—and heart—linger long enough and consider the grieving mother, lost in the darkness, bawling for her dead baby.

There was no question that Josiah felt akin to the unknown beast, knew the loss. But he also knew that something didn't have to be dead for a person to grieve. He missed Lyle more at that moment than he had realized. It was getting harder and harder to push the grief away, the homesickness.

And then there was the loss of his friendship with Juan Carlos, somehow reflected by the moonlight in the dead

calf's eyes. The old Mexican had held nothing but blackness and anger in his eyes when he'd ordered Josiah away
from the camp of shacks, threatening to kill him. It was
the end, an unquestionable finality, and that was just as
hard to take as far as Josiah was concerned.

"We need to find these rustlers," Josiah said.

"We're gettin' close," Scrap answered, as he climbed back
up on Missy.

A fire burned under a long overhang of limestone. An attempt had been made to keep the fire low, but
it was easily seen by two pairs of eyes that were looking
for anything out of the ordinary. Scrap and Josiah had
spotted the fire at the same time, and both of them were
surprised that they hadn't encountered any kind of resistance, at the very least a man standing guard on the perimeter.

A few sad moos reached up into the air, floating on a
cool breeze. The moon was at its apex, burning brightly,
like a torch held high in the sky. No stars could compete
with the yellow orb, at least ones close to it; only in the
distance were they able to be seen, and then they were faint,
pulsing dimly.

It was by the luck of the moon and clear sky that Josiah
and Scrap had been able to travel for so long into the
night. Once they had found the trail of the rustled longhorns, there was no mistaking it. Josiah had some tracking
experience and had learned, over the years, the signs to
look for, but in this instance, Scrap had proven invaluable,
and remarkably levelheaded.

Both men dismounted and tied their horses to a tall oak
tree that stood alone.

"This is makin' me nervous," Scrap said in a low voice,
trying to deflect any of the sound by lifting his hand up to
his right cheek.

"Seems a little odd," Josiah said, standing next to Scrap.

"Think it's a trap?"

"Could be, but what choice do we have? Wait them out if that's the case?"

"Wait until the sun breaks, maybe."

"We could do that, but it's the men we're after. These cows aren't going anywhere fast."

Scrap nodded. "I suppose you're right."

"Why don't you circle around to the top of that outcropping, and I'll slide in as close as I can get to the camp and see what's going on. If there's no man on the perimeter, then maybe they were a small outfit, short on men."

"You recognized that Mexican?"

"I did, but that doesn't mean anything."

"It means I'm not gonna be in much of a mood to ask a lot of questions," Scrap said.

Josiah cast the boy a glance and was about to tell him to keep a cool finger on the trigger, but he heard another coyote yip in the distance. Only this one didn't sound like the one that had alerted them to the dead calf, it sounded like a man trying to sound like a coyote, alerting somebody to Josiah and Scrap's presence.

CHAPTER 29

Josiah and Scrap immediately split up. The swivel holster Josiah wore was unsnapped and at the ready. He carried his Winchester '73, fully loaded and ready to fire. A Bowie knife also rested on his hip, and his gun belt had a full complement of bullets. He was as ready as he could be for whatever was coming his way. No group of rustlers was going to give up a hundred head of longhorns without a fight. Josiah knew that better than anyone.

Scrap was just as ready with his collection of skills and weapons. As far as Josiah was concerned, there was no better long shot in all of Texas than Scrap Elliot. No man he'd encountered could outshoot the boy. There were always contests of some kind going on when the two of them had been in the Frontier Battalion camps. That seemed like such a long, long time ago. The assignment in Corpus Christi was the longest amount of time Josiah had spent anywhere since he'd joined the Rangers in the spring of 1874, just a year before.

The coyote had gone silent, and Josiah edged along a

steady collection of rock, keeping the fire in sight. There had been no shadows. No movement. No sign of life around the fire. And that made Josiah nervous. He was almost certain that the second collection of yips he'd heard were man-made, not those of an actual coyote.

The cows were content, though, and that was something to be glad of. He could see them standing or settled down for the night all around the outcropping. The fire might have given them comfort, Josiah didn't know. But there didn't seem to be any nervousness about, anything that would suggest that the longhorns had been recently spooked.

Being as quiet as he could, Josiah managed to get close enough to the campfire to see for certain that no one was there. Scrap had not reached his spot on the outcropping to cover him, but that wasn't a concern . . . yet.

There was no gear, no sign of life, just a fire blazing away, like someone was getting ready to cook a good bit of beef . . . or send a signal. Certain now that the fire was a trap of some kind, Josiah edged back the way he had come, listening to everything outside of his own breath and heartbeat, trying to detect any kind of threat that he could.

The last thing he wanted to do was end up with a gun poked into his forehead, or get taken prisoner, or worse, die, recovering a small herd of cattle in the middle of no-where.

He'd had enough threats—especially in the last few days, what with Miguel tricking him at Agusto's cantina, and Juan Carlos ordering him out of the fishing camp at gunpoint. If anybody was going to be at the end of a barrel, it wasn't going to be Josiah. Not this time.

Back near the spot where they'd left the horses, he began to climb up on the mantle of rocks that Scrap had scooted along to get his position.

He whistled before going on, and Scrap almost immediately whistled back. There was a quick two notes, a pause, then two more that meant everything was all right.

Satisfied that Scrap had reached the spot they'd agreed on, Josiah climbed upward, until he stood on the crest of the rock, looking over the fire and down to the herd of longhorns.

The moon was high and bright, the face sneering at him, so much so that Josiah looked away from it. The bright light was a great aid to him, though, helping him see far into the distance. Beyond the light, darkness stood waiting like a mysterious black curtain, hiding all of the world, its secrets safe, or at least unseen, for the moment.

Scrap was waiting for Josiah, standing in the shadows, against a tall slab of granite, just above the fire.

"You see anything?" Josiah asked in a hushed whisper.

Scrap nodded yes. His eyes held a story, an urge to say something, but he restrained himself. There had been an odd air about Scrap since the stampede, since they'd left the fellas of the drive. It was like he was glad to be back on the trail with just Josiah, being a Ranger instead of a cowboy. Which made sense—all Scrap ever talked about was being a Ranger. He knew he could find work punching cattle, and he'd shown that. There was just something about the life that didn't appeal to the boy. Either way, Josiah was glad to find Scrap a little more tolerable and less antagonistic.

"What is it?" Josiah asked.

"Up around the corner of that rock," Scrap finally answered. "Two Mexicans with their hands and feet bound behind their backs, their necks both slit from ear to ear. Doesn't look like a shot was fired."

"Somebody didn't want to spook the cattle again."

"I 'spect so. Or else they was just killed because they was Mexicans. Maybe one of them minute groups did this?"

Josiah didn't flinch. "Could be. Show me."

Scrap did as he was told and led Josiah around the rock

he'd noted. Sure enough, it was just as Scrap said. Two men were lying faceup, their wounds both gaping. The blood was still wet, and looked black and vile in the shadows cast off from the moon. A pool of it surrounded the men, soaking into the ground. They were Mexicans all right. Even in their current state, there was no mistaking that.

Josiah walked around to the first man, a thin fellow with his eyes wide open and a pursed mouth that looked like it would explode if someone touched him. His clothes were ratty, and he hadn't been dead too long. Once daylight hit, the flies would surely make him a home for their eggs, and whatever else came along, critter-wise, would have themselves a feast. It was no secret to Josiah what a flock of buzzards could do to a man, how fast they could pick soft flesh off the bone. He'd seen his fair share of animals and insects helping themselves to the dead in the war.

"We're not going anywhere soon," Josiah said. "We best get to digging."

"Diggin'? I ain't doin no diggin' in the middle of the night," Scrap said with a scowl Josiah had seen more than once. "Besides, I ain't breakin' no sweat buryin' Mexicans. They might have been two of them that sought to raid Corpus. I say, leave them to rot."

"What do you suppose we ought to do with these two fellas? Prop them up by the fire and hope someone comes along and tells us what happened and who they are? They're meat. Food for more creatures than I'd like to think about. We don't have a choice but to bury them. It's the right thing to do."

"Says you."

"What should we do, Scrap? You tell me since all of a sudden you seem to have all of the answers."

"Are you gonna go orderin' me around again? I sure as hell haven't missed that much. I was thinkin' maybe we could get along as equals one of these days. That trail sure would be much easier to ride, instead of your sourness ridin' between us all of the time."

"Last time I checked I was still a sergeant."

"See, that's what I mean. Why can't you just treat me like a friend instead of somethin' that's beneath you, Wolfe? I ain't stupid, and there's things I can do better than you."

"Nobody said you were stupid."

"You might as well, always remindin' me that you're my superior. I know what rank is, darn it. We ain't in no company, haven't been for months. Not much has changed if you ask me, 'cept there's two dead men starin' at us, and I don't like the idea of bein' around them much. It could be me layin' there just as easily as it is these two strangers."

Josiah closed his eyes for a minute and held his tongue. There were times when he forgot just how young and untested Scrap really was. There had been no war experience to harden him, no relentless calendar of blood, day after day of looking into the eyes of dead men, even though some of them were still walking. Friends died all around him. Good boys. Soldiers who loved their mothers, who died instantly with a gunshot to the head.

Scrap still had a lot to get used to, a lot of death to see before he could see what it was. The worst part was the realization that your time could be up at any second. It was a violent, uncertain world they walked in. And it was growing more uncertain every day.

"I'm just asking you what we should do," Josiah said, looking as calmly as he could at Scrap. "Take it for what it's worth, but I'm serious. What do you think we should do, Elliot? I'm listening."

"I think we ought to wait till daylight. Poke around and see what we can, and try and figure out who these fellas are and what happened to them. Somebody had to sneak up on them to cut them like that."

"Somebody slit their throats. Killed them. They're dead."

"Then why didn't the person take these here longhorns? Round them up and ride off with them? And why
is there just two men? Two men might've been able to
round these cows, but they'd have to of been mighty good
at the cut, and I ain't never seen Mexcians that good on a
horse."

Josiah didn't say anything right away. Scrap's face was
red with anger, and he was as tense as a skunk about ready
to squirt.

"All right," Josiah finally said, "we'll wait until daylight.
There's got to be some gear around here somewhere. We
can cover them up with blankets. But once the light comes,
we bury them, and we get these longhorns back to the herd.
We've got to be in Goliad to meet up with Captain McNelly,
and I swear, I'm not missing that rendezvous. Is that clear,
Elliot?"

Scrap shrugged. "Clear enough. I'll go look for some
blankets."

"You do that."

Scrap started off toward the horses, then stopped suddenly. "There's thunder, you hear that, Wolfe?"

Josiah listened for a second, then scanned the sky. It
was free of any storm clouds. "That's not thunder."

"It's not is it? It's horses."

"Sounds like six or seven," Josiah said. "I knew those
coyote yips weren't real."

"Let's go . . ." Scrap ran up to the top of the ridge. "I
can't see 'em."

Josiah shook his head. "They'll be long gone before we
catch up to them; besides, it's too dangerous."

"Six or seven could have taken us, Wolfe. That don't
make sense if they was rustlers."

"Maybe the cows weren't what they were after."

"You mean the Mexicans."

"Maybe they were one of those minute groups. They don't

have any interest in cows. They just want to kill every Mexican they can find in the state of Texas."

Scrap exhaled loudly. "I 'spect it ain't right to let killers go, but you're right. It might be too dangerous."

"That's what I think," Josiah said, knowing full well that letting a group of Mexican-killers go free would be the easiest thing in the world for Scrap to do. His prejudice was loud and clear, even though he hadn't said anything of the kind. Somewhere in the distance, the coyote yipped again. Whether it was man or beast was a good question, but at the moment, it didn't matter to Josiah; if either came sauntering into the camp, he was going to shoot first and ask questions later. If it came to that.

CHAPTER 30

Scrap took the first watch after finding a bundle of gear stuffed under a slight overhang in the rock. He and Josiah covered the two men with blankets, then chose a lookout spot that gave them a wide view of the moonlit landscape. The dead men were completely out of sight but not out of mind. Rest did not come easy for Josiah, as he struggled to make sense out of the situation they'd found themselves in.

He had fully expected to find Miguel with the rustled longhorns, and not any sign of a minute group. But now that he thought about it, the guitar player had been anything but predictable. Josiah still did not know what the man was up to, but it was becoming clearer and clearer that Miguel was up to something, had a plan, or orders, or both.

Revenge as a motive was familiar to Josiah, and he was not going to hold any certainty as to whether it was Miguel and a gang or the minute groups that were responsible for the deaths of the two Mexicans.

Liam O'Reilly had been set on evening the score for Charlie Langdon's hanging and had even set a bounty on Josiah's head—which had led to his capture by two Comanche brothers and nearly cost him his life. But Miguel was a stranger, his only link was to Cortina, and then that was only an assumption. Cortina surely had bigger ideas, more pressing engagements, like rallying an army to take over Corpus Christi, than to take the time, and money, to avenge Liam O'Reilly and Pete Feders's deaths. Miguel had said as much, that that was Cortina's intent, but there was no reason to believe anything the man said, or implied, at this point.

Still, the idea of revenge made sense if Cortina had suffered a monetary loss of some kind when the channels to Austin, and within the Texas Rangers, were cut.

The night wore on with Josiah sleeping very little, his mind captivated by Miguel, the two dead men, and what it all meant.

Morning came slowly with no resolution or new insights, and Josiah relieved Scrap a few hours before dawn, when the night was at its darkest.

"You see anything?" Josiah asked quietly.

"Don't you think I would've woke you?"

"You're still sore at me."

Scrap looked away. "I'm gonna catch some shut-eye. We'll have our work cut out for us, getting all of these cows back to the herd, unless you want to track down that group of men we heard last night."

"I think you're right. We need to gather up the cows and get them back to the drive. It ought to be less than a day's ride."

"More like a full day, but I think we can make it."

Josiah stared at Scrap, tempted to apologize for whatever it was that was troubling the boy, but he decided against the gesture.

Scrap walked off without saying another word, and left

Josiah to settle into the same spot, and pick up his thinking about Miguel, home, what was coming next, and all that was before him.

The night air was chilly, and being without a fire left Josiah exposed to the breeze that kicked up now and again on top of the outcropping.

The coyotes, whether human or animal, had obviously decided that there was nothing to be had in the camp, and the herd seemed content.

Trouble is all the coyotes, real or otherwise, would have found, since Josiah was certain that Elliot was sleeping just outside of the fire with one eye open. Neither of them would rest until they returned the longhorns to the herd, and even then it would be questionable.

The upcoming meeting with McNelly weighed heavily on Josiah's mind. He did not want to return to Corpus Christi. He wanted to go home. He wanted to see Lyle and Ofelia. He wanted to be home more than any other time he could remember, with the exception, maybe, of when he had left for the war, gone on to Virginia, when the night-mare that was to come seemed like the Promised Land. Fighting man against man in the War Between the States was thought to be a train ticket to manhood, but it was less than that at times. Some days, Josiah felt like everything stopped for him the day he killed his first Union soldier. He froze from the inside out, learning nothing but how to for-get the death he'd caused, had a hand in.

Josiah rarely thought about those times, but he had seen a little of himself in Scrap when the boy reacted to the two dead men the way he had.

There was no question that Josiah had become jaded, that death was no longer a surprise to him. But all things considered, the recent events with Maria Villareal and ev-erything else, there was no way he could not feel a little more surprised by death than he thought he could, so maybe there was hope for him after all.

The full moon sank below the horizon, and the grayness of the new day began to creep up in the east, exposing a barren vista: rocky, dotted with scraggly mesquite trees and a herd of longhorns beginning to scavenge for anything green and tender they could find.

Certain that Scrap was still sleeping, Josiah decided to get a jump on the chore of burying the men. He eased away from the lookout spot down to the camp and found a small shovel in the gear.

By the time he had climbed back to where they'd left the men, the grayness on the horizon was becoming more visible, casting thin, narrow fingers of soft light into the black night sky. He could see a little better, and heard the first few bird chirps rise into the air in the distance. Spring brought a bounty of colorful birds north into Texas, looking for food and nesting spots. Some of them looked no bigger than a thumb and they were a myriad of colors. Josiah didn't know the names or the song of many of the birds—vireos, warblers, and such—but he couldn't help but notice them.

It was easy for Josiah to forget that it was the season of hope when the first chore of the day was burying two strangers, their throats ruthlessly slit.

The men had not moved, of course, were right where he and Scrap had left them, but the stink of death was starting to set in. The air was foul, and all of the taste buds on Josiah's tongue seemed to stand at attention in protest, and then retreat in full-out surrender as Josiah clamped his mouth shut and drew up his bandana to cover his nose.

Just as he had predicted, the flies had already found the bodies and were celebrating their cause, their way of life, and taking the opportunity to nest and feed as they saw fit.

Josiah found a spot with pliable dirt for the men's final resting place. But first he needed to take a closer look at them in the daylight, pull off anything that might be of use, like a gun or a knife, and see if there was anything that could tell him who these men were and what had happened to them. It was not a task Josiah was looking forward to.

He pulled the blanket off the first man just as the sun broke over the horizon. An insect, something as skinny as a pinky finger and black as the night, skittered away, under a rock. The flies were not afraid of Josiah or the light. He could hear them buzzing all around him and fought the instinct to bat them away. There was no use.

The first man was the skinnier of the two, and there was no sign of a gun belt, which told Josiah that anything of value had already been filched. He had to check anyway, but before he did, he reached up and closed the dead man's eyes. It was hard to call him a man; he was young, probably close to Scrap's age of twenty, if not younger. Another life cut short.

Josiah didn't know if he was one of the rustlers or not, but he guessed that he was.

Glad for the bandana over his nose as the rotting smell grew stronger, Josiah fished around in the man's pocket. The only thing he found was a locket with a picture of two young girls in it, probably around eight or nine years old, obviously sisters. The boy was too young to have a family of his own that age, so they must have been kin. Whatever the relation, the story of who they were and the dead man's identity would most likely remain a mystery that would go unsolved.

Disappointed, Josiah stuck the locket in his pocket and set about digging a grave.

Scrap showed up about an hour later. Morning was in full swing, and the moos and hollering of the long-horns overtook the sweet spring music supplied by the migrating songbirds.

"I got some johnnycakes cooked up for you and a bit of Arbuckle's left in the coffeepot," Scrap said.

The cool night had vanished as quickly as the darkness

had been overcome by the daylight, bringing with it a quick rise in temperature. Josiah was sweating. "We need to finish up here."

"You got the first one done and buried already?"

Josiah nodded at the rise in the ground next to the hole he was digging. "They were both stripped clean of anything of use. I've got no idea who they were or what they were up to."

"Mexcians is what they were. Rustlers, too. Stinkin' thieves who drew us away from a day's work and from bein' a day closer to Goliad."

"Maybe they were thieves. Maybe not. I doubt we'll ever know." Josiah tossed a couple more shovelfuls of dirt, then pronounced the hole complete. "You want to drag that one over here?"

"Not really."

"I've done most all of the dirty work, Elliot, and saved you from most of the stink and the flies."

"I don't like touchin' dead people."

"It's not my favorite thing, either, but it needs doing."

"Oh, all right." Scrap stomped over to the remaining man, who was nearly twice the size of the one Josiah had already buried. Scrap pulled off the blanket and let out a quick "Boy, howdy!" that probably could've been heard from a mile around. The smell must have ridden up on a quick breeze to Scrap's nose, because he began to choke and gag immediately. "That's the stinkenest thing I ever smelt," he yelled, burying his face in the crook of his arm.

This was not a situation that Josiah normally found humorous, but he had to turn away from Scrap to keep from laughing out loud.

Without another word, Scrap pulled the man to the grave, blanket and all, flies trailing after him like he was leading a parade.

Josiah helped roll the man completely in the blanket, then they eased him into the hole as gently as they could.

"You gonna say any words?" Scrap asked.

"Like Bible words?"

"Yup. I 'spect it don't matter if they were thieves after all. I guess every man needs a little send-off. Even a Mexican. I guess I ain't the last judge and jury. The Lord is."

"Don't know any Bible words to say. You?"

Scrap nodded. "My sister's a nun, you know. I think I might know a few if you have no objection?"

"Makes no difference to me." Josiah shrugged, then began to fill in the hole and cover the man up with dirt.

The other grave was covered with fist-sized rocks and bigger. There was a pile next to the new grave, waiting, that Josiah had found earlier.

A hawk circled overhead, then screamed, calling out playfully, riding the hidden currents in the sky.

Once the second man was buried and all of the rocks placed on top of the grave, both Josiah and Scrap stood back and removed their hats.

"Yea, though I walk through the valley of the shadow of death," Scrap began, "I will fear no evil . . ."

CHAPTER 31

———◆✕◆———

The sky was clear, blue as a bluebell could be, and offered no hint of rain or storms. It hadn't taken long to round up all of the longhorns, or at least most of them. There were less than a hundred head, but neither Josiah nor Scrap had bothered to count all of the cows. They searched high and low, did the best they could, then headed back east, toward the rest of the herd, with their wayward bovines.

Life would have been easier with a dog or two, and a couple of extra hands, but as it was, it was just the two of them driving the herd, one of them with far more experience than the other.

Josiah silently let Scrap take the lead. Cowboying was the boy's territory, and there was no way Josiah could command the herd, his own horse, and shoulder the responsibility of the success of returning the lost longhorns to Don Bowman with the ease that Scrap could. No use getting Scrap all riled up by challenging his skills or knowledge, making the ride back to the trail, and north to Goliad, any more uncomfortable than it already was going to be. Josiah had ridden with the boy long enough to know when to keep his mouth shut.

Every shadow caught Josiah's attention. He sat stiff in his saddle, expecting a shot to come from some hidden place, either taking him out or Scrap. At the very least, someone set on stampeding the longhorns again, or the minute group coming back to take revenge on them for burying the Mexicans.

Though there were not near as many head to run here, he had never before been in the midst of a stampede of two thousand frightened cows, bulls, and steers, and he hoped never to be again. It was an amazing amount of uncontrolled fear and power. Power with no conscience, or idea of right and wrong. The longhorns had just been spooked, pure and simple, and run willy-nilly to escape their fears.

Disappointed as he was that there had been no sign of Miguel, the instigator of this mess, Josiah was glad to be headed back to the drive. He was still a little nervous, all things considered. Cows were always nervous. One loud noise could send them running, and him, too . . . reaching for his rifle, needlessly or not.

The day progressed, and either the longhorns shared Josiah's desire to return to the larger herd or he was getting accustomed to hooting and hollering and punching a stray when he needed to. Still, there was no need for him to consider a change in the way he earned a living; he'd be no better as a cowboy than he was as a spy.

They didn't stop until they came to a rushing creek that needed to be crossed. The day was falling toward evening, and as much as Josiah had hoped they would reach the drive by the end of the day, it didn't look like that was going to happen.

Scrap rode up next to Josiah, his eyes hard and focused. He barely had any sweat on his brow, while Josiah felt covered with trail dust sticking to his own wet skin.

"We can cross 'em about a mile up, but we'll have to

cut through a thin pecan grove, or we can cross 'em here, but I don't like the look of the way that water's a-runnin'," Scrap said.

"Your call. Whatever you think is best."

"I don't like either option."

"How far off do you think the drive is?" Josiah asked.

"Hard to say, there's signs of them as far back as a mile or two. Patties are startin' to dry. Could be yesterday's."

"We need to push on then, squeeze as much daylight as we can?"

Scrap nodded, his attention drawn away from Josiah to the peak of an outcropping. He reached for his Peacemaker. "Looks like we got company."

Josiah followed Scrap's gaze. All of the longhorns were huddled together in a tight pack about a hundred yards from the creek. Beyond them was the start of a shallow canyon, the vegetation sparse, trying to grow in the spring bounty, and at the top were two men sitting on horses, looking down at the small herd.

The men were in direct sunlight, so it was hard to get a good look at them, hard to tell whether it was Miguel and a partner set on causing more trouble, or Indians, or someone else for that matter.

Josiah followed Scrap's lead, pulled his Peacemaker and chambered a round.

"The one on the right is mine, if it comes to that," Scrap whispered.

"Fine with me."

The longhorns ambled about, not distressed in any way or sensing any kind of a threat.

"You recognize them?" Scrap asked.

"Can't get a good enough look at them, but if they're any kind of shots at all, we're well within range."

"A blind man could hit us from there. Still, we're Anglos, so if they are a part of that minute group that killed the Mexicans, then we ain't what they're lookin' for."

"I suppose you're right."

"If they meant us any harm, we'd already know it by now," Scrap said.

"Maybe. Let's head that off at the pass." Josiah didn't wait for Scrap. The cowboying duties were over with. He urged Clipper on, tearing away from their spot, whistling and hollering, just like he was herding a stray calf.

Scrap followed closely behind him, and one of the men, the one Scrap had chosen as a target, waved back down to them.

The two men spun their horses around, galloped quickly out of sight, and reappeared moments later, rushing along the trail that led down from the canyon mouth.

Josiah brought Clipper to a full stop upon recognizing one of them. It was Hughes, the cowboy from the drive Josiah had ridden alongside before the stampede sent them chasing longhorns in every direction. He recognized the other man, a lanky cowboy with well-worn chaps and a dusty black Stetson set on his thin head, who he had also seen at the start of the drive.

Both men rushed toward Josiah and Scrap, not showing any weapons, just looks on their faces that spoke of relief.

Josiah holstered his Peacemaker. Scrap stopped Missy next to him but held his gun in his right hand, crossing it over to the left, relaxing a little bit but not completely.

"Looks like someone sent out a crew to look for us," Scrap said.

"Could be." Josiah squinted into the sun, checking the top of the outcropping for any more visitors. It was vacant.

Hughes reached them first. He rode a leggy paint mare that cut in and out better than any other horse Josiah had ever seen. There were times when Hughes, who was a thin, well-worn man himself, was at a forty-five degree angle with the earth when the mare was after a calf. Hughes had a serious face, a horseshoe mustache, and eyes that showed concern and agitation all at the same time.

"Glad we found both of you fellas," he said.

The other man rode up and stopped next to Hughes. They were all facing one another, two abreast. The second man didn't say anything, just nodded. He wore a black Stetson that was covered with trail dust, and carried a new-model Colt with pearl-handled grips that glimmered in the late afternoon sun. The gun was still strapped in, and neither man looked to be any kind of threat.

The longhorns mooed louder, moving off a little bit more toward the creek at the arrival of the two men, but they weren't too worried, just untrusting as usual.

"Don't imagine it took too much skill," Josiah said.

"You was easy enough to find, though I was doubting we'd find you by nightfall," Hughes said. "This here's Walt Burmer."

"Howdy, Walt. You know Sutton here?" Josiah said, remembering to use Scrap's spy name.

Burmer shook his head no. "No need to for usin' different names, Ranger. Bowman told us what was up. I saw Elliot ropin' a bit. Both of ya's look a little out of place."

"We were just getting our feet under us," Josiah said, not liking the man's tone.

Burmer shrugged. "Makes no difference to me what you call yourself."

"Well," Hughes said, "I'm glad we found you nonetheless, and I'm glad to see you got this here herd back together. Saves us the work. Where'd you find them?"

"'Bout a day's ride out, grazing in the scrub. Two men were with them, but they were dead. Throats cut from ear to ear. Weren't dead too long, but dead just the same. We figured you were the rustlers come back for the herd," Josiah said.

"Who were the men?"

"No clue. They were Mexicans, so I'm speculating that one of those minute groups from Corpus found them and killed them. They'd been stripped of anything of value."

Josiah unconsciously touched the locket in his pocket that he'd taken off the dead man's body. He knew there was no hope of finding out who was in the picture, to lead him to figure who the man was, but he hoped to anyway. If not, the locket was no trophy, no keepsake to hold on to to remind him of the journey or the way the two had been killed. He really wanted to forget the sight of blood as soon as possible.

"Bowman send you out after us?" Scrap asked. He fished in his pocket and pulled out a quirlie that he'd obviously pre-rolled, and lit it.

Hughes nodded. "Word is there's no Mexicans safe, which suits me just fine. You two need to head back north as soon as possible."

"Why's that?" Josiah asked.

"Bowman got word from your Captain McNelly."

Josiah flinched. "What do you mean word from our captain?" He still held on to the hope that Don Bowman had not exposed their cover, but it didn't look that way. This man knew something, and Josiah had a bad feeling growing in the pit of his gut that something was wrong. Bowman had been dead set on him and Scrap finding and returning the longhorns that were rustled, and now he'd sent a two-man crew out looking for them.

"There's no need to be coy, Wolfe. I know you're a Texas Ranger, not some hide trader turned cowboy named Zeb Teter. Elliot, too. Don't much matter to me who or what you are, though. I'm just followin' orders, fetchin' these beef hooves and returnin' them to the drive and sending you boys up north."

"North to Goliad?" Scrap asked.

"No," Hughes said. "North to Austin." He looked directly into Josiah's eyes. "Word came in that your son has taken ill. You need to get home as soon as possible."

CHAPTER 32

———◆◆◆———

Night fell a lot sooner than Josiah expected it to. Clouds rolled in from the west, covering the bright moon that had, just the night before, lit the trail late into the night and given Josiah and Scrap clear travel. The wind was strong, too, pelting Josiah's face with unseen dust rising from the ground. But he could barely feel the chill of the air, the pings of dirt hitting his face, or the wind at all. Josiah was numb with fear and anger, numb with emotions he didn't care to name.

All he wanted was to be home, to be rid of the four months he'd spent in Corpus Christi that had felt more like a sentence than an escape. He never wanted to hear the name Zeb Teter again, or think about being a spy. If that meant he was no longer welcome in the company of McNelly's Rangers, then so be it. It was way past time to return to Austin and face whatever waited there for him. No matter the price of his action, killing Pete Feders and making an enemy of the Widow Fikes, it was not worth losing sight of Lyle for long stretches of time.

Josiah was not a praying man, even when it came to the thought of losing his son to some mysterious sickness. He knew all about sickness and praying, knew better than most that there were no words, silent or spoken, that would change the natural cycle of whatever had caused the illness in the first place. He had buried too many of his loves to believe in magic, religious or any other kind.

Once Hughes had said that Lyle was sick, there was no stopping Josiah, no turning back. He tore out northward like a fire had been lit under Clipper's rump. If only the horse had wings.

Scrap followed after Josiah, keeping a respectable distance; close enough to let Josiah know he was there, not alone, but far enough away to discourage any conversation. The luck of good weather was all they needed.

Unfortunately, that brand of luck seemed to have run out. Not long after the wind stirred and decided to push straight across the rugged South Texas ground, thunder, lightning, then rain followed. Brief and intermittent at first, then the clouds unleashed every ounce of moisture they'd been saving up.

The season of opportunity was also the season of rain, of massive downpours and relentless storms, which was all well and good for wildflowers and farmers but not for a man fighting to get home to his son.

Josiah pushed on, taking little notice of the mud, of shallow puddles and rivulets forming in the dry ground. There was no hesitation to Clipper's gait, but the horse had slowed a bit, the ground harder to navigate, harder to get a thrust forward on from the last attempt to run as fast as possible.

Lightning danced overhead, disappearing as quickly as it spiked across the roiling sky, leaving the trail nearly black. Josiah's eyes were under constant strain to adjust, always looking for the way forward. Rain replaced the dust pelting Josiah's face, and though he knew he should stop, he just couldn't bring himself to.

There was no way he could reach Austin in an hour or a day, but one more step was one step closer to home.

Finally, he couldn't see past the night or beyond the rain, could not risk hurting Clipper, and decided to stop when a streak of lightning lit up the sky like it was daylight and revealed a thick stand of trees ahead of them. He slowed Clipper to a trot, the rain pushing the sweat and lather off the Appaloosa's firm but tired neck.

Scrap was next to him in the blink of an eye. "We can't go on, Wolfe."

"I know that," Josiah yelled back. "I know that." Rain streamed down his face. His heart raced so hard he thought it was going to jump out of his chest. His fingers were numb, the feeling long gone. The taste of salt stung his tongue, and it only took him a second to realize that he was tasting his own tears.

The fire was small but valiant. They had followed the creek north as far as they could, until it turned into a river with an outcropping that offered cover from the storm in a widening burst of limestone formations, just beyond the pecan grove Josiah had sighted.

Scrap took a ration of beans and a small pan from his saddlebag and set about cooking up some dinner to have with some biscuits he'd stuck in his pack the day before. Coffee boiled in a small pot. Both men had changed out of their wet clothes and hung them on a line Scrap had strung over the fire. Luckily, they both had another set of clothes along with them, tucked inside their slickers, for instances such as this.

Scrap smoked one of his quirlies as he tended to the beans, while Josiah sat at the edge of the rocks under an overhang, watching the storm play out to the east, losing its strength the farther away from them it got.

Thunder continued to boom, vibrating the earth under

Josiah's feet, and the rain was easing, from a downpour to just a steady drizzle. Beyond the light of the fire, there was only pitch blackness. It was like they were locked in a cave, even though it was a three-sided enclosure. Josiah felt even more trapped than he had in Corpus. His body ached, and he was tired, but the urge to keep going was strong. If it hadn't been for the storm, he knew he would have pressed on, regardless of the danger.

Clipper and Missy, who were far more comfortable in each other's company, huddled together not far from Scrap. They looked happy for the rest.

The smell of beans mixed with the smoke from the fire, but did little to rouse any hunger from Josiah. Not even when Scrap brought him a bowl and shoved it under his nose.

"Here, take this."

Josiah looked up, his eyes tinged with anger. "Eat it yourself."

Scrap stared at him for a second, started to say something, then walked off. He dumped the beans back into the pot, then found himself a comfortable spot in the shadows and ate his own dinner.

Josiah watched the storm roll on and felt just as much turmoil inside as out, but as the night drew on, and Scrap kept his distance, he began to realize that he was doing the best he could, that he could not get home any faster than he was.

A couple of hours after he'd rejected the beans, Josiah rolled out his bedroll, shuffled over to the fire, and settled in for the night. It took only a second for sleep to come and take him away.

Nightmares did not visit Josiah, only the darkness of deep, refreshing sleep. Surprisingly, the aches he'd felt the night before were gone when he woke. It took him a second or two to remember where he was, and why he was there, but once he did, he was amazingly clearheaded, and far less stricken than he was when he'd first heard the news that Lyle was sick.

The smell of coffee touched his nose, and Scrap had already been up and about, getting the horses, and himself from the look of things, tended to in the nearby river. He was fresh as a man could be who'd been on the trail for as long as he had.

"You're awake," Scrap said with a faint smile, easing into the camp.

Josiah's stomach grumbled. "Awake enough to be hungry."

"There's biscuits in the tin there."

Josiah looked to the fire, saw the tin, nodded, then hurried behind some bushes to relieve himself.

The only signs of the storm from the night before were soft, muddy, ground and the sound of a full-to-the-brim San Antonio River rushing not far from where Josiah was standing. Otherwise, the sun was rising in a crystal clear blue sky. The morning was cool, but it looked to be a warm day, not too hot to ride hard and fast in.

Done, Josiah went off to clean up, then returned to the camp to dress and eat.

"We ought to hit Goliad this afternoon, if I'm figurin' right," Scrap said, taking a spot across from Josiah.

Josiah sipped a cup of hot coffee. It was weak and tasted bad, but he wasn't going to complain. Campfire cooking was not one of Scrap's talents. Josiah just appreciated the effort. "Probably a day or so early to meet up with McNelly."

"Yup, probably so. We'll pass 'em on the trail to Austin, I'm sure of it."

"We can restock in Goliad, and I'll send a telegraph home to let them know I'm on my way."

"You think that's a good idea?"

"Why wouldn't it be?"

Scrap shrugged. "I don't know. Just might be some people lookin' out for ya that might cause trouble. It still don't make any sense to me that those rustlers were left behind with their throats cut and no sign of anything or anyone else. Why wouldn't the killer take the longhorns? Don't you think that was what they were after?"

"Hard to say. Maybe we came along and spooked whoever was up to no good. Stealing from a couple of thieves takes some courage. And there wasn't any sign of Miguel, the Mexican I saw shoot down and stampede the cows in the first place. I got to wonder where he's at, and what he's up to, but Ofelia needs to know I'm fine. Shadows and fear aren't going to keep me away from my son. Not now when he needs me the most. Not since I've been gone for so long." Josiah's voice cracked, and he looked away from Scrap.

"I know what this means to you," Scrap said.

There was nothing Josiah could say. Over the time he and Scrap had spent together, he'd told Scrap bits and pieces of his past, of the story about Lily and the girls. So Scrap knew that Lyle was all that Josiah had left in the world.

Josiah ate the last of a biscuit and downed his coffee. "You ready?"

"I'm just waitin' on you."

CHAPTER 33

————◆━◆⟡◆━◆————

Goliad came into view not long after noon. Josiah and Scrap broke off the trail along the San Antonio River and made their way over to the road that led into town. One of the first things they saw was the Presidio La Bahia, a dark gray stone fortress with thick walls and a church tower, adorned with a simple cross, rising into the clear sky. The building stretched on for a good city block, the shadows falling full on Josiah and Scrap, offering a dose of gloom that didn't need encouragement. Quietness surrounded them as they trotted by.

"A lot of blood on the ground here," Josiah said.

Scrap was riding alongside him. "I don't see anything."

Josiah shook his head. "No, in the past. A lot of men lost their lives fighting the Revolution. The first Declaration of Independence of the Republic of Texas was signed here."

"But it's a church."

"It is and has been here for well on over a hundred years."

"How come people are always fightin' in the house of the Lord, Wolfe?"

"Don't know. Probably because people think God needs a big building to live in."

"That's the silliest thing I ever heard."

"You asked. I answered."

"If you say so.

"I do."

Scrap eased Missy's pace to a slow gait and removed his hat in honor as they came to the far corner of the Presidio La Bahia. He didn't say another word until they were out of the shadow of the building. "I would've fought them Mexicans."

"From the look of things, we still are," Josiah said, looking over his shoulder at the fortress. "Maybe someday that war will be over."

"I doubt it."

"Me, too."

The main street of Goliad was not that much different than any other South Texas town. A row of buildings—mostly wood frame, though a few were constructed of brick—lined both sides of the street. The majority were two storeys, but a few were one, like the telegraph office just inside the proper entrance of the town.

"I'm going to stop here," Josiah said. "You go on up to the marshal's office and check in there, see if there's been any sign of McNelly, or any word from him. I'll join you when I'm done here."

"You ever stop to think that fella was makin' up the story about Lyle bein' sick?"

"Hughes? Why would he do that? And more to the point, how did he know about Lyle in the first place if he was making it up?"

"I don't know. Things haven't felt right since we left Corpus, if'n you go an' ask me. I was just wonderin', that's all. I'm not much for Mexicans, but I can't get those dead men's faces out of my mind, Wolfe."

"Well, we're a day's ride away, what would it have accomplished?"

"Coulda been nothin' more than a cause to get us away from those stampede strays so he could have 'em to himself. Lot of money there."

Josiah scrunched his shoulders. "I don't know, that doesn't make much sense to me, Elliot, but I suppose you could be right. We'll find out soon enough, once we land in Austin."

"What if we're not really supposed to go to Austin, and we're really supposed to meet up with McNelly like we planned? And we don't? That could be the end of my Rangerin' days."

"You're taking orders from me, right?"

"Suppose so."

"Then it'll be my ignorance that's the cause of falling for Hughes's trick—if it is that at all—not yours. You worry too much about losing your job."

"It's all I got."

"I don't believe that at all, Elliot. Not for a minute."

Silence fell between the two men. Josiah was heartened that Scrap had thought there might be something amiss with Hughes showing up and delivering the news about Lyle. But he doubted Scrap was right.

"We need to re-stock," Scrap finally said. "I'm plumb out of beans and coffee. I wasn't expectin' to be away from the chuck wagon so long."

Josiah nodded. "We're not going to get too comfortable here. We've still got about a hundred and thirty miles or so to travel."

"Fair enough." With that, Scrap flipped Missy's reins a bit, then turned and headed up the street to the marshal's office.

Josiah waited a second, then dismounted from Clipper and walked inside the telegraph office.

The telegraph operator was a burly man with white pork

chop sideburns and a clean-shaven face. He had suspicious eyes and looked Josiah up and down before saying hello.

"Need to send a telegraph," Josiah said, "and make sure there aren't any messages for me."

"What's the name?"

"Wolfe. Josiah Wolfe."

The operator thumbed through some papers lying in front of him. His desk was neatly organized, and the inside of the office was as clean as a freshly swept pen. "No, don't see anything here."

"You're sure?"

"If there was something here with the name of Wolfe on it, I'd sure as heck know, mister." The man was dressed in a typical black operator uniform with a black-billed hat, freshly starched white shirt, and a string tie. He spoke with as much authority as he looked like he carried. "I'll have you know I've been the operator here since the office opened. I know my job."

Josiah put up both hands, as if to fend the man off, even though he hadn't moved an inch or threatened to stand up. "No need to get all riled up, I'm just asking."

The operator studied Josiah's face, obviously looking for a sign that he was telling the truth, then bit the corner of his lip. "Who you expecting a telegraph from?"

Josiah sighed. He had spent the last four months of his life pretending to be someone else; it was hard to state his own business. "Might be something from Captain Leander McNelly. At least, I was hoping there was."

"The Ranger?"

"One and the same."

"You a Ranger?"

Josiah hesitated. "That I am."

"This official?"

"No, sir, it's personal."

The operator exhaled loudly through his nose and pulled the telegraph machine to him, an ancient Morse model. It looked to be an original, making it nearly forty years old. "Who you sending this to?"

"Ofelia Martinez in Austin."

"Address?"

"Sixth and Pecan."

"Go on," the telegraph operator ordered.

"Aware of Lyle's illness. On my way home. Day after tomorrow." Josiah stopped, looked down at his muddy boots, then back to the operator. "That's all," he said.

"You're sure?"

"I said that's all."

"Have it your way, mister. That'll be three bits."

"Three bits?"

"Four if you want to leave a message for Captain McNelly."

"I'm sure our paths will cross on the trail," Josiah said, digging in his pocket. He pulled out a handful of coins and tossed the telegraph operator three of them, just like he'd been instructed.

Arguing about money was the last thing he was going to do—or tell a stranger that he loved his son. The boy knew that was true. Josiah was sure of it.

At least, he hoped he was.

CHAPTER 34

❖

Josiah and Scrap left Goliad with a couple hours of daylight left to travel in. Weather, horses, and Scrap's attitude cooperated, making the departure quick and trouble-free. They'd gotten everything they'd come for: enough supplies to last until they reached Austin, and a telegraph sent ahead to let Ofelia know they were on their way home. The expectation, and hope, of making contact with Captain McNelly, did not materialize.

Josiah held more than a little quiet concern about not finding the captain in Goliad.

It was difficult not to let Scrap's doubt about Hughes enter his mind, but he continued to push his fears away. There was no reason to suspect Hughes of any wrongdoing, at least as far as Josiah knew. Maybe Scrap wasn't telling him everything he knew—which would be even more unusual. Still, it was rare for Scrap to have insight so deep into a situation and offer it up for consideration. Maybe the time in Corpus Christi, left to his own devices, had been good for Scrap, matured him in a way that Josiah hadn't thought possible.

If only Josiah could see, or feel, a positive outcome from his own experience in Corpus, then he might be in a different spot.

Missing McNelly gnawed at Josiah, caused him to worry more than normal, but they'd arrived early in Goliad, off schedule. Surely, Josiah reasoned silently to himself, they'd meet up with the captain, and the company, who were on their way to Corpus Christi to quell the uprising of Cortina's men and settle the minute groups who were set on killing any Mexican, good or bad, that they encountered. Even if there was something amiss, something foul about Hughes's intentions, the captain's assignment was true, either way. And rushing home was the only choice Josiah had.

He was glad to have Scrap along with him for once.

Cuero was the next town they'd come to, some thirty miles north of Goliad. There was no way they were going to make the town before nightfall, so they would have to camp along the way—which didn't matter as much to Josiah as when they'd first started out.

He felt a little more relaxed as Clipper pushed north as fast as he could. There was nothing left for Josiah to do but ride, after sending word to Ofelia that he was on his way home.

The rhythm of the ride was a comfort, the knowledge fully settled in Josiah's mind that he was finally heading north, finally leaving the tragedy of his time near the ocean behind him. If that was possible. His heart still ached for the death of Maria Villareal, and he still could not fully accept that Juan Carlos was no longer his friend, that the old Mexican would not show himself in the difficult times ahead. And, of course, Josiah could not even imagine the sickness that had stricken Lyle. He knew nothing of the details. Perhaps it was the fevers that had taken Lily and his daughters and had come to take his son away, too. Or maybe the sickness was something else, something that could be cured by medicine and knowledge. Maybe being in the city would help create a different outcome than when they'd been so far out by themselves, as they had been in Seerville. Josiah held on to that hope for as long as he could, that this sickness was different. That Lyle would still be alive when he reached Austin.

Miles passed, and night eased out before them as Scrap and Josiah rode straight into darkness.

The sun was quick to fall from the sky, and the moon was hesitant to show itself. Shadows, cast down from the hills, made the trail hard to see, and finally Josiah called to Scrap, bringing Clipper to a slow, easy stop. It was time to make camp as far as he was concerned.

Scrap agreed, even as the moon began to rise into the sky, struggling up from the distant horizon, like a flame hesitant to burn. The moon was almost full, offering a little more light as it broke free of whatever held it down on the other side of the earth. But the day was done, regardless of how much light fell on the trail.

Josiah took care of getting both the horses settled in, roping off a small corral, and offering them a hearty helping of oats that they'd picked up in Goliad. Scrap began to collect wood for a fire, his role as certain and unspoken as Josiah's. When it was just the two of them, cooking duties fell to Scrap. He was much better at it than Josiah was, which wasn't saying a whole lot.

Before long, everything was in place, the horses content, the fire rising and falling lazily under a pot of beans with a touch of fresh bacon. Both men sat before the fire, allowing the day to come to a quiet end.

"There's a creek that runs off the river, not too far to the west," Scrap finally said. "Be a good spot for a bath and a shave in the mornin', if we got time."

"I was thinking the same thing, if there's a spot where

the water's not running too fast and swift," Josiah said, sipping a cup of Scrap's still-too-weak coffee. "I sure don't feel much like myself."

"That's 'cause you've been goin' around tellin' people your name's Zeb Teter."

"I'm done with that."

"You sure?"

"As soon as I see McNelly, I am."

"You're quittin'?"

Josiah shook his head no. "I don't know what I'm doing, not for sure. I have to get home first before I make any more plans, see how things are with Lyle. But I'm going to tell McNelly that this spy business isn't for me."

"That makes two of us."

"There's men, like Juan Carlos, who're better suited to the kind of duty we were asked to do."

"If I were you," Scrap said, "I'd forget what that damned Mexican is better suited to. He threatened to kill you."

"He's still my friend."

"You're not his. Not now. Probably not never. That minute group finds him and he's a dead man, that's for sure."

Josiah decided to let Scrap have his say and not defend Juan Carlos. Maybe Scrap was right about the friendship, too, but Josiah doubted it. There were some things he knew about Juan Carlos that Scrap would never know. Like the kind of heart the man truly had.

Words retreated, and silence returned between the two men. No tension existed, just the reality that they could disagree and still remain in each other's company. Josiah did worry about Juan Carlos's well-being, though. Scrap was right about the minute groups.

The fire crackled and popped—the wood Scrap had scavenged was a little green. Smoke kept changing directions as a slight bit of wind played around the camp like a confused child. Insects buzzed about, legs sawing together in harmony, seeking mates, adding to the music of the night.

Somewhere in the distance, not too far away, a big cat screamed, a cougar making its presence known, and Josiah sat up straight, pulling himself out of the lulled state he'd allowed himself to fall into.

There was always a threat just beyond the darkness, but sometimes it was nice to forget, even if just for a minute.

Morning came much too soon as far as Josiah was concerned. Scrap had drawn last watch and was nowhere to be seen.

Spring offered cool mornings, and this one was no exception. The sky was still gray and peppered with clouds. The wind that had played with the fire the night before was still present but less confused and more certain of its direction. It was coming out of the southwest, bringing with it moist air that promised a day not of storms but of uncertainty. It didn't matter much. A hurricane couldn't have stopped Josiah from heading toward home.

He pulled himself out of his bedroll and tried the best he could to wake up. The first thing he did was make sure his guns were where he'd left them. Both the Peacemaker and the Winchester were within reach.

The flames from the fire had died, leaving orange embers breathing in and out, trying to stay alive, until the wind kicked up fiercely enough to return it to life. Josiah felt the same way.

He eased his way down the trail, the Peacemaker in his hand, heading to the creek to clean himself for the day, still only half-awake. A gunshot about fifty yards ahead of him got his attention and woke Josiah fully. He stopped, pulled the hammer back on his gun, and waited, trying to blend into the shadow of a tall oak tree.

The brush, not far from where the shot came from, stirred. Josiah raised his gun just as a rabbit broke free from the heavy thickets, running wild-eyed, straight at him.

Surprised, and relieved, Josiah took a deep breath, sighted the rabbit, and pulled the trigger.

The rabbit flipped back a few feet, somersaulting to a stop at Scrap's feet.

Scrap was panting, holding his rifle, an angry and perplexed look on his face. "I can't believe I missed the gall-darned thing, Wolfe. Damn it," he said, squatting to look at the rabbit. "You shot its head plumb off."

Josiah made his way to Scrap, a smile growing on his face. "Got lucky, I guess. Right place, right time."

"I can't believe I missed it." Scrap stood up and kicked the dirt.

"Looks like we got breakfast."

"Looks like."

Josiah reached down and picked up the rabbit by the tail, leaving the head for whatever would find it appetizing.

Scrap joined Josiah, and they walked side by side.

They crested the hill, which gave them a view of their camp and the world beyond. Dust rose in the distance like a coming storm. There were more horses with men on them than Josiah could count in a quick second.

He stopped, strained his eyes, and hoped like hell that it was Captain McNelly and the company of Texas Rangers, set on rescuing Corpus Christi and bearing news about Lyle.

CHAPTER 35

———◆·◆·◆———

McNelly led the company of Rangers straight into Josiah and Scrap's camp. Dust followed the riders, offering a fresh taste of dirt, but any fear that Josiah or Scrap may have felt about their impending approach was replaced by relief.

A look of surprise was plastered across McNelly's usually stern face. The horse he sat on was a big gray mare and made him look smaller than he was. Consumption showed on every ounce of McNelly's thin frame, but there was no weakness to be seen in his eyes. He was remarkably free of dust or dirt—somehow McNelly always managed to remain impeccably clean. He was dressed comfortably—no uniform was required even for a captain of the Texas Rangers—in riding pants and a button-down shirt, all perfectly aligned. There was no mistake that he was in charge of the thirty-some-odd men that had come to a stop behind him.

"Wolfe, Elliot, I thought I was to meet you in Goliad?" McNelly demanded, his voice echoing off in the distance.

Josiah stepped forward, the headless rabbit still dangling from his hand. "Bowman sent word from you while Elliot and I were out rounding up a herd of strays. Said that my son had been stricken with a sickness. I understood the orders, sir, but that news changed our direction. I was not going to spend one more second than I had to wasting time to get home."

McNelly slid off his saddle gracefully, landing on both feet at once. He held a cough in his chest and turned his head to let it out as delicately and unnoticed as possible before he walked up to Josiah, stopping inches from him. He was about a head shorter. "I do not know of any man named Bowman, Wolfe. You must be mistaken."

The company remained quiet; only the horses made any kind of noise—snorts and hoofs dancing nervously on the gravelly ground. All eyes were on the two men. Scrap stood silently next to Josiah, not daring to interfere, smart enough to avoid the conversation.

Josiah could hardly believe his ears. "What do you mean you don't know any man named Bowman? Is my son sick or not?"

"You need to watch your tone, Sergeant," McNelly said. "Or do I need to remind you of proper procedure? Surely, you have not forgotten the chain of command in your long absence from the regular Rangers?"

"Being a spy or away from Austin for such a long stretch was not my idea . . . sir." A pulse of energy tingled at the end of Josiah's fingers, and he fought not to curl his hand into a fist. Such an action would be a show of disrespect, and the consequences for his fist-making could be dire, regardless of intent.

"It was, however, your own volition that led to the assignment in Corpus Christi, Ranger Wolfe. I am not here to rehash that decision, and nor should you be. Your presence in Austin was troublesome. Just as I find your presence, at the moment, troubling. It seems a habit with you, Wolfe."

Silence settled between the two men, as they stared directly into each other's hard-as-steel eyes.

Josiah was angry and confused. The last thing he'd expected, once he identified the coming riders as McNelly and the boys, was a confrontation . . . and news that McNelly had no idea who Don Bowman was.

"May we speak in private, sir?" Josiah asked, through gritted teeth.

"I think that is a fine idea, Sergeant. You can leave the rabbit for a stew."

With his fingers still feeling tingly, Josiah had nearly forgotten that he was holding the meat for breakfast. Time had stopped for him, even though the sun was proceeding to march upward into the sky. He thrust the rabbit at Scrap. "Here, do something with this."

Scrap took the rabbit, holding it out away from him to keep the blood from dripping on his boots. He had an incredulous look on his face but said nothing, just glared at Josiah.

McNelly walked toward the crest of the hill. He didn't say anything until he'd reached the top and faced Josiah.

"Your son *is* sick, Wolfe. Seriously ill."

The tingling traveled from Josiah's fingers to his brain. He could barely breathe. "Why did you say you didn't know Bowman?" he asked, once he was able to mouth the words out loud.

"Because I don't. I sent word to the telegraph operator. How that information was parlayed to you was out of my field of knowledge. I just felt it important that you know. I also wrote that you and Elliot were to wait in Goliad for me."

"I was not given that information."

"You're certain?"

"I would not lie to you, sir. It serves no purpose. But I may have acted as I have, and headed to Austin, regardless of a charge of dereliction of duty. My son is all that I have left in this world, and nothing will keep me from rushing to him in an hour of need. Surely, you understand that."

"I do, Wolfe. But do you remember what I told you when I assigned you to Corpus Christi?"

Josiah nodded yes. "Trust no one."

"Exactly right. I am even uncertain of some of the men in the company, and whose allegiance they hold true to heart as we ride to face Cortina, to restore peace and order by dissolving the minute groups. They could be spies just as you were a spy. These are difficult times, and money is at the root of the troubles, while justice must wait, or be buried on the verge of showing itself."

Josiah craned his ear toward McNelly as the man spoke. His voice was raspy, and his words were difficult to understand at times. "How could you not trust all of your men?"

"The same way I do not trust you, Wolfe. Do not forget that. Or the fact that you have continued to make enemies in Austin, even though you have not been present to stir the pot."

"I'm sorry, I don't understand, Captain."

"The newspapers have not forgotten your name—thanks, in large part, to the Widow Fikes. And trust me, neither has Juan Cortina. You are well-known in parts of Texas that you don't even know exist."

"That matters little to me, sir. I only wish to continue home and see my son. What happens beyond that is out of my control."

"True enough. I will wish you well then. You are excused from duty, Wolfe. Ride fast to Austin. You are needed there," McNelly said, dismissing Josiah with a simple wave of the hand.

It didn't take long for a quick camp to be set up by the company of Rangers. The horses were properly corralled, with a fire roaring and men milling about, all of them anxious to get back on the trail, since they'd just reentered active service after nearly the entire winter off to do whatever they did when they weren't Rangering.

Josiah and Scrap were preparing to leave, to head north, instead of south with the rest of the company.

They were finishing up packing their saddlebags after a quick bite of breakfast. The planned baths in the creek had not materialized. They had lost more time than they had counted on, because of McNelly's arrival. Still, it was a relief to be free of orders to rejoin the fight in Corpus Christi. If that had not occurred, Josiah was ready to leave the service of the Texas Rangers right then and there. He was going home to Austin regardless.

Once he was fully prepared to leave, Josiah sought out McNelly. Scrap was right behind him.

They found the captain in a tent, staring at a large map. His forehead was sweaty, and there was a smell inside the tent that reminded Josiah of a saloon, of yeasty beer and liquor, but this smell was more like medicine than spirits.

McNelly looked up as Josiah and Scrap entered the white canvas tent.

"Wolfe, are you off now?" McNelly asked, wiping his forehead with a sopping wet white handkerchief.

"We are, Captain," Josiah answered.

"Do you have any intelligence to share before we journey into Corpus Christi, Wolfe?"

Josiah shrugged. "I was met by Maria Villareal, the spy on the inside of Cortina's organization. At least, she was supposed to be. I also met a man named Miguel, who I am convinced is a sympathizer of Cortina's and who may be directly, or indirectly, involved in the uprising. Agusto, the barkeep at the cantina where I spent most of my days, is dead, I am convinced at the hand of this Miguel, though I have no proof of it."

"What became of this female spy? This Maria Villareal?

She was very expensive to turn to our side, from what I understand."

Josiah did not answer straightaway. The words stuck on his tongue longer than he would have liked, only because he still felt responsible for the outcome. "She, too, is . . . dead, sir. Shot by an unseen man on a rooftop."

"And this death, you witnessed it with your own eyes?"

"I did, unfortunately. The woman was not killed straight out. I took her to a small fishing village to get help. She died there, later in the night." Josiah's voice cracked, and he looked away from McNelly. He did not want to have to re-count his loss of friendship with Juan Carlos. It was almost impossible for him to talk about.

"So you have nothing to help me, Wolfe?" McNelly asked.

"I failed, sir, I did not know Cortina's attack on Corpus Christi was going to happen." Josiah hesitated, shifted his weight. "I hope to never hold spy duty again, sir."

"I don't think that's a concern, Wolfe." McNelly turned his attention to Scrap. "And what of you, Elliot? In the months spent in Corpus, is there anything I should know before I lead my men into battle?"

Scrap stepped forward, and Josiah gladly stepped out of the way. "I'd say you need to seek out Sheriff John McLane. He's got his finger on the pulse of them minute gangs. Knows a lot of the fellas runnin' them. He ain't likely to be real happy to answer to a Ranger, but I found him to be a good man, Captain McNelly. He's one for law and order, and dead set against the minute groups. We might have seen their handiwork on two Mexican rustlers. I suppose those men didn't deserve to be killed."

McNelly nodded. "The minute groups are just as trou-bling as Cortina and his raiders."

Scrap withheld comment, and Josiah was glad. If there was anybody in the room who hated Mexicans as much as the men in the minute groups, it was Scrap Elliot.

"What became of this Miguel, Wolfe?" McNelly asked.

"I'm not sure, sir. I am certain he fired on a cattle drive, sending them into a stampede. My eyes are sharp, and I know a man when I see him. We went after the strays, Elliot and I, and found the two dead men he just spoke of, their throats cut. Rustlers, I believe, but cannot be sure. But there was no sign of Miguel. He vanished. Elliot and I were heading back to the herd when Hughes, one of the cowboys, sought us out and gave me the news about my son."

"Very well, then. I'm sure you are anxious to get on the trail to Austin." McNelly walked over to Josiah and shook his hand. "Be safe. I will keep my eye out for this fellow, Miguel. I would suggest you do the same."

Josiah withdrew his hand from McNelly's weak handshake, nodded, and turned to leave. Scrap turned to follow.

"Elliot," McNelly called out. "Where do you think you're going?"

"With Wolfe, Captain, to Austin."

McNelly shook his head no. "You'll be riding with us, Elliot, to Corpus. I need all the good shots I can find."

Scrap stared at McNelly, hesitated, then looked at Josiah, who gave him a quick, almost unseen, nod of approval.

"Yes, sir," Scrap said. "I'm happy to ride into battle with you." A sad smile crossed his face. He shook Josiah's hand quickly, uttered, "Good luck, Wolfe," then rushed out of the tent.

Josiah followed Scrap outside, not saying another word. He mounted Clipper, turned and nodded to McNelly, who was standing at the tent's door, and trotted the Appaloosa slowly until he was clear of the camp, then broke into a full run, not looking back as he went.

CHAPTER 36

———◆✕◆———

Austin came into view the following afternoon. The ride had been fast and focused. Josiah had barely taken time to rest Clipper, or himself, and done only what he had to do to keep going.

Clipper was showing signs of fatigue, of slowing unconsciously, but the horse continued to press on, continued to respond to Josiah's demands the best he could under the relentless push of his master.

There was an extra helping of spirit in the Appaloosa's heart, one that could easily be taken for granted, and had been on this trip. The bond between the man and the beast was as strong as any could be, but there was a scar on the relationship now, one that Clipper had no clue about. Maria Villareal's death—and the simple choice, retrieving his horse, that had caused it—would never be far from Josiah's mind, and because of the loyalty he felt for Clipper, he would always feel responsible for her death. Atonement seemed impossible, a lost cause, a regret to hang with the other violent moments of his life that held no hope of resolution.

It was difficult not to think about Juan Carlos, too, and of the anger and rage in his eyes as he pointed the rifle at Josiah and ordered him to leave.

Josiah wasn't sure how he was going to explain to Pearl what had happened with her uncle. Beyond that, there were other concerns to face. Returning to Austin meant facing the possibility that the populace and press, those that drove him out in the first place, would still be in the mood to see him hanged. He had to wonder if he would ever be able to walk the streets of Austin freely, or if everyone would continue to consider him guilty in the death of Pete Feders. It was not murder. It was self-defense. Even a manslaughter charge would fall flat, given the right venue.

The questions crowded his mind, but they did not stop Josiah's extreme pace. He had concluded that there was no getting away from the deeds he had committed in the name of service and employment by the Texas Rangers. His past was less a worry now, but he knew it would rise up to greet him at some point. He just didn't know when that would happen or where.

Josiah had journeyed far and fast, leaving the issues of right and wrong and fighting Juan Cortina in the hands of more capable men.

Oddly, he had missed Scrap's presence on the trip north, but he was certain that the boy was where he needed to be—and wanted to be: right in the middle of the fight with the Mexican interlopers. If Scrap had a chance to take Cortina's head, he would do so gladly. Rushing to Austin to see a sick child held little adventure for Scrap, and Josiah knew that. Still, the ride was far quieter than he was accustomed to.

The road into Austin was familiar now.

It was still hard to believe, but the city was his home—had been for nearly a year—but only because Lyle was there, waiting, hopefully still alive. The thought that the boy might be dead sent shivers down Josiah's spine.

He slowed Clipper as the road into Austin became Congress Avenue. The Old Stone State Capitol building stood centered at the end of the bustling avenue, lined with buildings of all sizes and for all purposes, good and bad. Fresh-cut lumber was not a scent Josiah had experienced while he was away, and the smell caught the attention of his nose right away, as did the sound of beating hammers.

Growth and prosperity had returned to Austin, the railroad and stagecoach lines providing a constant influx of new people, and money as well, obviously. Perhaps society had clawed its way out of the Panic of '73. Josiah hadn't noticed. He'd been too busy trying to be Zeb Teter to care about much of anything else.

The reality was that the state of the economy in the city mattered little to Josiah. The onslaught of building might be a result of the season, of the opportunity and hope that came with spring.

He sped up the avenue, looking for his normal cross street to get home. At this point, he wasn't concerned much about hiding his identity. He hoped that four months had been long enough for his face to fall out of the focus of hate, speculation, and rumor that he had experienced before leaving for Corpus in such a rush. Surely, it was someone else's turn. Another tragedy or scandal, a replacement for the rude accusations and speculation about his motives to kill Pete Feders—namely that he'd done it for the hand, and purse, of Pearl Fikes. Which was the furthest thing from the truth.

It was late in the day, and the sun was gliding down its unseen track to the other side of the earth. The sky was clear. The day had been warm. Warm enough for Josiah to work up a sweat pushing Clipper to ride faster and faster. He was covered, head to toe, in trail dust, and since the ride had been so frantic, there was still a layer of salt on his skin, a souvenir from the seashore. More than a couple of days of stubble covered Josiah's face. His clothes were stiff with filth. But his physical state didn't matter any more than the state of Austin's financial health. His heart was racing as fast as it could without jumping out of his chest, the closer he got to the little house at the corner of Sixth Street and Pecan.

He continued to try and steel himself for the worst news.

Josiah was not sure how he would react if he *was* too late. No matter the experience he'd accumulated over the years with facing the loss of those he loved, never seeing Lyle alive again was not something he could bring himself to imagine.

It would be too much of a loss to bear. The final straw. A snap of madness that would never heal. Josiah was sure of one thing: He would not survive the death of his one and only son. There would be no desire left inside of him to walk in the world any longer . . . No job, no amount of money, could ever take that pain away.

The house came into view just as the sun set beyond the horizon, offering up an abundance of gray light that only promised to grow darker. A buggy sat in front of the simple clapboard house, the single black lead horse tied to the hitching post.

Josiah pushed Clipper harder down the street.

The horse groaned but did as he asked, coming to a stop only when Josiah yanked back on the reins, tossing dust and dirt straight up onto the porch of the house.

He jumped off Clipper, his eyes blinded with fear, and rushed up to the porch. "Ofelia, Ofelia, I'm home. Lyle, I'm home," he called out.

A light burned in the window of the house, and to his surprise, Josiah found the door locked as he tried to turn the knob. He wrestled with the knob for a second, then began to beat on the door. "Ofelia, Ofelia, it's me, Josiah. Let me in." He beat on the door again, his fist stinging, his arm aching from the tension. "Let me in," he said, in a lower tone, his fear taking over, his resolve wavering, tears welling in his eyes. "Let me in," he whispered. "Lyle, I'm home." Exhaustion and fear had caught up with him.

Finally, he heard footsteps walking toward the door from inside the house. The doorknob turned slowly, and Josiah stepped back, expecting to see Ofelia, expecting to rush right past her to Lyle's bed.

Instead, the door swung open and there stood Billie Webb. "Lord have mercy, Josiah Wolfe, you have the patience of a rabbit." A head shorter than him, with shoulder-length brown hair, and summer blue eyes, Billie perched both hands on her hips and scowled at Josiah.

"Billie? What're you doing here?"

"Well that's a fine hello."

"I'm sorry, I wasn't expecting to see you."

"I bet you weren't."

Josiah peeked his head over Billie's, looked inside. "Lyle . . ."

"Is sleeping. Or, at least, he was until you started bangin' on the damn door like some darned fool intent on breakin' it down."

"I haven't seen him for four months." Josiah pushed by Billie, who remained firmly planted in the doorway.

"He's still sick, Josiah. Doc says he might be contagious until the fever breaks."

"I don't care."

Billie grabbed Josiah's arm and stopped him. "He might not know you. He's delirious sometimes and normal other times."

"I don't care," Josiah said, breaking free of Billie's grip. "I know *him*."

CHAPTER 37

The room was dark. A solid green blanket had been hung in the window to keep the light of day out. Now that it was nearly nighttime, the room was twice as dark as it normally would be.

Ofelia sat in the corner, at the foot of Lyle's bed, on the same stool she used to sit on in the kitchen.

The open door had let in a crack of light, enough for Josiah to see a tired set of deep brown Mexican eyes and a few new strands of gray hair on the woman's head. Ofelia looked up at him, forced a smile, then returned her attention back to the lump in the bed.

There was an odor in the room that Josiah recognized immediately. It was the smell of salves, tonics, and sickness. It was impossible not to remember that the same smells were the announcement of what was to come. The foul odor of death was not far behind. It had been that way with his three girls, Lily, and now, with Lyle.

Josiah closed his mouth, held his breath, and tried not to breathe in the smell, tried not to believe what his senses were telling him was true. Whatever unseen predator had attacked his family in Seerville had followed them to Austin. He squeezed his hands into tight fists.

Why don't you come for me, you bastard? Take me. Leave the boy alone. Damn it. Leave the boy alone . . .

Lyle was covered in blankets, a cold compress on his forehead. Only his eyes were visible, and they were closed. A small amount of movement at his chest was the only indication that the boy was still alive.

Ofelia held a pair of rosary beads in her hands and had stopped moving them as soon as Josiah walked into the room. He thought she might have been mumbling some prayers, but he wasn't sure and didn't care. There wasn't any tension between the two of them about Ofelia's belief in God, but they had a silent agreement not to discuss the subject.

"It is good to see you, señor," Ofelia finally said in a hushed tone. "The telegraph came. We were expecting you."

Josiah nodded and looked behind him. Billie was standing just outside the door in the shadows, her eyes fixed on him. He looked away, back to Lyle, then kneeled down beside the bed. "Lyle," he whispered. "Papa is here."

Lyle didn't move, so Josiah went to touch his shoulder to try and rouse him.

"No, don't, señor," Ofelia said. "We don't want you to get sick, too."

"I don't care."

"We do," Billie said, from behind him.

"I want him to know I'm here," Josiah said.

"He'll know when he wakes up," Billie snapped. "Now, let him be, and let him get some sleep. It took us hours and hours to get him calmed down in the first place."

"What was the matter?"

"He was calling out for you."

Josiah exhaled and stood up.

"It is all right, señor, I will watch over him."

Billie nodded. "You need a bath. You smell like a wet pig who's been drug, headfirst, through a pond full of swill and mud."

"I've been riding for days, trying to get here as soon as I could," Josiah said, as quietly as he could, through clenched teeth.

"I don't care what you've been doing, you smell. And you need a bath. Now, let's get on with it," Billie ordered with a point of the finger, out of the room.

The water was hot as it could be without scalding tender flesh. Josiah was up to his shoulders in the water, his eyes half-closed as he sat there, soaking. Billie, thankfully, had given him some privacy, but only after he had to chase her off, convincing her that he was more than capable of giving himself a bath. She'd looked spurned but had walked off, in a huff.

A little bit more dirt on his skin and the water would have been muddy. It had been a good while since he'd had a bath.

The tub sat under the overhang on the small porch just off the back of the house, and night had fallen. Clouds covered the sky, and there was a cool touch to the air. Insects chirped happily, a reunion of songs and desires set off by the arrival of spring. There were no frog calls, no songs of the woods that Josiah was accustomed to. Beyond the insects, he could hear the pulse of the city still beating: a piano clanking in the distance, a man screaming at his wife two houses down, a dog barking.

The bath felt good, but Josiah was still unsettled, his footing not certain, even though he was home. Finally home.

The kitchen door opened, and light filtered outside from the coal oil lamp that was burning dimly.

"Do you need anything, señor?" Ofelia asked, standing

off at a respectable distance, the rosary beads still in her hand.

"No, I'm fine, thank you. Is Lyle still sleeping?"

"*Sí. Como un ángel.* Like an angel, señor. Like an angel."

"Please don't say that."

"I am sorry, señor. I meant nothing by it."

Josiah laid his head back on the rim of the tub and looked out to the sky. "I know. I just can't think of him being any way other than how he was when I left. I can't lose him, Ofelia."

"Neither of us can, señor."

Josiah turned his attention back to the short, round Mexican woman and realized that he asked a lot of her, and Ofelia had given him even more. She loved Lyle like he was her own.

"How did Billie come to be here?"

"The señorita, she show up one day looking for you. Months ago. Not long after you leave for your duty. I tell her that you are gone, and I don't know when you come back. She comes to see me and Lyle, *cada vez en un tiempo*, every once in a while. But when she saw Lyle was sick, she stayed to help me. I am grateful for her help . . . but . . ."

"But what?"

"She thinks she live here now. Comes in the door without knocking." Ofelia pointed to her chest. "I knock when you are home, señor. This is not my *casa*."

Josiah wasn't sure what to make of what Ofelia was telling him. It made him even more uncomfortable. "She has a baby of her own . . ."

"*Sí*, the baby stay with someone at her boardinghouse. She don't bring him here to Lyle's sickness. You like this *chica*?" Ofelia was leaning on the doorjamb, her face serious and concerned.

"I helped her and she helped me. I think it's as simple as that. I hope so, anyway."

"It is *not* that simple, señor."

Josiah exhaled deeply. "I know."

"*Tener cuidado*. Be wary."

"I'm too tired to be anything else. But why do you say that?"

"She is a nice girl," Ofelia said, bringing her voice even lower than it was. "But I think she is looking for something that is not here most of the time."

"Like what?"

"A papa for her *niño*."

Josiah nodded. "Thank you, Ofelia. You are a good friend. I don't know what I would do without you."

Ofelia laughed, as if it were the only reaction she knew to make but she wasn't quite sure it was the right one. "There is no need to worry, señor, I am not going anywhere anytime soon."

CHAPTER 38

———◆◆◆———

"I'll see you home," Josiah said to Billie.

A curious look crossed Billie's face. "You don't have to. I've walked that walk a ton of times, thank you very much."

"No, I'd like to."

"Suit yourself."

Billie walked out the front door, wrapping a white shawl around her shoulders. Josiah followed after her, closing the door behind him softly.

Lyle was still sleeping and probably would continue to for the rest of the night. As was her custom when Josiah was away, Ofelia had slept in the bed opposite Lyle's, albeit with one ear and one eye open. Though Josiah was back, due to Lyle's state of health, rather than return to her own lodgings in Little Mexico, Ofelia was staying put, sleeping now on a mat just outside the door to the boy's room.

The bath had revitalized Josiah, and a couple of healthy servings of Ofelia's *menudo* had sated his appetite. He had changed into a set of clothes that had been left behind four months prior, and they fit him loosely. Ofelia had said he looked like an *espantapájaros*, a scarecrow.

It was good to be home, but Josiah felt different, almost like he was waiting to catch up with himself. Clipper had been put away in the livery down the street where the horse was usually kept, and everything else, as much as possible, had been put back in its place—with the exception of Lyle, who still had not woken to find his father home, and Billie, who needed to be escorted to her own home.

Night had fully enveloped Austin. There were none of the new gaslights on the street Josiah lived on. Those were saved for the main thoroughfares. With the clouds thick in the sky, there was no moonlight to navigate by, but Josiah knew his way—and so did Billie. She walked five feet in front of him, her pace rapid, her arms wrapped tightly around her, to keep warm in the chilly air, Josiah supposed.

The air felt good to him. It was nice to be on solid ground, off the back of a racing horse.

"Billie, would you slow down?" Josiah asked, walking even faster to catch up with her.

They had walked about two blocks.

Billie stopped abruptly and turned to face Josiah. "I'm so mad at you I could just spit. Haven't you figured that out, Josiah Wolfe?"

Josiah stopped, too, about a foot from Billie.

There was music still playing in the distance, a raucous melody rising into the night air, mixing with other saloon music emanating from Congress Avenue. Cowboys from the trail were either taking a break, getting ready to head out, or coming back. Regardless, there was always something to celebrate. But Josiah was not in a celebratory mood and wanted nothing to do with saloons, liquor . . . or angry women, for that matter.

"Why would you be mad at me, Billie? I haven't been

here to do anything," Josiah said. His voice was firm, and he stared her in the eye.

"Just like a man to think you have to be here to make a woman worry and fret over you."

Josiah stuffed his hands into his front pockets. "I didn't ask you to fret over me, Billie," he said softly. "I did what I thought was best for everybody. I had no choice but to leave Austin if I wanted to stay a Ranger."

"You left that little boy, Josiah. And now he's sick. You ever think he needs a daddy more than you need to be off traipsin' around bein' a Ranger?"

"It's my job. I don't know how to be anything else."

"Well, it ain't right, and you damn well ought to figure out how to be somethin' else."

The veins in Josiah's neck tensed up. "Come on, Billie. Let's get you home. We're not doing anybody any good standing here hollering at each other." He grabbed her arm as he began to walk forward, but Billie pulled away. Josiah could see tears welling up in her eyes.

Billie stopped suddenly, then turned and lurched forward, throwing herself into Josiah's chest.

She wrapped her arms around him, holding on to his waist like she was about to drown.

At first, Josiah stood stiffly, his arms at his sides. This was not the first time Billie had surprised him by jumping into his arms. Each time was uncomfortable for Josiah, and this time was no exception.

Billie turned her face up to Josiah, her eyes wanting, almost begging him to kiss her.

The feel of her pressed against his body began to awaken something in him that had been dormant since he'd left Austin. The simple desire for a woman, to feel needed, to want something more than a piece of information, a drink, or a ride home. He wanted to be needed, and he wanted to feel alive again, know what it meant to be intimate for more than a fleeting moment.

"I worried about you. About your son," Billie whispered. "Don't that mean somethin' to you?"

Josiah kissed her then, felt her welcoming and desire, and matched it with his own loneliness and forgotten needs. It was a long, deep, passionate kiss. The outside world around them disappeared, and if the air swirling about them had been cold when they first walked out into the night, then between them now it was warm, hot, and growing hotter.

Billie moaned and leaned into Josiah, pressing against him even harder, grinding at the waist.

He felt her, could taste her desire, and for a moment, he was glad to let himself go. It was nice to be wanted, to feel what he had been missing. But somewhere deep inside of him, he heard Ofelia's warning, heard the reminder that Billie was after something—a father, a husband, a life—he might not be able to provide. And then he thought about Pearl.

Josiah pulled away from Billie then, ignoring his own state of arousal, ignoring Billie's unspoken offer to love him, to show him a way to pleasure that could last, if he wanted it to.

"What's the matter?" Billie asked, a look of shock and concern crossing her face.

Words stumbled to the end of Josiah's tongue and stayed there. He didn't know what to say, so he said nothing, just looked down to the ground, kicked the dirt, and turned sideways, letting his embrace of Billie fall away and pulling out of hers at the same time.

"It's that other woman ain't it? The one you can't tell whether you love her or not?" Billie demanded, her face all twisted in a growing rage.

Josiah nodded yes. He didn't think about trying to not answer her or acting as if what she said wasn't the truth. It was. Billie had hit the nail on the head—mostly. He was afraid, too, of getting into something that he couldn't get out of. He didn't know Billie that well; he felt obliged to her for helping him escape from O'Reilly and the corrupt sheriff in the town of Comanche, but he'd already done as much as he thought he had to do to thank her. He was having a hard enough time being a father to Lyle; he wasn't sure taking on another child was something he could even consider.

He had yet to see Pearl since returning to Austin, and he didn't know where they stood, or if she would even see him. He hadn't even sent her a letter in all of the time he'd been away.

Taking up with Billie, running off into the night for a moment of pleasure, no matter how desirable, was a mistake he was not about to make. He had enough new regret to wear, he wasn't about to add more, if he could help it.

"You could've had anything you wanted, Josiah Wolfe," Billie continued. "Anything, I tell you. I would've loved you till the moon fell out of the sky. But now you ain't gettin' nothin'. I never want to see you again. Ever, you understand me? I never *ever* want to see you again."

Before he could answer, and before he could reach out to touch Billie to try and calm her down, she tore away from him in a full run, disappearing quickly into the darkness. The only remnant of her presence was the echo of her sobs, rising into the air and mixing sadly with the saloon music that played on as if there was not a care in the world.

CHAPTER 39

❖

Josiah did not chase after Billie Webb. He stood there for longer than he should have, staring after her, wondering if that was truly the last time he would ever see her. It felt like an end, one that he wasn't all that sad about, more confused than anything else.

Darkness engulfed Josiah, and as tempted as he was to chase after Billie, he knew it was best that he didn't. They both shared a weakness that, if breached, could cause them both a lot of problems. Problems neither of them needed. Billie was still grieving, still trying to find her way after losing her husband, Charlie, and for some reason, she thought Josiah was her way to a new life, or, at least, a direction to take.

What Billie didn't know was that Josiah carried his own grief. Not only from losing his family—that was always there—but from being responsible for Maria Villiareal's death, and for leaving Lyle for such a long stretch of time.

One thing was for sure, Josiah was done with spy duty,

with long assignments. He would make that clear to Captain McNelly the next time he saw him. It would either be agreeable, or that would be the end of his Texas Ranger career, plain and simple.

After taking one long and deep look down the street, into the darkness as far as he could see, making sure Billie was truly gone from sight, Josiah turned and headed back to the house on Pecan Street.

His pace was slow, and he was able to focus on the steps ahead of him. He was a couple of blocks away from home, and the street he was on was lined with houses, all built about a foot from one another. None of them had yards, and like his own house, each one had a simple porch that faced the street. Hitching posts dotted the street, and there was no boardwalk, just the dirt from the road. Most of the houses were dark, and being aware of the lack of privacy and how it felt to be invaded by curious eyes, Josiah ignored the goings-on in the houses as he passed by if there were lights in the windows.

About a half a block down, Josiah caught a whiff of smoke. Not chimney smoke, or smoke like Scrap's quirlies, but cigar smoke. He was certain of it. When he looked behind him, just passing an alleyway, he was just as certain that he saw the shadow of a man skirt away, just out of sight, and disappear into the darkness.

Josiah picked up his pace, and just as he was about to turn onto Pecan, he glanced over his shoulder again. The hair on the back of his neck was raised, like someone was watching him, trailing him. It was a well-defined sense, born in the War Between the States, and it had saved his life on more than one occasion. Josiah trusted his intuition more than his sight at times. This was one of those times.

Out of the corner of his eye, he saw a glowing red orb, and the figure of a man about a half a block behind him. Now he was sure someone was following him. Instead of turning left on Pecan Street, he turned right, and eased his hand down to grip his Peacemaker. A quick jerk up, since he wore a swivel rig, and a spin, and he'd have the man covered—as long as the man didn't shoot first.

Maybe there was more than one, Josiah thought, fearing he might be walking into a trap. He stopped then, the barrel of the gun aimed automatically at the figure's chest.

The figure, almost certainly a man, stopped, too. They were about fifty feet apart, facing each other. The stub of the cigar glowed deep red as the man drew a drag from it.

"You wouldn't shoot an unarmed man, would you, Wolfe?"

Josiah recognized the voice but couldn't place it right away. "How do I know you're not armed?"

"I suppose you just have to trust me." The cigar dimmed like a shooting star fading from sight. But there was no question that the man was coming closer now, moving toward Josiah.

With his thumb, he eased back the hammer of the Peacemaker. "I'd stop right there, fella. I've got my gun on you."

"I figured as much, but you'd be making a big mistake shooting a newspaper reporter, out for a stroll, just doing his job."

The man continued to walk forward, and his features were coming dimly into view. A splash of light fell on him as the clouds parted and the moon shone onto the ground briefly, then disappeared, offering up another dose of darkness.

It was then that Josiah fully recognized Paul Hoagland, the short, mousy-looking reporter from the *Austin Statesman*, who had pursued him out behind the capitol building after Josiah had given his testimony to McNelly, Jones, and the adjunct general.

"You owe me a story, Wolfe," Hoagland said, coming to a stop about a wagon's length from Josiah.

"I'm not sure I owe you anything, sir," Josiah answered,

easing the hammer back to its place. He kept his hand on
the grip of the Peacemaker, though, just in case . . .

"I saw you to freedom in exchange for an interview, or
have you forgotten?"

"I've been away for a while."

"Trust me, Wolfe, there are those in this fair city of ours
who are still interested in knowing what has become of you.
You were gone, but not forgotten, as they say."

"I have been serving the Texas Rangers, as I have done
for nearly a year now."

The smell of the cigar was pungent and thick as Hoagland
stepped even closer to continue the conversation with Josiah.

Josiah stepped back, not wanting to have the conversation at all. His mind was still buzzing from the emotional
confrontation with Billie. The last thing he wanted to do
at the moment was have an exchange with a man whose
business was the use of words and, as far as Josiah was
concerned, the spreading of lies and gossip.

"It seems so," Hoagland said. "Your whereabouts were
obviously considered a secret once General Steele issued
his statement clearing you of any wrongdoing."

"What is it you want from me, Hoagland? Can't you
leave me and my family to ourselves? I'm a simple man."

"I only want what you promised me—the story from
the horse's mouth about what happened to Captain Peter
Feders. Was it really self-defense?"

"I have answered that question to the only court that
matters."

"You most certainly underestimate the court of public
opinion. They ran you out of town once, and they surely
will again."

Josiah stepped forward, ignoring the cigar and his re-
pulsion to it. Hoagland stood his ground. He didn't flinch,
didn't show a quiver of fear.

"Who do you really work for, Hoagland? Who really

wants me run out of this town once and for all? The Widow Fikes?"

Hoagland chuckled. The bowler he wore trembled and almost fell off. "Really, Wolfe, you have been away for a long time. The Widow Fikes has no power of persuasion in this city. She has no property. No standing at all. She's lost everything, or didn't you know?"

It was as if the air had been sucked out of the world. Josiah's thoughts immediately turned to Pearl. There had been no communication between the two of them the entire time he was in Corpus Christi. To be honest, he didn't know if Pearl Fikes was dead or alive—but he suddenly wanted to run to the estate and beat on the door, rouse Pedro, and prove the newspaperman wrong.

"Oh," Hoagland said, "you didn't know." Obviously judging by the look on Josiah's face.

"No," Josiah whispered.

"You have enemies here, Wolfe. Enemies that hold more power than Elvira Fikes could ever hope to hold."

"I have enemies everywhere."

"You sound proud of that."

"It's a talent I have, acquiring enemies."

Hoagland chuckled again. "I like a man that's not afraid to make enemies. Maybe that's why I find you so interesting."

"I'd rather be left alone." Josiah turned to walk away, and got a few steps off before realizing Hoagland was just going to follow him. "You're not going to give up, are you?"

"No. I'm not."

"Then here's what you need to know: I killed Pete Feders. It was self-defense. Him or me. And it was one of the worst days in my life . . ."

CHAPTER 40

———◆◆◆———

Morning pushed into the green blanket covering the window. The edges around it glowed with soft golden light. Beyond the window, the world began to wake. A few horses clip-clopped down the alley that ran behind the house. A rooster crowed, even though the sun had already poked up over the horizon an hour or so before, and the ground rumbled with the power of a train waiting on the tracks as it built up steam, preparing to depart the station two blocks away.

Josiah sat up and wiped the sleep from his eyes. The smell of coffee, of really good coffee, greeted his nose, and he knew immediately that he was home, not on the trail with Scrap, whose coffee was weak and nearly tasteless. Complaining about such a thing never have crossed Josiah's mind, but he had sure wished Scrap had taken some coffee-making lessons from Ofelia.

Lyle was still buried in a bundle of blankets in his bed. The boy was breathing slowly and steadily, nothing to give Josiah any more concern than he already felt. The only other noise in the house was Ofelia as she shuffled about quietly in the kitchen.

Standing hesitantly, pushing the night fully away with a stretch and a reach to the ceiling, Josiah was not too anxious to start the day. The run-in with Hoagland had left him feeling unsettled and unsure of what to do next. In the end, the man had left Josiah standing on the street with no promises and his demand still in place. Josiah owed him a story. It was that simple—even though Josiah didn't feel like he owed the man anything, much less a story about shooting Pete Feders or what had happened since. The past was the past. As haunting as it might be, Josiah wanted nothing more than to move on now that he was home, in the same room with Lyle, who, when he was well, knew nothing about the past. The present was the boy's only concern.

Josiah was anxious, however, to make a visit to the outhouse. First, he checked on Lyle, peeked over the lump in the blanket to see his son's face. Before he could catch a breath, he yelled out, "Ofelia, come here!"

Josiah immediately plopped down on the bed next to Lyle and, carefully as he could, rolled the boy over to face him. The bed was wet from top to bottom. Perspiration dripped off Lyle's forehead as he flickered his eyes open.

"Papa," Lyle whispered, struggling to pull his arms from underneath the heavy trap of blankets piled on top of him. "Papa, Papa, Papa. I dreamed you were here."

"What is it, señor?" Ofelia asked, rushing into the room, wiping her hands nervously on the apron she always wore.

"He's soaked," Josiah said, a worried tone in his voice.

"Move, move," she said, more demanding and authoritative than normal.

Josiah stood up out of her way, and Ofelia slid into his spot, her hands removing the blankets, running over Lyle's face and chest like an expert prospector looking for, and finding, gold. "His fever, it broke, señor."

"That's good, right?"

"'Felia, I'm hungry," Lyle said, wrapping his arms around her neck. "Papa's home. Papa's home." A smile grew on the boy's face, and his eyes locked onto Josiah, promising not to leave. "I dreamed him, 'Felia. I did."

Ofelia smiled, reached over to the small table next to the bed, grabbed a rag that had been used for a compress, and began to wipe the sweat from Lyle's face. "You did, Lyle. I tell him to hold a picture of you in his mind before going to sleep every night. *Le prometí a él hay magia.* I promised him no magic."

"It is *magia*," Lyle said. "I made Papa come home in my dreams." Lyle struggled one last time, pulled his arms out from under the blanket, and thrust them up in the air, begging Josiah to pick him up.

Josiah wasn't sure what to think. "That's good news, right? He's going to be okay, Ofelia?"

"The doctor says if the fever breaks, that is good. But it can come back. *Niño* is still weak, and the sickness may not be gone. I have seen this happen many times before, do not get your hopes up."

"When the girls got sick, the fevers never left. Lily, too."

"I remember," Ofelia said, a hint of wistfulness in her voice.

"So maybe Lyle is better? This is different?"

Ofelia smiled, then nodded, yes. "I hope so. By all that is *ponderoso*—um, mighty, I hope so."

Josiah matched her smile then, a wave of relief washing over him. He turned away from Lyle, not wanting his son to see the tears welling in his eyes. There would be no burial, no death to consider, no madness to face, not today anyway, and hopefully, not anytime soon.

Then just as quickly, he wiped away his tears, turned around, and pulled Lyle up from the bed and into his arms. He hugged the boy as hard as he could without squeezing the air out of him. Lyle did the same.

* * *

There was no question that Josiah's mood was lighter. The sight of Lyle—though clearly not up to the usual gregariousness of a boy his age—returning to health pushed all of Josiah's concerns and worries to the back of his mind. Still, once the day wore on, and with Ofelia hovering over Lyle like a happy but overly concerned mother, Josiah felt he was ready to face one more uncertainty that awaited him.

He wanted to see Pearl.

Not one to take another man's words for the truth, especially a man like Paul Hoagland, Josiah fetched Clipper, who was well rested now, and made his way to the Fikes estate.

The ride was slow, as Josiah wanted to take in the day, get a sense of the city since he had been gone. He had noticed the continued growth upon arriving, the new buildings going up, and now that it was later in the day, the hammers pounded furiously, trying to outlast the daylight. As he passed St. David's, an Episcopal church with Tiffany stained glass windows glittering in the sun, the bells in the tower rang out, striking three times.

Josiah urged Clipper on, taking no notice of passersby, if they stared at him, recognized him, or not.

Lyle was alive, and the fevers were gone. There was nothing that could take away the relief he felt. What other people thought, what had happened in the past, before he left for Corpus Christi, were the least of his concerns. He rode down the street, sitting square in the saddle, his back straight, his shoulders pointed to the sky, like any other man with nary a care in the world.

It didn't take long to arrive at the estate. He had to pass the governor's mansion on the way, and he barely paid any attention to the traffic around it or the Old Stone Capitol building not too far away—horses, buggies, wagons, all hitched or waiting for something or other. Voices rose into the air, and they mixed together in a loud mumble, one that Josiah could not decipher, nor did he care to.

He was at a slow trot, and at the first glance of the lane that led down to the grand house that was the heart of the Fikes estate, Josiah knew that Paul Hoagland had told him the truth.

The house was vacant. Weeds sprouted from the fertile ground and lined the lane, growing haphazardly, without worry or care, promising to overtake the entrance given time and half a chance.

Ivy vines and bindweed flourished, taking fence posts as their own. The fences that surrounded the estate normally saw a fresh coat of whitewash every spring, but they had not been tended to recently. The sun and winter had faded and flaked the wood, showing bare and gray spots in a myriad of places.

Josiah rode up to the house anyway.

A sash was broken, hanging cockeyed off the window above the double front doors that led inside. The entryway was worthy of grandness. The doors were heavy, the wood mahogany, hand-carved with intricate designs that had seen the likes of governors, captains, and maybe even kings, for all Josiah knew. But now the doors were covered with boards, crisscrossed, barring entry of any kind, to man or beast.

Josiah stopped Clipper and eased off the horse, leaving him to his own volition, not hitching him up.

Clipper, of course, found a fresh patch of wild clover and made a snack out of the misfortune of the Fikeses and what remained of their once beautiful home.

A slight wind skirted across the open paddock to the south, drawing Josiah's attention to the pond that lay just opposite the house, just beyond where Clipper grazed. The spot in between had been used for any guests to park their wagons or hitch their horses, and was already dotted with weeds and wildflowers, all struggling for their rightful place.

The pond was where he and Pearl had had their first kiss. It was a fine memory, as clumsy as it had been, and at that moment, Josiah realized that he had no idea in the world where Pearl was, or even where to begin to look for her. But he knew he had to find her. He had to see her again . . . if that was even possible.

CHAPTER 41

———◆◆◆———

Josiah made his way back to the governor's mansion, hoping to find someone he recognized, or at the very least someone who could tell him what had happened to Pearl once she left the estate. It was the only place he knew to go.

Finding a spot for Clipper was difficult, but Josiah squeezed the Appaloosa in at the very end of the hitching board. Certain the horse was secure, he headed up to the mansion, past a teamster steadying a four-horse team of heavy-footed draft horses. Sweat on the animals' backs gleamed in the sunlight, the lather suggesting the load of the now empty wagon had been heavier than normal.

"Sure is a lot of activity for such an ordinary day," Josiah said to the teamster as he passed by.

The teamster was a plump man with a short gray beard, floppy felt hat, and droopy eyes that reminded Josiah of a lazy cat's. "Gettin' ready for the Spring Ball or some such thing. I don't know what they call it. I just deliver their kegs and bundles of goods. A comin' out for the girls, or some such event. Don't know nothin' about such fancy doin's myself. How about you? Got a delivery to make yourself? You're empty-handed."

Somewhere in the distance a crow called. It was an un-usual sound in the city, and it unconsciously drew Josiah's attention to the sky, but he saw nothing of concern. "No, just looking for somebody," he said, continuing on past the teamster.

The teamster said something that sounded like "Good luck," but Josiah couldn't be sure, nor did he think the teamster could help him find Pearl, so he didn't bother to ask.

An open set of ten steps, about ten feet wide, led up to the front door of the governor's mansion. The house, a Greek Revival–style place, bore a flat roof and was fronted by six massive pillars. The pillars were pine timbers hauled up from Brastop, a reminder to Josiah of the heavily wooded forests of his boyhood home, and how tall the trees were there. There were no such trees in and around Austin. It was a forest of buildings, none of them too tall, all host to crit-ters, but mostly unseen. Maybe it hadn't been a crow call after all.

The mansion was white with black shutters on both sides of the tall windows. Unlike the Fikes house, it looked fresh and well kept. The glass windows gleamed in the sunlight, with the odd swirls of thinness even more apparent in the glare of the day. Gas lighting had been recently installed in the house, a modern convenience that seemed worrisome to Josiah, but he understood the desire for immediate light, and the disregard for the smell, residue, and trouble offered by the use of coal oil.

Caged birds were kept in the kitchens, songbirds mostly, caught in the wild and sold as warning alarms. If a bird was found dead on the floor of the cage, a gas leak was the first suspect in the death.

The door to the mansion stood wide open, and a tall,

older black man, dressed from head to toe like he was about attend to a funeral, nodded at Josiah. "May I hep you, misser?" There was no distinction in the man's tone—Josiah could have been the most important man in the world for all it mattered to the manservant, who was obviously on door duty, to direct the deliveries of the day. He stood square in front of the door, barring entry.

"I'm looking for someone," Josiah said.

"Does you have an appointment or a delivery to make, misser? I needs to see papers either way, you unnerstand."

"No, no, I was just wondering if you could tell me what became of the Fikeses. You know, the house down the way. It's empty now, and I'd like to get in contact with them, check on their circumstances, you might say."

The black man studied Josiah curiously. He wore a goatee, and it was pure white, like a thick hedge had sprouted on his strong chin and been dusted with a heavy snow. The contrast of the white, curly but finely groomed facial hair against the man's skin was so stark that he almost glowed.

The servant glanced quickly down the street, toward the Fikes' estate. "You got bizness with them folks, the Fikeses, misser?"

"I'm a friend. At least I think I was."

"You looks familiar to me."

"I don't think we've ever met."

"What's your name, misser?"

Josiah hesitated, then looked the man directly in the eye, searching for malice, or contempt. He answered when he was certain he saw neither. "Josiah Wolfe, sir. I doubt you know me. I'm just a simple man, greatly concerned about the loss of the Fikeses. Now, if you could just tell me the fate of the women who once lived in that grand house, I'd be mighty grateful. Then I'll be on my way. Looks like you have a busy day going on here."

"Oh, I know who you is, yes, I do. You's that Texas Ranger that kilt the other Ranger some months back, aren't you?"

Josiah didn't flinch, didn't move, didn't imply one way or the other if the servant was right. He had hoped that time would wash away the notoriety he'd gained by killing a captain in the Texas Rangers. But, from his meeting with Paul Hoagland, and now this mention and recognition of the act, it looked like that had not happened. His reputation preceded him wherever he went. It was something to keep in mind.

The black man shivered, or shimmied, or trembled, Josiah wasn't sure which, from head to toe. Whatever the reaction, Josiah was certain he didn't like it much.

"You waits right there, Misser Wolfe. You jus' waits right there." The old black man vanished inside the mansion like he was on a predetermined mission and would stop at nothing to reach his destination. Josiah knew that kind of determination when he saw it.

The street behind Josiah was busy with traffic, and the noise was growing by the minute, something he was not too accustomed to. He'd spent most of his time in Corpus Christi in Agusto's cantina, and there were not as many people in the seaside town as there were here in Austin. At least, it hadn't seemed so. Silence suited him more so than he'd remembered.

He stood stiffly at the door, growing more nervous by the second, waiting, with no idea what the black man was up to, whether it was good or bad, and who he went after. If that was it at all. He just didn't know.

Maybe I should just leave, he thought.

Under normal circumstances, he would have already hurried off after the black man had disappeared into the mouth of the mansion, but Josiah was becoming more and more concerned about Pearl. She could be anywhere in the city. Anywhere in the state or country, for that matter. There was absolutely no sign at the estate that gave him a clue to her present whereabouts. So he waited, albeit uncomfortably.

Footsteps echoed toward Josiah on the finely polished walnut floor of the mansion's foyer. He looked up to see two figures moving toward him, both identities lost in shadows and the darkness of the clothes they wore. From his walk, there was no mistaking the black man who was clearly returning with another man, oddly of about the same height and willowy build.

The day had warmed, but Josiah still wore a short jacket, a jacket long enough to conceal, to a degree, the Peacemaker on his hip. He also wore a thin knife strapped in his boot. Austin made him just as wary as the barren trail, and being prepared was a matter of survival, regardless of the location. Out of instinct, he eased his hand to the top of the pistol grips. It would only take two heartbeats to drop his hand the rest of the way, finger on the trigger, and swivel the gun forward for a clean shot.

As the sun reached inside the house, Josiah saw that his instinct to reach for his gun had been sheer overreaction. The man walking alongside the black man was Pedro, the manservant from the Fikes estate.

He stepped forward to meet the tall, still impeccably dressed Mexican—he was dressed in the same black getup as the doorman.

A broad smile crossed Pedro's face, and he grabbed Josiah's hand and shook it heartily. "Señor Wolfe, I heard you were back in town, but I did not expect to see you so soon."

Josiah returned the handshake, his grip firm and happy. "It is good to see you, too, Pedro. I'm lucky to find you here."

Pedro withdrew his hand, staring at Josiah, the smile fading from his face. "You have been to the house, then?"

The black man stood back, retaking his post by the door, but watching every move the two men made.

"Yes," Josiah said. "What happened?"

Pedro shrugged. "I know little of the details, señor, but

there was less and less money. One day word came that we would all be forced to move, that we were free to work elsewhere. I owe that family everything I have, señor, an education, a livelihood for more years than I can count. I was the last to leave, and only then when I was forced to."

"But you have a job here."

"I do, and I am grateful for it, but I miss Pearl and Madame Fikes regularly."

Josiah stared back at Pedro, searching the man's face, surprised at the emotion he saw, the loss that was obvious in his voice. "What has become of Pearl, Pedro? I only came here in hopes of finding out what happened to her."

"She is here, in Austin, still. I do not think she could go anywhere else."

Josiah exhaled audibly, and Pedro smiled again, seeing his relief. "I'm happy to hear that."

"There is an all-women's boardinghouse on Second Street, Miss Amelia Angle's Home for Girls. She is staying there for the time being. She is finishing up her lessons to become a schoolteacher." Pedro looked away for a moment, then faced Josiah again. "She must learn a trade to earn money, señor. There is little money left to live on."

"What of her mother, the widow?"

"She is in a sanatorium. Her health is in severe decline, and she is unable to care for herself."

"I'm sorry to hear that."

Pedro nodded, and Josiah stood there staring at the man who had almost single-handedly run the entire operation for the Fikeses. It must have been difficult to start over, but there was nothing Josiah could find to say, so he kept quiet. Instead, he stepped back and said, "I need to see Pearl."

"The rules are very strict, señor, at Miss Amelia Angle's house," Pedro said, looking to the sky. "You will not be allowed to enter by the time you get there. Her room is on the top floor, in the north corner." He had lowered his voice, so the black man would not hear him.

"Thank you, Pedro," Josiah said, turning to leave. But he stopped; he had one more question. "How did you know I was back in town, Pedro?"

"The newspaper, señor. There was a big mention of your arrival on the front page. Everybody knows that you have returned to Austin."

CHAPTER 42

———◆✕◆———

Miss Amelia Angle's Home for Girls was not hard to find. It was a quick ride to Second Street. The house was three storeys, not that old, built in the most recent style: high peaks, gingerbread lattice tacked to the eaves, a red brick turret on the ground rising up past the second floor, most likely hosting a parlor, and a long wraparound porch, the woodwork just as fancy as the lattice. A black wrought iron fence ran all the way around the property, which took up about a quarter of a block from what Josiah could see.

Everything was green and fresh from the spring rains. The trees looked well pruned, and urns with fancy flowers dotted the porch. Smaller urns lined the steps that led up to the double front doors. There was no way of knowing what kind of flowers were in the urns, but they were fragrant. Bees buzzed about, all the way out into the street, intoxicated like they had just left a saloon after a long binge. The air smelled like it was perfumed with the most expensive toilet water in the world.

Josiah sat comfortably on Clipper, off to the side of the

street, trying not to draw any attention to himself. There was still a lot of traffic making its way over to Congress Avenue.

He had hoped to catch a glimpse of Pearl, but all he saw was a big sign on the gate: "NO VISITORS AFTER 5 P.M."

A quick check of his pocket watch told him he was too late by about twenty minutes. Pedro had implied that the rules at Miss Amelia Angle's Home for Girls were strict, so there was no thought of trudging up to the front door and possibly making trouble for Pearl. He didn't know her circumstances, other than they couldn't have been comfortable.

As nice as the house looked, surely adjusting to life in a boardinghouse was difficult for Pearl. She was accustomed to servants and cooks and having the run of the big house. It was hard for Josiah to imagine the changes Pearl must have faced, but he certainly understood the curves life could throw at a person. If Lily and the girls would have lived their full lives, Josiah knew he'd still be at home in the piney woods of Seerville, living, in his own mind at least, happily ever after, trying to eke out a living as a farmer and maybe a lawman of some kind. Maybe a Texas Ranger. Maybe not. It was impossible to say and really didn't matter anyway.

Josiah knew that Pearl Fikes was resilient, a strong woman—though he didn't know the extent of her strength and will. Losing her way of life, her place in society, would surely be a test of all her attributes.

A soft tinkle of piano music began to emanate from the house. It sounded like the music was coming from the turret, and it was well played, classical; a waltz of some kind.

Josiah eased Clipper's reins and kneed the horse gently, moving him forward so he could get a better look. He wanted to see if he could peek into the window from atop his horse in the street, without alerting whoever was playing the piano of his presence.

It was difficult, but there were heavy curtains pulled to each corner of the window, allowing a slight view in the form of a V. Josiah craned his neck and, to his disappointment, saw that the piano player was not Pearl. It was a young woman with flowing auburn hair.

There was nothing he could do now but wait and hopefully see Pearl coming or going, or bide his time until dark came. If it came to that, then he'd try and rouse her by tossing a small pebble at the window that Pedro had said was hers.

Another piano competed with the one in the turret, only this one wasn't playing a waltz, it was playing a familiar saloon song, "Camptown Races." The music drew Josiah's attention away from Amelia Angle's house. He let Clipper know he wanted to go, but it was like the horse already knew it was time to move on before Josiah tapped him with his heels. The Appaloosa bounced his head and began a slow trot forward.

There was a time in Josiah's life when he would have never considered spending idle time in a saloon, but sitting on his horse outside a house, pining like a lovesick boy, hoping to catch a glimpse of a girl, was something he'd never considered he'd be doing either, not at his age.

The trip to Corpus Christi had changed a lot of things in his life, and his return to Austin, now that Lyle seemed to be on the mend, was an announcement of that fact. The city was different, too. More hectic, more vibrant. It was like there was a current of energy running under the dirt streets, pulsing like some unseen force, urging movement to continue on indefinitely.

The ride was short, and the saloon was easy to find. It stood about two and a half blocks from the boardinghouse, just at the edge of the residential section of Cypress Street. It was an odd place for a saloon. Josiah couldn't remember ever seeing the saloon since he'd moved to Austin—but he had been away a lot of the last year.

The saloon was tucked in between a mercantile and a haberdashery, with a small sign over the door, "EASY NICKEL SALOON," and no batwings. The solid door was standing wide open, and the music flowed out into the street.

Josiah tied Clipper to a hitching post. There were plenty to choose from; the nearest mount, a black gelding, was three doors down in front of a doctor's office, waiting patiently.

He looked up to the sky, checking the position of the sun. It was out of sight, and the grayness of twilight was a promise on the eastern horizon. Then Josiah checked his Peacemaker, made sure it was tight in the holster. He didn't expect trouble, but walking into a saloon brought a fifty-fifty chance of finding it.

The inside of the saloon was dark. Only a few sconces flickered on the walls, and a few hurricane lamps burned at the bar. The overhead collection of lamps, set on an old wagon wheel, had not been lit yet.

Only the piano player, a scruffy, bespectacled man with a bald head, and a barkeep were present in the saloon. The barkeep was tall, thick-armed, and barely glanced up when Josiah walked inside. Without saying a word, he made his way to the bar.

"What can I get ya?" the big barkeep said.

"Whiskey," Josiah replied.

"One?"

"That'll be enough."

The music played on, slightly picking up pace, starting all over at the beginning of the song. It was like the piano player was trying to get something started but didn't have the will, or power, to fully see it through.

Not far from where Josiah stood, a newspaper lay open on the bar. The headline, *McNELLY RUNS CORTINA BACK TO MEXICO*, caught his attention. He was tempted to read the article, but he could just about recount the episode from his own experience in Corpus—and he knew Scrap Elliot would be right in the thick of things. For some reason, that thought gave Josiah a bit of comfort. There had been no need for Scrap to accompany him back to Austin, though there did seem to be something missing since the boy's departure.

"Kind of lonely in here," Josiah said.

The barkeep slid the whiskey onto the counter. Josiah plopped two coins on the bar, picked up the glass, and swigged down the whiskey in one long gulp. No matter how much he tried, he still did not like the taste or burn of whiskey. But he was after neither effect, just the immediate result. He was after the slow calm, not the rowdy burst of energy that came from the drink. For him, how liquor affected him depended on the mood and the environment of the moment.

"Night falls, it'll bring in the coin," the barkeep said. He had a slight German accent, but it wasn't real strong. Josiah wondered why the man didn't work at one of the German beer gardens around town, but he failed to ask. The barkeep didn't appear to be in the mood for conversation, and truth be told, neither was Josiah. He was just building his nerve to see Pearl.

Not knowing what to expect when he found her made him nervous. Assuming that she would even want to see him was pure presumption on his part, and that was an odd feeling. Especially since he had pushed a willing Billie Webb out of his life—at least for the moment. Something told him that he hadn't seen the last of Billie, and he wasn't sure how he felt about that.

"You want another?" the barkeep asked.

Josiah shook his head no. "Just going to stand here for a bit if that's all right with you?"

"Suit yourself. Joe there only knows two or three songs."

"Thanks."

Joe the piano player nodded, smiled, then went back to banging the keys.

It didn't take long before Josiah became annoyed at the music and the loneliness of the saloon. He was looking for a distraction, something to take his mind off Pearl. Instead, he had an empty feeling in his stomach, and a growing sense of dread.

Without thanking the barkeep, who was busy shining glasses with a white towel, Josiah walked out of the saloon.

Night had fallen, but the darkness was not pure yet, not thick—the world was covered in shadows, not the blanket of pitch-black night. Still, he had waited long enough. He was going to find Pearl, or he was going home.

He unhitched Clipper, settled into the saddle, and turned to head back the way he'd come.

But a feeling came over him that slowed him down, like a pair of eyes was burning a hard hole into the back of his neck. Josiah looked over his shoulder quickly, reacting to his instinct.

He was certain he saw a man slip into the shadows of a thin alleyway between the doctor's office and the mercantile. With a swift jerk, Josiah turned Clipper back around and stopped at the mouth of the alley to get a better look. He eased his hand back and gripped the Peacemaker, ready to pull it if he had to.

There was nothing there. No sign of man or beast—a cat or a dog, maybe—intent on doing him harm.

Josiah exhaled lightly then, knowing his senses had been dulled a bit by the shot of whiskey and heightened at the same time by the experience of the night before, encountering Paul Hoagland in the street. The reporter's threat, that they were not through with each other, still weighed heavily on his mind.

It wouldn't have surprised Josiah to catch the reporter trailing after him, hoping for more of a story.

Unsure whether or not that was the case, Josiah spun Clipper back around and headed straight to Miss Amelia

Angle's Home for Girls. He wasn't going to start living his life in fear that he was being spied upon by a worthless newspaper reporter.

He needed to see Pearl Fikes. Plain and simple: He wanted to get on with his life, and nothing was going to stop him. Not now.

CHAPTER 43

———◆◆◆◆◆———

A light burned in the window at the back of Miss Amelia Angle's Home for Girls. The light was not smoky and muted, but steady and bright. It appeared Miss Angle's house had been outfitted with gas lamps. Obviously, gas, used as an everyday fuel, was spreading to the farthest reaches of Austin; an occurrence that Josiah found interesting, but less notable than the presence of the moving shadows in the room of his focus. If Pedro had been correct, then it looked like Pearl Fikes was where she was supposed to be.

Josiah scrounged up a few suitable pebbles and tossed them up at the window. The house was three storeys, and the first couple of throws missed the window entirely, bouncing off the wood siding with a shallow, almost inaudible, thump. After a couple of more tries, he pinged a small rock off the window, light enough so the fragile glass didn't shatter.

Instead of tossing up another rock, Josiah waited. He could feel his heart beating in his chest even faster now. There was still a slight taste of whiskey in his mouth, as foreign as it was welcome. Wasting time in a saloon had become a necessary evil in Corpus Christi; now it seemed he had no aversion to the act like he'd had in the past. Not that he thought about the aversion a lot, but the change in his own attitude was a surprise to him.

A shadow moved forward in the room. Josiah palmed a rock and readied his next throw, determined to get Pearl's attention. He worried less about drawing anyone else's attention, and he was sure he wasn't the first man to toss pebbles at the boardinghouse windows.

Pearl appeared at the window, the steady gas light behind her. Her long blond hair glowed like golden straw. She wore a curious look on her face, but it didn't take a sighting scope to see recognition burst across it and curiosity change to unbridled happiness once she laid eyes on Josiah.

In response, Josiah waved, urging her to come down, and Pearl disappeared abruptly from the window.

The last time he had seen her was in the coach outside of the capitol building. Pearl had whispered to him, *I need you,* after which he had disappeared for the next four months and offered nothing in the form of communication. No letters, no telegraphs, nothing. He was fully undercover, taking his spy assignment from McNelly as seriously as he could. Ultimately, he didn't know what kind of reception to expect from Pearl, especially considering the changes that had occurred in her life while he had been away.

Josiah paced then, walking in and out of the shadows in the alleyway that edged the back of the boardinghouse.

Lights from the windows of the house shone down on the gravel, and the moon peeked in and out of the clouds overhead, providing a reasonably clear view of everything around him.

There was still noise about, even louder piano music from the saloon and a moderate amount of traffic pacing by on the main streets that intersected at the corner lot the boardinghouse sat on. Josiah could barely hear anything, his mind full of jumbled words as he searched for the right thing to say to Pearl.

I'm sorry.

Maybe, he wasn't sure. Duty had called, and it had seemed the best thing to do, getting out of Austin, letting the hubbub die down.

I love you.

He wasn't sure. It was a hard thing to say, even though Billie Webb was pushing him to say it aloud one way or another. He knew Billie had her needs for him to say so, but it just wasn't that easy. He loved Lily. Always had, always would. How could he love, Pearl, too?

I missed you.

That was the truth. He had barely given Billie a thought when he was in Corpus Christi, while Pearl had been on his mind almost every day. Pearl, Lyle, and Ofelia. That counted for something, he thought. *I missed you* would be the truth; easier to say.

Emotions were not a foreign territory to Josiah, but he preferred simpler terrain than he was standing on now. As it was, he knew he had to see Pearl, and that was that. Maybe he would know what he felt as soon as she appeared.

As it turned out, Josiah didn't have to say anything. Not at first.

Pearl rounded the corner, her hair flowing behind her unbound as she ran to him. She was dressed to be alone in her room, ready for the night, her bedclothes on, a fine robe, too, open and unbuttoned, fine red satin fluttering about like a flag on a windy day.

Josiah stopped pacing and grabbed at a breath, because the sight of Pearl immediately took it away from him.

Not only did he feel alive, but he saw the desire for him in her eyes even in the grayness of the night. He had not felt wanted in a long, long time, at least that he recognized. Not since he was with her last, on the night before leaving Austin. There was no comparison of how he felt with Pearl to his feeling in the company of Billie Webb. Billie made him nervous, and with Pearl, Josiah was beginning to feel like himself.

Pearl ran straight to Josiah, uncaring about where they were, or if anyone saw them—wordless, her eyes glistening. The force of her body against his knocked Josiah back two steps, off balance. He had to reach for Pearl and pull her close to him to regain steady footing.

Josiah buried his face in her neck. She smelled like a field full of Texas wildflowers: bluebonnets, Indian paintbrush, daisies, and indigo. And her skin felt like velvet. He had longed for her touch without fully realizing it.

The world around them disappeared, and for a brief moment, it was as if they were the only two people who walked on the earth. Josiah was transported to the last moment they had truly touched, back to the barn on the estate, when they had made love for the one and only time.

Pearl was breathing heavily, and though he couldn't see her face, he could feel the wetness of her tears against his skin.

"I missed you," he whispered.

Pearl pulled back and looked Josiah in the eye, their noses an inch apart. He didn't wait for her to respond. He could not restrain himself any longer. He kissed her as passionately and as deeply as he knew how. Happily, Pearl responded in kind.

Time stood still, and it was only when they both heard the clopping of a coming horse that they broke apart and scurried, holding hands, into the shadows of a carriage house.

A buggy passed by, heading out to the main street, its sole occupant a man dressed in dark clothes and a high hat, who paid them no attention at all.

Once the buggy was past, Pearl broke into a laugh. "I feel like a schoolgirl."

Josiah smiled. Even in the darkness her eyes were alive and happy. "You look like one, too."

"I am improper, Josiah Wolfe. And you should be ashamed of yourself for not calling on me at the appropriate hour."

He was certain—almost certain—that she was playing with him, and he was very happy to find her in good humor, instead of scolding him or holding him in contempt for his absence.

"You look just fine to me, Miss Fikes."

"You are a scoundrel. With whiskey on your breath, no less. How am I to be sure that this is the Josiah Wolfe I know?"

Josiah looked away, then, breaking her gaze. "I had to go away."

"I know that. I understand. I also know you were on an assignment."

"How did you know that, Pearl?"

"I still know people, Josiah, no matter that my circumstances have changed."

"I'm sorry about that. I know it must be hard."

"Hard?" Pearl asked, tilting her head curiously. "Hard was not knowing if you were dead or alive, or if you would ever come back to Austin for longer than a minute to retrieve your son and then disappear again."

"I could never be in this town without seeing you. Unless you would no longer want to see me."

"You've changed." Pearl ran the palm of her hand across his cheek, letting it linger before pulling away.

"I'm sure we both have."

The sound of a window being pushed open caught Pearl's attention. She put her index finger to her lips and moved in closer to Josiah, pressing against him, like she was trying to disappear into his body.

Josiah pulled Pearl closer. Her head fit comfortably under his chin, and he was able to see a person, an older woman, looking out the window, up and down the alleyway. It didn't take asking to know that Pearl was breaking the rules by being outside of the house after dark, not to mention in the arms of a man. She would most likely be put out on the street if she were caught.

Satisfied there was nothing outside, the woman closed the window and disappeared.

"She's still watching," Pearl whispered.

"I had to see you. I couldn't wait another day, another hour," Josiah said.

Pearl smiled, then leaned up to kiss him. Josiah responded, though still tense with the thought that someone might be watching them.

Finally, Pearl pulled back. "I should go back inside."

"I'll call on you tomorrow. If you'd like."

"I'd like that, Josiah. I'm anxious to see what's become of you in the daylight."

"I'll try to behave myself."

Pearl started to pull away, but hesitated. "How'd you find me?"

"Pedro. I went to the house first . . ."

". . . But no one was there."

"It hardly looked the same."

"I imagine not. I have not returned since the day I left."

"Pedro told me of your mother's health. I was surprised that she was in a sanatorium."

"We have been most fortunate, Josiah. A benefactor has seen to our means, or else we would surely be out on the street. There was no money left. Nothing of my father's to hold on to to see us through difficult times."

"Your mother was staking her future on Pete Feders."

"She was wrong, Josiah. And that is the last I will speak of that. Do you understand? I am happy here. I would have been chained to Peter, if he had gotten his way. I have freedoms now that I never thought possible. I am in training for a teacher's position, and it is the most rewarding occupation I can imagine. There is no longer the need for me to be the belle of the ball, and you must know how much I hated that."

"I didn't know, but I do now."

They were talking in whispers, and every ten seconds or so, Pearl would look over her shoulder at the back of the boardinghouse to make sure she wasn't being seen.

"I really have to go, Josiah. I cannot jeopardize this life I have now, no matter how much I want to run off with you."

"I understand. I'll be on the doorstep at the first appropriate hour."

"Is that a promise?"

"Yes," Josiah answered. "I promise."

CHAPTER 44

———◆◆◆———

Josiah watched Pearl disappear into the house, then waited for her to appear in her window. She never did, but the light went off after a few minutes. He saw shadows in the room and was certain he saw her waving him off. She was probably trying not to be seen by anyone, coming, going, or motioning to him. After a few minutes he felt comfortable enough to leave.

He had hitched Clipper about a block east of Miss Amelia's, so he had a little jaunt down the alleyway, up a half block, then back to where he'd secured the horse. Hurrying was not in the cards. Josiah felt full and happy, like he'd just eaten the best dinner of his life.

Pearl wasn't angry with him and still wanted to see him. That was heartening, encouraging. Maybe with everything that had happened, he could court Pearl properly now. Maybe it would be easier since she was no longer gracing the society pages, or bound up in a world of manners and money that Josiah could never compete with.

It was difficult, even in his moment of euphoria, to be happy for someone else's misfortune. Especially if he concentrated on it long enough and saw his own hand in the demise of the Widow Fikes. There was an accounting to be had for killing Pete Feders, and Josiah felt he'd lived with it long enough. At least outwardly. He would hold on to his set of responsibilities for the act, privately, for the rest of his life. But even in his own mind, given the current economic state of Texas and the country, the lack of luck and the load of misfortune that had fallen on the Fikeses, he could reason that even if Pete Feders had married Pearl, the result might have been the same. There was no way to ever know, though.

Josiah turned north, off the alleyway, and was headed happily toward Clipper, when he heard a set of footsteps fall in behind him. His heart dropped. He was certain that Paul Hoagland, the newspaper reporter, had followed him, had seen the exchange between him and Pearl. The last thing Josiah wanted the entire city of Austin to know about was his continuing relationship. It was fragile enough. Notoriety might just be enough to wreck any chance he had to properly court Pearl.

The happiness he'd felt was obviously fleeting, and that riled Josiah to no end. Anger boiled from deep within his soul, and without missing a step, he spun around, ratcheted up the Peacemaker from the swivel holster, and aimed directly at the figure who was trailing him.

It only took a second to determine that he was wrong. There was most definitely a man following him, but it wasn't Paul Hoagland.

"Hey, there, brother, you look familiar."

Josiah heard the voice and knew immediately it was Edgar Leatherby—Leathers, the ex–Trappist monk he'd met in Ingleside.

Leathers's thin, angular face came into full view then, as

Josiah stood there, surprised and curious at the same time. He kept the Peacemaker trained on the man more out of habit than distrust.

The man stopped, and they were facing each other about fifteen feet apart. Leathers wore a black felt Stetson, to cover his bald head, and an open duster. The duster was black, too, and Josiah could barely see the man's pale white hands. They hovered to his sides, within easy reach of the guns on both hips. He was a thin man, his most remarkable feature how stark yellow his teeth were from all of the cigarettes he smoked.

"I knew a man by the name of Zeb Teter who looked an awful lot like you," Leathers continued. "No, make that exactly like you."

"Maybe you're mistaken," Josiah answered. "Or maybe there's more than one man that looks like me."

"So you're sayin' you're not a lowly hide trader from down Corpus way?"

"I'm not saying."

"Too bad. Seems to me a Texas Ranger ought to be able to speak the truth about himself. Who he is and what he is, brother."

Josiah shrugged. He inched his finger closer to the trigger. "You come here looking for trouble?"

"I came here lookin' for Josiah Wolfe."

Tired of the charade, Josiah didn't hesitate to respond. "Well, you found him. How's that?"

"I know that, Wolfe. I knew it from the moment I saw you in Corpus Christi. I knew who, and what, you were."

"So you say, Leathers, so you say." Josiah had always gotten mixed signals from the man. Could never figure out if he was a friend or a foe. He'd had an inkling to consider the man a friend, but that inkling was running pretty thin at the moment.

Leathers returned the shrug. "You gonna keep holdin' that gun on me? No way to treat an old friend, is it?"

"I'm not feeling real friendly at the moment."

"I don't imagine you are, brother. I never did believe your story."

"You kept digging at me."

"You didn't break, though, I'll give you that. You never smelled like a hide trader. You smelled like a spy."

"How'd you find me?"

"Here? Or in Ingleside? I was outside the livery when the marshal suggested you join up with the cattle drive. I was a good spy, unlike you."

Josiah remembered back to the moment Leathers spoke of, and he'd been sure he heard somebody, but hadn't seen anyone when he checked. He thought he was just overreacting at the time. "That was you?"

"That it was."

"How'd you find me here?"

"Newspapers are a wonderful thing. It seems the folks in Austin find you interesting."

Josiah caught his next words and didn't respond with any anger toward Hoagland, who surely didn't know what he had done by leading Leathers to him. "How would you know what a spy smelled like, Leathers? More to the point, why would you care?" he said, in an even tone, regretting that he only had one gun on his side, fully loaded. His only other weapon was the knife tucked in his right boot.

"Man's gotta make a livin', there, brother."

"I'm not your brother. And, at the moment, I'm starting to think your story about being a monk who left the abbey is about as fictitious as my hide trader story."

"Oh, it's the truth, all right. I *was* a monk. But I broke one of the commandments. There was no forgiveness after that."

"Really, which one?"

"Thou shall not kill."

Josiah nodded. "What are you doing here, Leathers? That is your name isn't it?"

"Does it matter?"

"Not really."

"I didn't think so."

"So you want to tell me why you're here? You obviously had a reason to come to Austin."

"You're my reason, Wolfe."

"Really? Is there a bounty on my head? It wouldn't be the first time."

"It'll be the last."

Josiah didn't answer. He was in a much better position than Leathers was to win a shoot-out. At least, it appeared that way. The man was awful calm.

"Did you really think Cortina would come after you himself?" Leathers asked. "Once I knew you were joining up with the cattle drive, it gave me time to make a plan. I got myself hired on as the cookie to be closer to you, so I'd have a shot at killing you. I was low on money, too, and Cortina isn't much on bankrolling his hired help. The reward would be there when I finished the job, so with what little money I had left I hired a couple Mexicans I knew to help rustle the cows at the start of the drive. I knew I could stampede the cows by taking advantage of the messiness of the start; those cowboys were some of the lousiest greenhorns I've seen—including you. Then I'd catch up with my rustler friends after you were dead and finished, sell the cows to Cortina, and collect the reward all at once."

"But you missed me."

"I did, regretfully, and was nearly shot myself. That helped me stay in Bowman's good graces for a while, and gave them somebody to go after. I guess with me standing here, it all worked out. Just took longer than I thought it would."

"How did you kill the rustlers?"

Leathers looked at Josiah curiously. "I don't know what you're talking about. I stayed with the drive until I reached Austin. Otherwise, Bowman would've known I was up to something. I much prefer being a religious man to a cook, Wolfe."

"And you lost the cows."

"Pity. But I can still get the reward for you."

Josiah took a deep breath. Maybe he and Scrap had been right all along and the rustlers were killed by a minute group. It was the only explanation he had at the moment.

"I guess Cortina wouldn't come after me himself, would he?" Josiah said.

"He knew there were spies in Corpus. More than just you. Maria Villareal turned on him, and she paid the price."

"You killed her?"

"This is not a moment of confession, Wolfe. Those days are over for me. I was hired to rid Corpus of spies and their ilk. You figure it out from there if I killed that female traitor or not. You were a slippery quarry. I've come to settle my claim. Cortina doesn't want you dead or alive. He wants you dead. Period. Takin' you alive was O'Reilly and Feders's mistake. It won't happen again."

Now things were starting to make sense to Josiah. Leathers was a spy hunter for Cortina. He had taken advantage of Josiah's mistake when he'd gone after Clipper and shot Maria Villareal, then followed him and Scrap to Ingleside, and beyond, to the cattle drive. The last time Josiah had seen Leathers was right before the stampede.

He recalled Agusto's death, and it could have been at Leathers's hands, too, now that he thought about it. But the constancy of Miguel puzzled him. Miguel had disappeared before Maria was shot, only to reappear at the saloon in Ingleside, briefly. He was also the cause of the stampede, after shooting down into the herd. And then there were the two rustlers that Josiah and Scrap had found with their throats cut. Something told him Leathers was behind those killings, even though he couldn't quite figure out why at the moment.

"So it's just you and me?" Josiah said.

"I'm a hired killer, not a gambler, Wolfe," Leathers said. "You got your finger on the trigger, but I promise you, you won't dare shoot me."

"Why's that?"

"If I don't show up alive after this is all said and done, then your precious Pearl Fikes will be dead as dead can be. Be a pity to see such a pretty young thing flayed open at the gullet like a simple chicken. Either way, I win. Lower your gun, Wolfe. Lower it now," Leathers commanded, calmly pulling two silver six-shooters out of their holsters and aiming them directly at Josiah.

CHAPTER 45

———◆⬦◆———

Josiah eased his finger off the trigger of his Peace-maker. "If anything happens to Pearl Fikes, I promise you, Leathers . . ."

"Promise me what? You're a dead man, Wolfe. Don't you get it? This is it for you. The end of the line. I'm talkin' to a dead man."

The grip of the Peacemaker slipped out of Josiah's hand. "You're like a cat, Leathers. Playing with your prey before you kill it?"

"I think I liked you better as Zeb Teter. You weren't so confident and mouthy. Pride is a sin, you know, there, brother."

Josiah exhaled, thought about diving to the right or to the left, but either way he was still a clear shot for Leathers. At least he'd go down with a fighting chance, instead of just standing there, waiting for the man to pull the triggers of his two guns. If Pearl hadn't been involved, that was exactly what he would have done, taken his chances, at that very moment. But there was more to gamble on now that he knew that Pearl was, somehow, in danger.

"I think you're bluffing, Leathers."

"Think what you want. I told you, I'm no gambler."

There was only one thing Josiah could think to do, and that was dive straight toward Leathers, tuck into a roll, and come up shooting. Hopefully, the monk wouldn't expect that.

Piano music played furiously in the distance; the barkeep at the Easy Nickel Saloon had obviously been correct in his prediction that business would pick up once darkness fell. The piano player was on another round of "Camptown Races."

Overhead, the moon slipped behind a cloud, a deeper darkness falling to the ground in a collection of shadows that were as dense as a midnight storm.

Leathers's cheek twitched. He was about to make a move.

Josiah took the twitch as a sign, the only chance he could see to save himself, and he dove forward, just like he had planned.

The dual explosion of Leathers's six-shooters going off at the same time was deafening as thunder, and in the midst of his tucked roll, Josiah was certain that he saw the quick release of bright orange light from the end of both barrels, directly toward him.

There was no pain, at least not yet, as Josiah came out of the dive, reaching for his own gun and sliding it upward. At that moment, he was certain his ploy had worked and he'd escaped without being shot. For the moment.

Only having six shots, Josiah had to make sure each one counted. As he came up, his finger on the trigger, another shot rang out—but this one came from behind him, catching Leathers just above the right knee.

Josiah fired, too, hitting Leathers square in the chest, just a half a second later. Unsure of who fired the shot from behind and what he was up against, Josiah fired again, hitting Leathers just at the base of the throat.

Josiah came to a full stop in a crouched position then, the Peacemaker aimed directly at Leathers. He was saving the remaining cartridges.

The ex-monk looked stunned and surprised as he stumbled backward, one of the guns falling to the ground with an audible thump. Blood exploded from all three wounds, the most visible being the final one from Josiah. He must have caught one of the man's main arteries. It looked like he had just been gutted, as blood spewed like a fountain from his throat.

Leathers fell to the ground on his back, the other gun popping out of his hand, far enough away for the man not to be an immediate threat.

Josiah spun around, yanking his Peacemaker out of the holster, his eyes searching for any movement. He wasn't sure if the shooter behind him was friend or foe, and he sure as hell wasn't taking any chances.

"Wait! Wait, señor! It is me, Miguel!" The short Mexican guitar player stood about ten feet beyond Josiah, just to the left of a collection of heavy bushes, his hands up in the air, his Walker Colt, with the fifteen-inch barrel, teetering heavily. The barrel was pointed toward the ground, not at Josiah. "Don't shoot. I am here to help. I swear."

Josiah lowered the Peacemaker, then turned sideways, keeping Miguel in sight, as he edged over to Leathers.

The ex-monk was dead, his eyes fixed upward. Blood still drained out of his neck, but it was slowing. Josiah leaned down and took the man's pulse—there was none there.

He stood up and faced Miguel. "How do I know I can trust you?"

"Because McNelly said to trust no one, didn't he, señor?"

"He did say that. More than once."

"Then you have to trust that I know the captain, that he

said it to me, too. Would it surprise you that a Mexican could be on the payroll of the Texas Rangers?"

"You started a stampede, Miguel. Two men were killed."

"*Sì*, señor, I shot down at the cows, but I saw what you didn't. The gringo, there, was about to shoot you. You couldn't see it. It was the only thing I could do to save you. I had nothing to do with the dead men."

"Then the minute group must have killed them. I hope Scrap and McNelly find them and bring them to justice."

Miguel nodded. "I cannot say for sure, but I stayed behind to keep an eye on the man, just in case I was wrong. He intended to start that stampede, señor, I am sure of it."

"Leathers said as much."

"We will never know for sure who killed those rustlers, but this Leathers was a very bad man, señor. I am glad he is dead."

Josiah hesitated for a second before he said anything else. "McNelly put you in charge of looking after me?"

"Of looking after you all."

"He killed Maria."

"I know, I know. I failed."

Josiah looked up and down the street, glad that their shots had not drawn any attention. At least not yet. "I failed, too, but Leathers put another woman in danger. We have to make sure she is all right."

Before Miguel could say a word, Josiah rushed down the alley, into the shadows. All he could think about was seeing that Pearl was unharmed.

All of the lights were off in Miss Amelia Angle's Home for Girls. Josiah and Miguel eased around the house, looking for any sign of trouble, any sign of duress. Nothing looked out of place. There were no horses tied to the hitching posts in front of the house. Music from the nearby saloon still played on, and all of the doors and windows of Miss Amelia's were closed.

"What are you going to do, señor?" Miguel asked, as quietly as he could.

"Go in," Josiah said.

"Go in?"

Josiah nodded. "Got any other ideas? Leathers said if he didn't show up here, then Pearl would be killed. I have to get upstairs without being heard."

Miguel smiled. "Come with me, señor," he said, digging into his pocket.

Josiah followed Miguel up onto the long porch that ran the length of the house. A board creaked as Josiah stepped up. They both stopped, looked around, and listened, to make sure no one had detected their presence.

Satisfied, Miguel walked up to the door and stuck a slender piece of metal in the keyhole. "All good spies are good thieves, too," the Mexican whispered, as a click echoed and he eased the door open.

"Stay here," Josiah ordered, entering the house, his Peacemaker in hand, ready to fire at the first suspicious thing that moved.

He stopped inside a wide, open foyer and let his eyes adjust to the darkness. A clock ticked not far off, probably in the parlor. There was a sweet smell in the air, a mix of perfumes and the fragrance from the spring flowers planted in the urns on the porch. A settee sat just inside the door, along with an umbrella butler and a tall coat stand. The stairways were straight in front of him, and Josiah made his way up one of them, as easily and quietly as he could.

He looked over his shoulder before turning up on the first landing, just to make sure Miguel was still in his place. He was.

Josiah headed upward, past the second floor, onward, up to the third floor. The only creature he saw was a red tabby cat that was sleeping on a windowsill. The cat opened its eyes, looked at Josiah curiously, flipped its tail, then closed its eyes as Josiah passed by, paying him no mind.

Once he got to the third floor, he had to stop and figure out what room was Pearl's.

He counted the doors and was certain that out of the four doors that faced the alleyway, the second to the last was the one that he had seen Pearl standing in.

He listened for any sign of life, heard a few light snores beyond the doors, then made his way to Pearl's room and stopped just on the outside of the door, his gun pointed straight up in the air.

It was then that he heard the scoot of a chair leg across the floor, and took it as a sign of duress.

Time had run out. Whoever was working with Leathers was about to do their deed.

Josiah jumped back, kicked the door in, and aimed his gun at a shadowy figure moving from a desk by the window to the bed.

A woman screamed. It wasn't Pearl.

"Pearl?" Josiah yelled out.

The woman screamed again. And a series of lights started popping on behind him, thanks to the wonderful installation of gas.

Standing before Josiah was an unknown woman, dressed for bed, obviously coming from the desk that sat in front of the window, with a closed diary on it.

She screamed again. Doors popped open. Feet scurried. And Josiah turned to flee the room, only to be met by a woman who looked like a boulder with a broad mop of gray hair stuck on top of it, covered in a flowery nightdress and carrying a big club angled up in the air.

"Don't!" came a familiar voice. The hallway was full of girls now, and Pearl pushed her way through the crowd. "Josiah Wolfe, what on earth are you doing here?"

Josiah lowered his gun. The woman, whose room he had broken into, screamed again.

"Maggie, would you please stop screaming. There's no danger here," Pearl said.

Josiah looked at Pearl curiously, relieved. "You're sure. No danger?"

"Do you know this man, Miss Fikes?" the boulder-sized woman asked.

"Yes, Miss Angle, I do."

"I thought you were in danger, Pearl. I'm sorry." Leathers obviously *was* bluffing. "I need to go." Josiah turned to the screaming woman and said, "Sorry, ma'am, I didn't mean you any harm."

He made his way past Miss Angle and stopped in front of Pearl. "I'm sorry, I'll explain tomorrow." He kissed her quickly on the cheek and hurried off, not looking behind him to see if she was blushing or angry. All he knew was that all of the girls were giggling hysterically, and their attention was focused on him, thankfully, rather than on a killer.

By the time he'd seen Miguel off, it was nearly midnight when Josiah returned home. Once again, he made his way as quietly as he could into the house. This time not looking for danger, but the sight of a recovering, happy little boy. He found him just where he'd thought he would, in bed, with no fever, completely unaware of the dangers of the world.

Ofelia was asleep on a mat on the floor, not willing to take the bed that was Josiah's when he was home.

Something would have to be done about that, he decided, as he left the room.

He was far from sleepy, too wound up to go right to bed himself, so he went back outside and sat on the porch, letting the night air wash over him and the silence of the city settle around him.

The first thought that came to Josiah's mind as he sat down, letting go of the events of the day, was simple, and one that surprised him: *It sure is good to be home.*

EPILOGUE

―◆◆◆●――

Josiah welcomed the smell of the ocean as it touched his nose. He eased Clipper along the beach, riding just inside the surf, listening to the waves crashing, staring at the small fishing village in the distance. It was never a question whether he would ever return to Chipito, it was just a matter of when.

The blue-roofed shack came into view, and Josiah kneed Clipper gently, asking him silently to pick up the pace. The Appaloosa responded with a head shake, then he grunted, like he was enjoying himself and was hesitant to leave the easy gait anytime soon, but he obliged, kicking up sand and water as he sprinted toward the village.

It was midday, and a large fire burned in the center of Chipito. Thin black smoke rose gently into the air against the perfect azure sky. The fires were used to smoke fish, and the smell, mixed with ocean, was welcome. Josiah was hungry, but he had other things on his mind.

He and Clipper made it to the village quickly.

All of the boats were gone, out to sea for the day. A lone

woman, one he did not recognize from his previous visit, was busy scrubbing some clothes in a tub outside her shack. The woman, her skin dark as leather, watched every move Josiah made with suspicious eyes, as they should have been.

He dismounted from Clipper as easily and nonthreateningly as possible, and instantly unsnapped his gun belt and tossed it over the saddle. He extended his arms straight out, showing the woman he wasn't armed, and walked over to her. The suspicious look on her face did not change.

"I'm looking for Juan Carlos. Is he still here?"

The woman nodded and pointed to her left, out to sea.

Josiah followed the tip of her finger and saw the figure of a man standing knee-deep in the water, about two hundred yards away. "Thanks," he said, and walked away.

"You a friend of his?" the woman called out.

"I used to be."

The woman nodded and went back to scrubbing her clothes. "He has no friends here. I doubt you'll be welcome, either."

"I'll take my chances."

Josiah walked slowly toward Juan Carlos. The old Mexican was net casting; tossing the net out, reeling it back in hand over hand, each time the catch empty. He seemed oblivious to anything around him. There was no bucket on the shore to contain his catch. It looked like he was just whiling away the time.

Sneaking up on a man like Juan Carlos was not wise, so Josiah stopped just short of the water, took off his boots, and rolled up his pants. "Hey," he yelled loud enough to be heard over the crash of the surf.

Juan Carlos turned around. He looked even older and skinnier than the last time Josiah had seen him. It seemed to be difficult for him to stand against the taller waves, but the old man fought for a foothold, and won every time, though Josiah wasn't sure how. A good, stiff wind could have blown the man straight north to the Dakotas.

A tense, angry look fell across Juan Carlos's face as he recognized Josiah. "I told you I'd shoot you if you ever came back here."

Neither the look nor the words slowed, or stopped, Josiah's approach. "I'm unarmed."

"You don't think I've shot an unarmed man before, señor?"

"You might as well shoot me then."

"I don't have a gun on me." The net dangled from Juan Carlos's long fingers, his grip loose. "Why are you here?"

"To tell you how sorry I am for not being there for Maria Villareal. I made a bad decision, and I will pay for it for the rest of my life. Her death was my fault. I am sorry."

"And that is all?"

"That, and I have a question to ask of you, too."

"Sorry will do you no good."

"Let me explain myself."

Juan Carlos shook his head no, then reared back and tossed the net solidly into a rolling wave. He jerked back, closed the net after it hit the water, and started pulling it back in. "There is nothing to explain. Maria is dead. It is that simple." The net was empty as he pulled it up to check it. "What is your question? What is so important that you came to a place you're not wanted, and that is very dangerous for you to be?"

"It's about Pearl," Josiah said, staring directly into Juan Carlos's deep blue eyes. "I'd like your blessing to court her properly."

A wave crashed against Juan Carlos, nearly knocking him down. He fought to regain his footing, tipping his hand into the water to steady himself, then said, "And if I say no?"

Josiah shrugged. "It's not just up to you. Pearl has a say in this, too. Her father is dead. You're the closest thing to that she has. She has lost nearly everything else in her life, and if we are to start making something of our lives, I want to do it right. Do I have your blessing or not?"

Juan Carlos exhaled deeply, stared back at Josiah, and abruptly handed the net to him. "Here, see if you remember anything I taught you."

Josiah took the net, situated it properly in his hands, eased back, watched the waves for a school of mullet, then tossed the net as hard as he could.

The net splashed into the water in a perfect circle and sank completely out of sight. He yanked back, felt a little tug and resistance, and pulled the net back toward him with all of his might, sure that he had caught something.